by Andrei Codrescu

POETRY

Alien Candor: Selected Poems 1970–1995 (1996)
Belligerence (1991)
Comrade Past & Mister Present (1987, 1991)
Selected Poems: 1970–1980 (1983)
Diapers on the Snow (1981)
Necrocorrida (1980)
For the Love of a Coat (1978)
The Lady Painter (1977)
The Marriage of Insult & Injury (1977)
A Mote Suite for Jan & Anselm (1976)
Grammar & Money (1973)
A Serious Morning (1973)
Secret Training (1973)
the, here, what, where (1972)
The History of the Growth of Heaven (1971, 1973)
License to Carry a Gun (1970)

FICTION

A Bar in Brooklyn: Novellas & Stories 1970–1978 (1999)
The Blood Countess (1995, 1996)
Monsieur Teste in America & Other Instances of Realism (1987)
The Repentance of Lorraine (1976, 1993)
Why I Can't Talk on the Telephone (1971)

MEMOIRS

Road Scholar: Coast to Coast Late in the Century. Photographs
      by David Graham. (1993)
The Hole in the Flag: an Exile's Story of Return & Revolution (1991)
In America's Shoes (1983)
The Life & Times of an Involuntary Genius (1975)

ESSAYS

The Dog with the Chip in His Neck (1996)
Zombification (1994, 1995)
The Muse Is Always Half-Dressed in New Orleans (1993, 1995)
The Disappearance of the Outside (1990)
Raised by Puppets Only to be Killed by Research (1989)
A Craving for Swan (1986, 1987)

TRANSLATION

At the Court of Yearning: the Poems of Lucian Blaga (1989)
For Max Jacob (1974)

EDITOR (with Laura Rosenthal)

Thus Spake the Corpse: An Exquisite Corpse Reader 1988–1998,
      Volume 1, Poetry & Essays (1999)

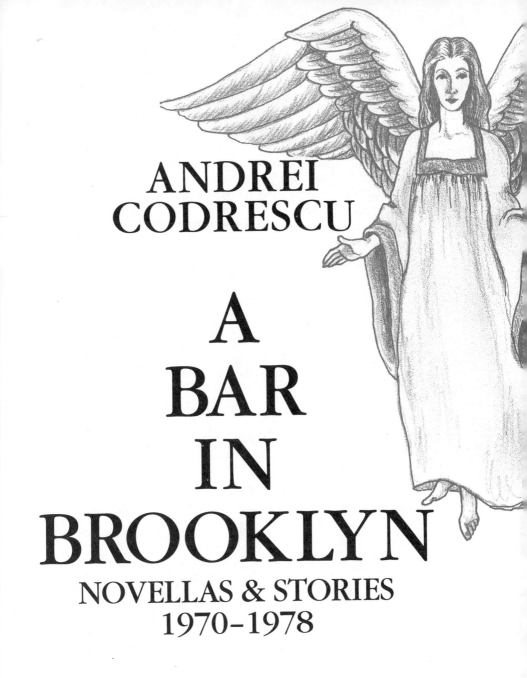

ANDREI CODRESCU

A
BAR
IN
BROOKLYN

NOVELLAS & STORIES
1970–1978

BLACK SPARROW PRESS
SANTA ROSA 1999

ACKNOWLEDGMENTS

The author thanks the editors of the following publications in
which some of these works first appeared in earlier versions:
Coffee House Press for "Monsieur Teste in America"; *The Paris
Review* for publishing "Monsieur Teste in America, and Samba
de Los Agentes"; *New Directions Annual* for publishing "The
Herald"; *Departures* for publishing "The Old Couple"; *The
Painted Bride Quarterly* for publishing "Julie"; and *Hot Water
Review* for publishing "A Bar in Brooklyn." "Samba de Los
Agentes" also won the Pushcart Prize and was published in
Pushcart VIII (Pushcart Press), and in the Avon paperback
edition of the same anthology.

Black Sparrow Press books are printed on acid-free paper.

LIBRARY OF CONGRESS CATALOGING–IN–PUBLICATION DATA

Codrescu, Andrei, 1946–
    A bar in Brooklyn : Novellas & Stories 1970–1978 / Andrei Codrescu.
      p. cm.
    Contents: Word to the reader — Monsieur Teste in America — Samba
de los Agentes — Three simple hearts — Tenderness — Perfume —
The herald — The old couple — Petra — Julie — The babysitter —
A bar in Brooklyn.
      ISBN 1-57423-097-2 (paperback)
      ISBN 1-57423-098-0 (cloth trade)
      ISBN 1-57423-099-9 (signed cloth)
     1. United States—Social life and customs—20th century—Fiction.
2. Immigrants—United States—Fiction. I. Title.
PS3553.03A6   1999
813'.54—dc21
                                  99-22178
                                  CIP

TABLE OF CONTENTS

WORD TO THE READER

My first fictions in English date to 1970 when I wrote and rewrote a novel called "How I Became Howard Johnson," and kept a fictitious journal alongside a real one. The novel was an attempt to make myself over into my new language and I was excessively sensitive to criticism. When the three friends who read it pointed out various flaws, I rewrote the whole thing. Since I used a manual typewriter and only type with one finger, the rewriting was endless. In 1971, "How I Became Howard Johnson" was bought by a publisher in Berkeley. This was a respectable children's book publisher who decided, for reasons having to do with his hippy son in Amsterdam, to publish "hip" adult fiction. The man didn't understand a word of my book, which he bought along with six other titles, in the hope of luring the wayward son back to the family business. My novel was surreal, full of odd syntactical constructions, fresh impressions of America, and long conversations between baffled (or stoned) protagonists. The manuscript underwent thorough copy editing, typesetting, and jacket design. The week before it was supposed to go to press, the wayward son returned from Amsterdam and showed no interest whatsoever in his father's "hip" conversion. The guy was a junkie, interested in heroin not literature. Daddy cancelled the whole hip venture and there went "How I Became Howard Johnson," never to see the light of day again.

The fictitious journal was started in New York in 1969 and was continued through 1971 in California. I wrote the entries in the morning in coffee houses. They described the day as if it already happened, noting in minute detail various adventures. In the evening I wrote the real journal, noting the day's events as they had actually happened. The idea was that, years hence, I would compare the two diaries and see how fiction held up to reality. Years hence I did that and, to my surprise, I could barely tell what was fictional and what was real. Life in those days had a fictional quality about it anyway. The fictional diary might note, for instance, an encounter with a mysterious young woman in a dress shop where I helped her make a decision, then aided her in trying out the dress. In the real diary I find a similar encounter, brought on perhaps by the earlier fantasy, or pre-existent in some way.

In 1973 I wrote a series of surreal story-poems and published them in a mimeograph chapbook titled *Why I Can't Talk on the Telephone.* The stories were attempts to explain my awkwardness with the telephone but were aimed, more generally, at the interface between humans and machines. In those days, machines hadn't quite taken over humans as resolutely as they have now. The machines under my scope were things like typewriters, telephones, television, electrical appliances (and electricity itself), airplanes, and the immortal Vegomatic which made its first appearance in television advertising around that time.

In 1973–74 I also wrote another novel, called "Meat from the Goldrush." It was a book influenced by Garcia Marquez' *One Hundred Years of Solitude,* which had just appeared in English. In my book, a family of Eastern European butchers figure out a way to transport bodies from history with the help of a time machine. These bodies, fresh from battlefields, are then converted into delicious cuts of meat to which everyone in America becomes addicted. The citizens begin to eat their own ancestors and history becomes circular and it short-circuits. This novel fared surprisingly well with editors I sent it to, and it came very close to being published by Harper & Row. "Meat from the Goldrush" remains my good friend Pat Nolan's favorite fiction of mine.

In those same years, my friend Tom Veitch and I resolved to write a thousand-page novel called "The Hippie Termites." We wrote together every day for about four months, just like Joseph Conrad and Ford Madox Ford, but had to give up at around 250 pages because our "hippie termites" were beginning to run dry. A beautiful comic book of several chapters of "The Hippie Termites" was illustrated and published by the late, brilliant Greg Irons.

The writing of brief stories ("minute stories"), prose poems, and even nearly conventional short stories, went on right alongside my "real business," which was the composition of poems. I always looked on fiction as a form of relaxation, a vacation from the rigorous art of modern verse. In a scale known only to true artists, fiction comes much lower on the rung of creation than poetry. At age sixteen when being a poet was the highest calling available, a fellow teenage poet looked me earnestly in the eyes over a cup of cognac-laced Turkish coffee at Flora Café in Sibiu, Romania, and said: "If you ever write a novel, I will never talk to you again." He hasn't.

Even then, however, I was secretly harboring dreams of fiction. By the time my poet friend had threatened me in that manner, I had already penned some adventure stories and I was working my way into some absurdist fiction à la Urmuz, the great Romanian absurdist and grandaddy of Dada.

In 1975 I published a slightly fictionalized memoir entitled *The Life and Times of an Involuntary Genius* with the prestigious house of George Braziller. I did not consider this a true work of fiction though, because I had used too many true facts of my life. My true break in fiction proper came in 1973 when George Plimpton accepted my novella, "Monsieur Teste in America" for the *Paris Review*. George had his assistant, Fayette Hickox, call me up to ask me to cut the story in half because it was much too long. "The only thing this long we ever published was Philip Roth's *Goodbye, Columbus,*" George told Fayette to tell me. I said that we should discuss this and I suggested that we meet at the Lion's Head in the Village. Fayette got there before George and said, "My God, I think this is the first time George came downtown in ten years!" George showed up eventually and we had a few drinks and I defended my story, and then George said, "OK, we'll run the whole thing." So there it was, in the *Paris Review,* as long as *Goodbye, Columbus.* The next year I published another novella there, almost as long, entitled "Samba de los Agentes." These two novellas are collected here.

I found the form of the novella congenial. Halfway between a short story and a novel, it was just the right size for what I had to say. In France, novella-size books of 100–120 pages are called "novels" and accorded the dignity of that form. American publishers, for some reasons (practical ones, no doubt) loathe such short books. The American novel is supposed to be thick, voluminous, filled with long stretches of character-development. What's more, American publishers prefer these thick volumes to be realistic, drearily realistic, as if American readers were schoolchildren and they had to be pedagogically numbed by the tedium of description and the minutiae of psychology. Unfortunately, this penchant for the realistic Big Book has become a self-fulfilling mode: American readers have been rendered childlike and disciplined, unable to make leaps of imagination, or fill in for themselves what they already know only too well.

I have also collected here two other novellas, dealing with one of my constant themes, the mystery of

10

polymorphous sexual magic. "Three Simple Hearts" refers to Flaubert's "A Simple Heart," and at one point I'd hoped, like Flaubert's *Three Tales*, to gather three novellas in a single book. There are four novellas here instead, alas.

The stories that follow these novellas are all written from the point of view of women. They are shorter and more experimental because I was working out various modes of access to the female psyche, and I didn't yet feel at home inside its voices.

These fictions, novellas and stories were written between 1970 and 1978 and represent themselves well, although some of their concerns can be found in later novels, notably, *The Repentance of Lorraine, The Blood Countess,* and *Messiah*. The esthetic hierarchy established in my adolescence has not been entirely toppled. Poetry is still the highest of the arts, but much is possible in the more generous spaces of fiction.

Andrei Codrescu
October 9, 1998

A BAR *in* BROOKLYN

NOVELLAS & STORIES 1970–1978

Monsieur Teste in America
an arrival and the necessity of it

At twenty-nine years of age, completely satisfied with the gentle fall outside, with vast stretches of contentment ahead of me in an unbroken mellow yellow greenery, I took my head in my hands and I considered my position. *I was bored in heaven!*

At first, unbelieving, I tried to go on with my daily routines; just at the moment when they could have secured my nights, they got blasted by this realization. "Oh, daily routines," I cried at them as they filled with void, "please do not abandon me! I am only trying to conquer my ambitions, to set my greed to rest in the cool shade of its immediate demands, to give my need for worship a little rest and nostalgia (R & G), to lure the beast of my lust back into the zoo where it belongs, to silence my mind to the point where stupidity *will* be my strong point, to shut up in general, and to shrink physically in particular." Unresponsive to my passionate plea, the daily routines began disintegrating.

With this crisis pending and with the rains not far off, I opened the part of my brain containing the past and let it spill in great globular formations across my closed eyes. My past, tied in neat bundles, each bundle with its own conclusion written in red ink on the face of it, obeyed me gently like a river when the Pacific Gas & Electric plant moves away. Or closes shop.

Who was I? Was I bored in Heaven because I was not I? Or was I bored because Heaven wasn't I? Was I boredom or was I Heaven? Was I in Heaven for being I on Earth? Or was I to be on Earth as the conclusion of Heaven? It was hard to decide.

When I came to America, to Norte America, I needed someone to counsel me in the simple secrets. I did not know such a person. Older exiles who, as myself, had come here without speaking a word of English, guarded their simple secrets carefully because their vampiric ambitions depended on them. A man might have three simple secrets by the age of forty-five if he emigrated at the age of twenty. A sixty-year-old man who emigrated at fifteen might have six simple secrets. I didn't have any and no one gave me theirs. I had to go at it alone, something I have a horror of. I don't even like going to the bathroom alone.

O Lord! I cannot imagine living without simple secrets!

Well, it took me three years to learn it (a history of academic excellence) but I did. Here it is:

America is exactly the way it seems to be. There are no hidden intentions.

To a European, this is inconceivable. The whole idea denies the fundamentals of experience. It is like listening to a dog laugh. Notice the old Hungarian lady waiting for the bus. She does not wait for the bus in the square clearly marked BUS STOP. She runs ahead of the bus before it has even stopped. The black bus driver shoos her away furiously. She goes back to the allotted area for boarding (she still does not believe it!), gets on the bus and starts a long harangue about the driver's rudeness. "I know my place," she says, "you should know yours!" As you can see, she is speaking about human places. Hers & His. Nowhere does it occur to her that there is *a place for boarding*. She does not believe that objects mean what they say. Her definition of objects is *that which is put in front of a woman to mislead her*. If

16

you ask her who put the object there she will laugh. Other people, of course. The hidden intentions of the sign BUS STOP are as clear to her as his watch is to the driver. BUS STOP in her country does not mean BUS STOP. It means also: *crowds, place, age, a public appearance, social position, a lady, engagements.*

Take this same lady and say "chocolate" to her. She will immediately have a vision of rare pleasure. Take the nearest American and say "chocolate" to her. It will mean only *a trip to the drugstore.*

On the other hand, if you seriously pull this lady aside and say "Jim" to her or "Elma" or "Gertrude," she will naturally ask the real questions: is he/she married yet? Do they have children? What are the latest scandals? It would never occur to her to impute an area of shadowy intentions to a person. Objects are the only guilty party. People are blameless to the extent that, although they put the objects there, they understand that it's only a game.

So, the first simple secret that it took me three years to learn was, as I have said, this:

America can be taken for granted. The obvious is very serious about itself here.

In Europe, I knew, the obvious did not exist. It had been riddled with holes there. An intelligent person is supposed to look through these holes before taking a step. And in Europe everybody is intelligent. Except the peasants, of course. But then they are objects anyway.

This one simple secret seemed to me so precious that for the next six years or so I did nothing but bathe in the sunny obviousness of America. (I made quite a bit of money, too.)

Then I became suspicious again. Here was I, twenty-one years old. If America is so obvious, I thought, how does she do it? A fatal question, friends, and I only hope for your sake that you are all Americans and never have to ask that. I looked at the ads for edification. I turned on the television. My living room floor was littered with newspapers. I took apart the house appliances. Then I didn't look at ads, TV, newspapers or appliance innards any longer and I instantly forgot what I saw in the ads, TV, newspapers and appliances. And thus, with the swiftness of electroshock, I comprehended a *second* simple secret:

Don't look back! They might be gaining on you!

This is when I began my long affair with the American language. If everything was obvious and firmly progressive it meant, naturally, that the language was a virgin expanse of snow on which my footsteps, if firm enough, could lead the rescuing party to me. So you see the psychological basis on which this affair thrived: I planned to use, yes, use the innocence of the language to further my aims which were neither more nor less than cracking the safe holding all the simple secrets of America. (Think of all the money I was going to make!)

O what a language! Contagious words imbued with mass-market meanings like a sponge full of ink crowded my mind to dictate their grammar to me! This grammar I was, of course, cautious to disregard as any lover would disregard his beloved's family if they didn't approve. Grammar did not approve of me so I didn't approve of grammar, and I continued in spite of its protestations to love the language to distraction. With one move I would suck the structural juice of grammar and spit it on the ground while with another move I would gather brilliant clusters of adjectives to my bosom and caress them into action. I discovered, o tender passion, that one is never alone with words in America. Vast masses of people accompanied each word to its place in the dictionary. These masses did what I did, ate what I ate, thought what I thought. The words of America's language brought me an incalculable dowry. They put at my disposal all the natives of the Norte America continent to dispose of as I saw fit. I was not anxious to hide from these folks even though I could never be intimate with my beloved. I despise intimacy and the bourgeois heart of it. I loved to sit still, surrounded by words truly open like transparent glass buildings without any doors in and out of which thousands of people jumped into their obvious business.

"If I could just have your words forever, my tongue," I whispered, "to fit them to my good intentions like silencers to guns, I could, conceivably, own the continent."

Above my bed, during this affair (we rarely left the bed, my darling and I) stood this injunction by Bill Knott:

People who get down on their knees to me are the answers to my prayers.

But, alas, no human passion is made to last. Like eggs, passions must be stuck in a refrigerator of the spirit, and this I was not willing to do.

At the age of twenty-four, I began to lose my enchantment. (And I wasn't making any money. A good agency of the government [welfare] understood my plight and saw to it that I sat in bed but it didn't pay much.)

Also, around this time, a tremendous nostalgia began to quake in me. I could barely remember my native tongue and I missed the fabulous capacity for abstraction that I had had before coming to America.

In this depressed state I moved into the wilderness, resolving to never speak, want or ask for anything. The wilderness had served this purpose until today when, looking at the purple and gold noose in the clouds above the ocean, I realized this horror: *I am bored in Heaven!*

There was someone I knew who had the cure to my ills. It was the mentor of my youth, the man most

19

responsible for setting the tender bones of my mind in the position in which they are now, the man who inspired me with his shining example, the man to whom I owed my ability to think: Monsieur Teste.

Summoning the remains of my strength, I dragged myself to the tiny post office of the nearest forgotten community (a nouveau old town inhabited by the nouveau poor) and I dictated the following telegram to the startled postmistress whose siesta had never until then been interrupted:

> MONSIEUR TESTE STOP PLEASE COME TO STOP AS STOP YOU ALWAYS STOP HAD STOP PARIS STOP EUROPE STOP

Two days later, the postmistress, terrified, unable to control her gothic features from glowing in the moonlight, appeared at the window of my modest treehouse and handed me the following:

> ARRIVING STOP IN NEW YORK STOP BY BOAT STOP APRIL 13 1974 STOP MONSIEUR TESTE STOP

I was twenty-nine years old that day.

Δ

New York with its usual disagreeable sense of humor lay under the general strike like an actress under a Foreign Legionnaire.

It was an ominous sign and downright depressing when I realized that Monsieur Teste had arrived but could not get off the boat because nobody would lower the gangplanks. There I sat, straining my eyes past the Statue of Liberty, trying to catch a glimpse of my savior among the black dots the fog jotted around the liner *Calypso*. The America Monsieur Teste was going to step on at the end of the strike was not the America I had found at my arrival. In my time, in 1966, America was a cluster of bubbles fighting to boil its human stew in a combination of exotic spices: Buddhism, mysticism, Marxism, etc. Now, in 1974, the ground was solid, the stew had been eaten and the people of America lay on their backs digesting quietly while murmuring, in unison: *Down with eccentricity! Back to realism!* Only realism did not upset the stomach. God was not in fashion any more. Survival was.

I was curious to see how Monsieur Teste would take it. He was not used to politeness. And originality was on the wane.

When I finally had the chance to say, "Welcome, Monsieur Teste," three days later, and hand him the bag of grapefruit I thought would stand for flowers, my curiosity had reached its boiling point.

He walked slowly across the deck, tall, skinny, grim-faced, dressed in a three-piece suit with an artificial zinnia in the lapel. Although he was walking in my direction, he looked insistently to his left side as if he had dropped his watch in the water. When he came close, he lifted a pale blue set of eyes, planted them into my own brown ones, and took the bag of grapefruits out of my hand without a word. I took his suitcase, which was very light (Monsieur Teste travelled, as he had always, with only a toothbrush, an aluminum canteen filled with mineral water and a complicated mathematical instrument laid carefully at the bottom of a small velvet-lined case) and he took my hand, which was very sweaty (since my earliest childhood) and thus, hand in hand, we put our four feet at once down on the New Land. I had the curious feeling that I too was arriving in America for the first time. Everything looked unfamiliar. It's Teste's immediate influence, I thought. Without a word he had already begun teaching me my old ways.

21

"Well, what do you think!" I said, including, with a sweeping gesture, the tall towers of Manhattan, the deserts of Nevada, my treehouse in California, my efforts at understanding and my present bafflement.

He didn't answer. He didn't make a gesture, either, because he had, as I knew, killed his puppet as far back as 1923. I would have given my kingdom just then for a clenching of his fist.

Later, sitting in one of those "luncheonettes" for which New York is justly famous, I ordered two bowls of blood red cabbage borscht for Teste and myself. In silence, with a collective mouth, we set ourselves upon the blood red liquid and shlurped intimately at each other like waves lapping on a beach. We were off to a good start. Monsieur Teste rose.

"The unknown makes me shit well," he said, by way of his first words in Norte America.

While he did his business in there I let contentment spread through my bones which together with the warmth generated by the borscht squeaked in utter delight. My bones! It was the first time since coming to this country that I had thought of my bones. Like a loose screw within the machinery of my own body, I had been malfunctioning without knowing it. How could a man live without feeling his bones? I had missed everything.

Teste returned, we paid and, in the taxi taking us to the airport where our plane for California waited, I leaned my tense head on Teste's bony shoulder and watched the neon of New York light up. It was going to be an idyll between us, yes, sir. No one and nobody would come between us.

"How long are you going to stay, mon Teste?" I said.

Wordlessly, he pointed to the meter of the taxi which was just then hovering between twenty-nine and thirty, miles or dollars I don't know, and when thirty finally became firm, he lowered his index finger. Ah, thirty ... But thirty what? Thirty days? Thirty weeks? Thirty years? Thirty minutes?"

"Thirty times," he said.

"Oh?!"

"I will stay until you have insulted me thirty times. Then I will leave."

"I will never insult you, Monsieur Teste," I cried out.

"One," he said.

Δ

On the plane I kept silent, calculating feverishly the many ways in which I would keep myself from insulting Teste. I would never refer to him without the polite Monsieur before his name. I would never talk politics. I would ignore the strangeness of his body. I would this and I would that. I had twenty-nine times left and I planned to use insults sparingly. I wanted Teste with me as long as possible. And if, I thought with cynical smugness, I got tired of him I can always insult him really fast twenty-nine times in a row and hasten his departure tremendously. But then I felt so guilty for allowing this thought to cross my sorry mind that I grimly clenched my smugness and pulled out a lock of my hair in self-retaliation. Teste was silent also. It was hard for me to tell whether he enjoyed the quiet night flight or whether he was listening to some internal rumbling. Before I could decide, the stewardess approached inside a teased platinum blond cloud and handed us glasses full of Coca-Cola like red rain out of the fullness of her heart. I could have kissed and embraced her for her gesture but I refrained when I saw Monsieur purse his lips, close one eye, put the straw behind his ear and spill the Coke. If I hadn't seen the deliberateness of it I might have thought the incident accidental. But I was sure he had done it on purpose. Why?

To make me insult him? Absurd! Presently, the platinum blond cloud folded in neat halves and two white branches shot out of her plumpness and began groping blindly at my feet with a yellow paper towel, the end of which looked like a sail and, suddenly, I understood! Monsieur had created the incident in order to make me see that other things beside platinum clouds filled with red raindrops existed. There were, in this marvelous world, also platinum blond clouds filled with red rain navigating at our feet with yellow sails. Oh, Teste!

Not much else happened on the plane and soon we saw the blue lights of San Francisco carpeting the earth like a cemetery of fresh ghosts signalling to the stars which were, you've guessed it, us.

Ah, what times awaited us! What mounds of blueberries! What terrors of filament! What corrections! What complete misuse! What tremendous erections! What filmy collaterals! What love! What caprice! What torrents! What torrential injections! What adjectives! What perceptions! Raining upward, the lights of San Francisco filled me with the elan of a god whose immortality rests in insults! A human whose love depends on a shut mouth! A monster whose ears must stay open all the time! A Lilliputian tied to the head sperm in the spermpack of a giant about to shoot his load in the belly of time! What felicity!

Δ

The coffee was cozily percolating, the sunlight lanced the dust motes in the air. We were sitting on the rug, in my pleasant little San Francisco apartment (I keep one in the city), Teste and I, exchanging significant glances though their significance was vastly increased, no doubt, by my interpretations of them. I read a thousand meanings in his slightest movement and each one of these meanings enriched my life enormously, inexplicably. When, finally, we decided to talk it was at a level decidedly lower than the one I had just experienced.

"What's your watch worth?" I said, noticing an expensive gold watch on his wrist.

"It is the most expensive watch in the world," he said. "It is my one and only admission that the world exists. An expensive admission. One must never admit anything, but if one has no choice, as in the case of time, one must not admit cheaply."

"An admission is an admission," I said. "What does it matter if the signature under a man's confession is set with diamonds or not? He has confessed, that's all."

"You are wrong, *mon chou*. If a man could sign his confession in diamonds, he would lend magnificence to his admission. He should, at least, sign with great care and a feeling of the absolute.

"Value," he continued, "is a defense of the unattainable. All things must be expensive. Things are an admission of man's impotence. They must not come cheap."

"The people are poor," I said.

"The people are bored," replied Monsieur.

"At least they aren't private," I countered.

He thought about this for a moment then reminded me of a fact I had forgotten:

"I am minding my own business."

With great pleasure I proceeded to describe to him how minding one's own business was not possible in America and how this wasn't really a bad thing because while it was true that others delved into one's business it was also possible for one to delve into others' business and *that,* you will grant, is the supreme pleasure of a democracy.

"What about music?" he cried. "And dance?"

"That is true," I readily agreed. "In America all art

forms are in the service of literature. Their job is to fatten up the words."

I showed him gorgeously illustrated art and music magazines in which the language, obviously inspired by the fact that no one had been there before, took off in fat and happy ways, exploding here and there around a comma only to redress itself and masturbate endlessly. I showed him dancers kneeling before reviews of their own work as if seeing themselves in a mirror for the first time. There was no endeavor, creative or crafty, that did not aim its crippled heart at the dartboard of print.

Monsieur Teste showed no sign that he saw what I was showing him. He said, "These people speak in complete sentences!"

There was so much contempt in his voice. I did not understand.

"The infinite," he said, "is a great influence on unfinished sentences."

That is true. I had been blind. Infinity was demanding my apologies. I turned toward the coffee maker which sat on the window sill and, looking vaguely at the gorgeous clouds, I murmured my excuses.

Δ

April 16, 1974
I masturbated as I got up. Monsieur Teste said:

"You are getting old. Instead of strangers, you fantasize about great lays of yesteryear."

"I beg your pardon," I said. "There was, in all those lays, a stranger I hadn't noticed at the time."

At breakfast, Monsieur Teste had a raw egg and a carrot. I asked him why.

26

"Entrusting your discoveries to language is like giving information to the wrong spy."

"But how else could you answer my question?"

Swiftly, he half-rose from his chair and plopped the yet uneaten raw egg into my face while, with his other hand, he thrust the carrot in my mouth which had fallen open from shock and surprise.

I told him, as I wiped off the goo, that it's possible to fool the language without resorting to action. He looked at me contemptuously and got himself another egg from the refrigerator which he left open to stare into for the rest of his breakfast.

During the afternoon, I was so exhilarated to have him unveil the simple secrets of America for me, that I told him, "This will be a fruitful time for me. Thank you."

"In the first place," he said, "don't ever thank me. The Japanese have seven ways of saying 'thank you' and each one implies a certain degree of resentment. In the second place," he continued, "I like the word 'fruitful.'"

He proceeded to tell me the story of a conference he had once participated in. "After having said many things to each other during the conference, the gentlemen bowed their various heads and took off for parts unknown, some to bus stations and some to little restaurants in the neighborhood.

"It had not been a lost day. It had been fruitful and each and everyone carried the fruit of it in his heart. Some carried pears, others carried figs, others draped limp bananas over their biceps while yet others could be seen with mangoes. 'Seen,' that is, through the look in their eyes. But the hearts these gentlemen carried inside were all identical. Each heart carried four chambers and each chamber was loaded with fruit.

27

"When the gentlemen played Russian roulette, later that afternoon, they aimed their hearts at their heads before squeezing the trigger. Death, for the winners, consisted in fruit taking root in the brain. 'Life is a fruit in the heart of a targeted brain' was the motto of this session. Death, therefore, is a last minute rush for vitamins.

"Every time a fruitful conference takes place the gentlemen age a little and this conference was no exception. It seemed that other gentlemen's emanations made the gentlemen older. If the gentlemen could be left alone from birth to death, aging would not occur. But nobody grants the gentlemen solitude, least of all the gentlemen them-selves. So the gentlemen want to be wolves. Can you blame them?"

"My God," I said, "it occurs to me that information works for death."

"A hired hand, cher."

"But what was the subject of this conference?"

Monsieur Teste lit a cigarette, looked at me with undisguised pity and said, "Anyone found frowning on the new god Chemistry will not be pulled out of the crucible in time for the party." Then slowly, he added, "Two."

Δ

April 17
I had a horrendous dream last night. I dreamt that Monsieur Teste wasn't real. I was terrified. But then the following solution offered itself to me: *Unreal people never exercise benevolence. They exist in the interim.*

There was a poem in the newspaper today. Monsieur and I read it together:

28

It's tough to be doing what you don't
find easy
it's easy it's really easy
to do what you want
the body takes the lead
over the head
the heart swings the whip
the body is hip
the head is dead

I expected Teste to fly out in a rage. "Teste" means *head* (in my opinion) and I thought the poem insulted this part of the body. Instead, Teste was rather pleased. He said that Teste does not mean *head* and it never meant *testes* but it will always mean *taste.*

I thought I noticed a spark of eroticism in Teste. But I was mistaken. He was merely sticking his tongue in and out of his mouth to see how far it would go.

Last night, as we lay on our bunks, Monsieur Teste told me his opinion of truth. He told me of the high regard he had for the truth. It is precisely because of this regard that he lied all the time. But, in his own words:

"I lie in order to hide the truth from morons. It's the morons I have to keep in the dark. Did you ever notice that when a moron steps into the light from a, let's say, dark room, the light doesn't seem to matter any more. The moron brings the darkness with him. All morons carry dark rooms. Why did the moron tiptoe past the medicine cabinet? There are people who claim that enlightening the morons is the greatest thing anyone can do. These people are morons themselves. Crypto-morons. And it's because there are crypto-morons around that one has to hide the truth at all cost. The crypto-morons love to get to the truth in order to pass it on to the obvious morons who then proceed to draw conclusions. This is how you can tell a moron from a non-moron. The morons always draw conclusions. Whenever there are more than three humans in a room the moron among them will reveal himself by drawing conclusions. This is all detailed in my pamphlet: *How to Catch a Moron*. Some morons are so eager to draw conclusions that they don't even wait for something to draw conclusions from. They pull them out of thin air. These particular morons are not dangerous. They draw their conclusions and, if left alone, they will not bother anybody. But if they have even a single fan, watch out! It's the morons who work over a bit of material, however, that are to be most feared. Scientists are the foremost example of this type of moron ..."

Δ

April 18
I must admit, after he'd gone to sleep, I became worried about Monsieur Teste. He might not survive his sojourn in America. He'd barely been here five days and he had already begun to abandon large portions of the language. I could not for example, induce Teste to say "Pepsi." That he hadn't yet abandoned the entire American language was due, no doubt, only to the resiliency of a few abstract words for sentiment which weren't much in vogue and on the backs of which Teste hoped to slide unobserved by the everawake collectivism of the language.

"Don't worry," Teste said when I dropped my angst on him next day. "My real ally is the resiliency of subjunctives. I am not, properly speaking, abandoning the language, I am merely watching the language abandon itself after it passes through the torture chamber in my lower belly."

Good for the subjunctives! They had a lot of nerve. I

would hate to lose Teste at this critical stage in our relationship.

He didn't say a word all afternoon. We took a walk and, thinking to please him, I pointed out several objects and repeated their names like a child: "Trolley car. Salami. Chevrolet."

I knew what he was thinking. He thought that I was deliberately setting out to destroy the uniqueness of objects by naming them.

When we got home he gave me a demonstration of how to deal with names. He pointed to the coffee maker and said, "floor," to the fruit bowl and said, "foot." Then he looked smug and satisfied. Since there were no morons around I felt insulted. I'm not a moron. I know a fruit bowl from a foot. The strangeness of our state hit me. Here I was, stepping lightly through polysyllables in order not to insult him and with every insult he dealt me I felt myself to be more and more successful. The more he insulted *me* the less capable I was of insulting *him*. He was denying the laws of communication.

In the evening we had visitors. The swinger couple Johnson. The two of them are the embodied American principle: *Both Sides of the Question.* This principle, taken from television, took in the Johnsons the appalling form of a tremendously fast rush to make decisions followed immediately by counter-decisions. An evening with the Johnsons amounted to nothing in the end because as soon as the Johnsons did something they analyzed it instantly. They were swingers who swung away from each other. As soon as the male Johnson took of his clothes, the female Johnson put on her coat, and, as neither Teste nor I did anything, he hastily put his clothes back on as the female Johnson walked out of hers. As soon as she took her clothes off I took off mine and looked as she put hers back on only to be followed by the male Johnson dutifully taking his off at which point I put mine back on and watched as the process swung inevitably toward futility, all this time keeping an eye on Teste who opened the refrigerator door and began what now amounted to an addiction with him: staring into the depths of it.

It was, I thought, a delightful way to spend an evening but Monsieur thought differently:

"You've been doing the wrong thing," he said to me. "You've been trying to be human. It is better to be a root or a stalk. The point is that you can't trust the world with your understanding of it."

"But how then," I said in utter astonishment, "can you entrust the world to your understanding?"

"You can't," he said and laughed—the first time I have ever seen him laughing because, if you remember, he never laughed with Valéry.

In the middle of the night I got up, careful not to wake Monsieur, and I began to write in my journal. But he woke up and spoiled my pleasure.

"Aha!" he said. "You don't believe that the world exists!"

"What do you mean?" I feigned, knowing only too well what he meant.

"Writing stands squarely in opposition to the world; it is an addition to perception, an ordering process, a way of forcing unnatural connections, it is an inaccurate description for the sake of sanity ... You're afraid of going mad ... You think that you're allowing visions to surface while in reality you are putting a verbal lid on your unconscious ... You are perpetuating a system on which the mind bases its arrogance against nature ..."

He was absolutely right. I burnt my notebook.

Δ

April 19

American poetry came to lunch today. Many poets were missing but I made do with the ones who were there. The poets there were mostly from the New York School, a school which I attended in the hope of finding out the simple secrets the ignorance of which so handicaps a foreigner in America. These poets knew a great number of simple secrets which they spread around generously, unlike the rest of the schools which bored me to death with their European pretensions. I had learned, among others, such notions as "Clear the range!" (Ted Berrigan), "If it fits in your mouth, it's natural!" (Ted Berrigan), "Take it easy!" (Anne Waldman), "What's up, Doc!" (Tom Veitch), "Why not Egypt?" (Dick Gallup).

For lunch I cooked a whole favorite menu of mine composed of fifteen dishes:

Entrée
New poetry movements. (I am an expert in these because I made up most of them. Aktup, Metabolism, the Bowel Movement and Syllogism. All have me as one of the founders. I have also furthered Actualism, Essentialism and Infantilism. American poets, with their pragmatic sense of craft and their ferocious drive toward respectability, are afraid of labels. This is because labels, traditionally, have been put on them by critics. So, at some point in American poetry, there began a race to elude critics. The widest range of cultural eclecticism was brought into play in every poem in order that the poet place him or herself beyond

criticism. The exceptions to this are the conceptually inclined, who paste on their own labels and elaborate their philosophy at leisure. See Isidore Isou's Lettrisme through to Aram Saroyan's Minimalism.)

Soup

Pure meaninglessness does not exist, only misdirected intentions. Nobody has yet written a perfectly obscure poem. Sit down, Clark Coolidge. Is it because nobody has yet committed a perfectly arbitrary act? I would think that a complete student of the abstract does not exist either, because he or she would have a body, hence a cliché. In the form of a body everybody inhabits a cliché. The question, naturally, is: Is the Universe arbitrary? And the answer, depending on your prejudices, commits you to a cliché. But nothing, *nothing* can stop you from reshuffling it, regardless of point of view.

Pâté de foie gras

Ted Berrigan and Tom Veitch.

Ted Berrigan (who has Dada and is basically innocent) reshuffles the language we speak every day in order to present himself to us disguised as us, but from an unexpected angle, that of hearing our own words in his mouth on a page cut in talk patterns. Tom Veitch (who has God and is essentially anxious) reshuffles concepts like death, love and sex in order that they leave their conceptual skins to throw us into fits of self-examination. Tom uses a lofty and aristocratic place from which things are small enough to be manipulated but big enough to scare the wits out of us. Ted, on the contrary, is possessed by one instrument, his voice. Ted is a purer writer than Tom because the philosophy of a situation only interests him if it is incomplete, i.e., human. Tom reaches for harmony with higher forces and is, in this sense, a

34

magician. Purity, one sees, is really the degree of dedication to one's obsession. Ted is obsessed with voice, Tom with God, and each of them does it by shifting things out of their conventional places.

Gravy
I see reality through a grid.
Each little square in the grid is an action
preceded by *Don't*.
Outside the grid is the world of *Do*
so if I were looking in from the outside
I would be so busy I wouldn't even
perceive the grid
hence no poems

A Medium-Sized Suckling Pig with an Apple in His Mouth
There are poets with a distaste for reality.
These poets are insane, meaning that they have no defined territory toward which to reshuffle their world, so they wander through their imaginations and bring out things that, on first sight, nobody has ever seen. These poets have to be intelligent, however, and if they are, they usually notice that what they brought back resembles some quite common thing that everybody sees every day. At this point, they form a method by bringing intelligence to bear on romanticism. These poets have no style. They are mechanics of celestial pornography. Michael Brownstein is one of these. I have never seen anything of his in which a subtle apology isn't made to some secret search. All his works say: *Look, I am sorry, dear God, but as I was coming through the stratosphere half of you burned up so I put a shoe in the missing place.* John Ashbery does the same thing but he keeps his terms abstract. This is a terrible disadvantage because abstracts tend to make one re-examine one's shakiest assumptions and,

if this were done, it would take twelve years to correctly read a John Ashbery poem.

Steaming Spuds
The search for meaning is an instinct, especially if the poem suggests that meaning should occur. But no poem, as said before, can help *but* suggest it, because language is a machine of control. The language of poets like Brownstein and Ashbery is, usually, international. The Surrealists were of the same mind and ended up creating the first international poetry idiom.

Fruit: Peaches, Melons and Blackberries
It is a monument to the stupidity of American criticism that all references to the New York School have, so far, spoken of a collective voice when, in truth, it is precisely the New York School that has brought the largest number of methods, attitudes and trends into a scene dominated by uniformity and boredom. There are at least fifteen poets in this set who embody essentially fifteen major philosophies.

Drugs: Cocaine, Yoga and Pot
The politico–literal–sexual waterfall of Anne Waldman, John Giorno, Tom Clark and Lewis MacAdams. In this case, the personalities of the poets are in constant demand and the steady intensity becomes a special therapy, models of which could be made and sold at political conventions.

Napoleons, Rhum Babas, Eclairs and Baklava
Informational accumulation in view of a massive collapse of the senses; Peter Schjeldahl's monomaniacal recording of dreams, Scott Cohen's fascination with large statistics, Alice Notley's collection of bizarre colors and rare flowers, Kenneth Koch's lyrical efforts to eat the vocabulary, etc.

36

Cigars
Aram Saroyan and Joyce Holland. Minimalism and Essentialism.

Coffee
The wonder world of Joe Brainard. This is the Look what I found! school and is, uniquely, American.

Honey
A school of cultural refinement organized around obscure but exciting quarrels with all kinds of Alexandrian poses, eclectic decadence and transcendental irony. (Transcendental irony is, naturally, the opposite of bourgeois or proletarian irony. It is irony with the superior term in another world.) Tony Towle, Carter Ratcliff, Ron Padgett (sometimes), Kenward Elmslie, Bill Berkson.

A Final Joint
None of these exist in a pure state. See Dick Gallup.

Whipped Cream
There is a lot more. Some resident critics would now be in order. Poets, as a rule, see themselves as defined by their works and the critical intelligence brought to bear on their contemporaries is almost always oral. America is, however, in great need of some new directions and a translation of these poetries into easy-to-follow computer programs could, conceivably, save the world a hundred years of sterility.

Everybody relished the food immensely and when we were all full, we began to sing songs made on the spur of the moment and write collaborations.

Later, Teste and I washed the enormous pile of dishes in silence. Throughout the evening, Teste had been terribly quiet, unimpressed with all the gaiety around him. I did not want to press him for an opinion of the evening but, shortly after, he said, "I find collaboration like youth: chatty and arrogant."

Pressed for clarification, Monsieur said the following (which I am going to use as an introduction to the collaborations of the previous evening): "As the Nazis knew, collaboration helps the Empire. It is a sad reflection on our times that instead of fucking, people collaborate. Do you know how many drugs you consumed last night?"

"No," I said, "I don't remember."

"The hipper among your readers ..."

"The *hipper*?!"

"The heap there, of readers, will, no doubt, be able to identify what drugs went into each one of these sad works and, god knows, there was hashish, speed, coke, opium in alcohol, alcohol in glasses, etc., going in at the rate of two grams per poem."

"The Surrealists," I said, "like the late New York School ..."

"Ended up dead and in books."

"Collaboration was quite the rage in Alexandria too in the sixth century ... Alexandrine verse originated in two heads ..."

"Which goes to prove that, being homosexual, the great Alexandrine writers convinced the better-looking boys to pick up the warm pen and finish their thoughts ..."

Teste smirked and, without apparent connection, added savagely, "I am *not* from Romania."

"Each one's Teste is from wherever each one is," I said, but he didn't laugh.

"I am an embodiment of the third person," he said.

"The hell you are," I countered. "You're the second or nothing."

We had our first quarrel.

"Big words are the mark of small minds," he said.
"Up your ass."

Tonight we made up. We looked at the immense sky filled with stars and felt at peace with each other. Teste did not need any prompting to feel at peace but I had to repeat to myself William Carlos Williams' famous lines:

I have discovered that most of
the beauties of travel are due to
the strange hours we keep to see them

before I too felt a cosmic grace and boundless happiness. My heart, at 3 AM was full and in harmony.

Δ

April 20
This morning I realized the difference between me and Teste. He is at least twenty years older than I am because he is French. I overheard him murmuring, as he was shaving:

"Understanding is for old folks. Young ones should fight."
    I can't say I disagree. But can you trust the old fogies?

"Being as full of ideas as you are," said Monsieur, disdainfully, "you will not have failed to notice that I never think about sex."
    "I have noticed," I answered curtly. "At your age ... I understand ..."
    "You understand nothing. I am the opposite of sex."

We went to the ocean.
    "Isn't it beautiful?" I said.

"No," growled Teste. "It's obvious. I like my beauty elusive, a little perverse if you please ..."

I was beginning to wish Teste would leave. Slowly, a hooded executioner rose from my archetypal pool bearing the shiny tools of his trade: insults, conspiracies and anxiety. I knew, however, that I could not, at this time, execute Teste without eliminating myself in the bargain. I proposed a vacation instead.

To my surprise, Monsieur agreed. He was already taking walks by himself, he would simply prolong one of these and walk for a whole day and night. He packed up very carefully the three items he carried and left without words.

Δ

April 21
A blissful day. Not a thought. I had steak and eggs for breakfast.

Δ

April 22
"Money," I said. "Money, Teste." He didn't understand. "I can't afford to keep you any longer. I ran out of money."

Teste regarded me, squinting. "What you mean to say is, you are afraid of what I *think* about money?"

"I know you *don't* think about money. You merely understand its principles. You know, for example, how it operates, what it's used for and how it can be transferred from one pile onto another. You are a brilliant economist, Teste, but what I'm saying is: I don't have a penny. We need cash."

"OK," said Teste. "Here is what you do. You go into

a big department store and buy a steam iron or a power drill. You pay for these, go to your car, put the drill or the iron on the front seat and then return to the store with your bag and receipt. In there you get another steam iron power drill, walk up to the cashier and say, 'I'm sorry. I just remembered that I already have one. I would like my money back. Unfortunately, I don't seem able to find the receipt. But you remember me, I was here a moment ago.' She'll give you money; you go back to a similar department store where, since you have the receipt, you can get more money."

I was astonished. Monsieur Teste, Monsieur Teste, where did you pick up that kind of detail? That is utterly unlike you.

"I picked that up," said Teste in answer to my thoughts, "in Monterey. I like scams. Scams are forms of relaxation."

And think of it, only yesterday I had been tired of him. And today, today, he started talking native. Simple secrets, "scams" he calls them. Our relationship was squarely back to its original purpose: accelerating my enjoyment of simple secrets. Which is not to say that Monsieur Teste is practical. He is not. He is an aristocrat. I must describe his face in case you missed him: like a doll torn up by traffic, his face bears the scars of a thousand typewriters. But over it, a sort of plastic mold has settled, fixing his features in place, a mask of serenity. An aristocrat does not move without reason. I need Teste. He is the logic of my childhood. I must defend my life from prose.

"Which direction should we go?" I asked him in the morning as we were about to take a rare common walk.

A cement mixer, across the street, began its infernal whirring. Monsieur listened intently.

"It sounds like it wants to hurl us north."

Monsieur liked to leave the impression that his decisions were dictated by the advice of inanimate objects in his surroundings. Perhaps they were. After all, he had *really* listened to that cement mixer.

Teste has a vast understanding of literature. Like a cement mixer his mind can hurl together disparate fragments of various books to create the continuous paste of interest on which his presence is founded. People always ask him, he told me, how is it that he loves writers that he, only a week before, castigated for cheapness and stupidity. That is, Monsieur Teste replies, because a week ago he hadn't read them. "I was castigating them for not coming to my attention. There is no reason in the world why I should love somebody I never read!"

He generally manages to give a psychological slant to his knowledge, which is a pity, really, considering that what makes reading great is lack of editorial attitudes.

We quarrelled over fiction. Fiction, in my opinion, should divest itself of psychology. Description is really psychology so, please, no description. Dialogue is generally nonsense so, please, don't say anything.

What remains then? Why, the subjunctives, of course.

Teste heartily agreed but said this: "Do you like people or not?"

"Well, I do, sort of ... of course ..."

"There you are," he said. "You need psychology to eliminate the threat to your reputation."

I really don't know what to make of Teste. On one hand he says that it is better to be a root or a stalk. On the other he recognizes the human dimension. Then I

42

remembered what he thinks of writing, in general, and I realized: my God, he is tremendously real, he is over-real, he is here and oh, perhaps he has no plan, after all.

I was mad. But Teste had already curled up in a chair, with the refrigerator door open, staring into what to him must have amounted to the heart of Universe.

Δ

April 23
I woke in panic. I thought, for a moment, that Teste had packed his swift bag and left in the middle of the night. I was happy to hear him say, "Your genes are like the layers of an onion. None of your ancestors had enough imagination to make himself God."

"Actually," I began tentatively, "my grandmother ..."

"Cut the crap," he said. "There is no purposefulness in you."

"You mean purpose?"

"No. I mean 'purposefulness,' like stature. I have watched you get up in the morning. Every morning is different. Sometimes you wake up feet first, sometimes you lift your head up and, at times, you feel the air with your hand like a cheap viola in search of a Nazi."

"You mean—no consistency?"

"I mean well," he said.

"And yet," I replied, pointing to the piles of manuscripts lining the tops of our heads on shelves set high enough so the cat wouldn't piss on them, "there is consistency in those. I want to tell the world about the prejudices of my time and how my personality reacted to them."

"Ha ha ha," said Teste, "You don't even claim resistance. Or distance. You are a lost soul."

Looking like a bishop, Monsieur joined his hands and

put the mitre of his tangled fingers in my face. They smelled, slightly, of garlic and asparagus.

In order to prove my humanity, consistency and reality I worked all afternoon on a *Dictionary of Received Ideas* to spring on Teste when he returned from the walk he had now gotten into the consistent habit of taking by himself.

I quote from the rather lengthy work:

If you look at fire long you'll pee in bed.
The underground's been forced there by mean weights.
The excess of reason makes monsters of boredom.
White flowers are funereal.
Black flowers are erotic.
Academia is taxation without imagination.
Carfax Anthrax.
God is partial to ferociousness.
Birds filled with lead.
A sense of humor is a sense of authority.
Closeups don't have any sense of humor.
Truth sits in an autobiography like a bird dog in an
  underground hospital.
The Exterminator is after the facts.
A man's name is his cage.
A miracle is the shortest explanation.
Intuition is the daughter of miracles.
Baby irony is transcendental.
Geriatric irony is worldly.
Worlds meet at ironic junctions: the resulting clash is a
  miracle.
Mommy means I want, Money means I don't need her.
Heraldry is structural horniness.
The Penis is a barricade.
Poetry is mistranslation.
A discovery is followed by silence not applause.

I wrote hundreds of these but when Teste came home I didn't dare show them to him for fear he would open the refrigerator door and say nothing. Teste is not rude, he is just superior. Without him, I wouldn't even know there are better things in this world.

Teste is a gourmet. I won't mention all the things he brings home from his walks: fragments of old fire escapes, snails without shells (slugs), dirty socks, meteors.

Δ

April 24
Today, as Teste lay silently on his bunk looking at an incipient spiderweb, I planted myself by the door and broached the subject of insults. Every day since he had arrived, I had become more and more insulting, yet he did not seem to notice. I had broken my own rules a hundred times. I had done him endless little bad turns. I had made him gulp America while I held his jaws open. I had been a miserable tormentor to this man whose sublime dislike of history made him a saint. I had been horrible and yet, like a flower enjoying the crassness of a florist, he had withstood my grossness with a lighter and lighter head. He must like it here, I thought. And if he does it will be *I* who must move out ... I am the one carrying dissatisfaction. Teste is spotless. He has grown more real while I have grown more insecure.

I blurted, "Teste, mon cher, I think it is impossible for me to insult you."

"You will find a way," he said.

"I'm stuffed up with thoughts like a swan with pomegranates," I confessed.

Feigning innocence, which he despised, he said: "You sure know your Latin!"

The funniest thing happened. Teste was coming home when, suddenly, two burly men grabbed his thin arms, pushed him into a doorway and emptied his pockets. He had nothing on him except the mathematical instrument at the bottom of the little velvet case in his vest pocket.

"What's this?" one of the men said, holding the tiny tentacles of solid brass to the street light.

"Allow me," said Teste. He took the instrument from the man's hand and began turning the black tentacles.

"Hey," said the other man, "I hope that thing ain't ..."

He finished with a howl of pain. His companion began to also howl and as they howled Teste stepped neatly through the thin part in the middle of their pain loop and exited into the sunlight where a wino greeted him.

"How did you do it?" I asked.

"Simple," said Teste. "They were looking into my eyes."

"And?"

"They understood."

Δ

April 25

I have chanced upon the ultimate insult. I will put Monsieur Teste in a novel. It had been Paul Valéry's way of subduing his Teste and I have no proof that it won't work.

I mapped my attack or "my novel." My novel would have no relationships. This is difficult since not only characters but also words stand in certain relationships to each other. It is in the nature of relationships to delegate ownership to the wrong party. Of course, only *natural* relationships are at ease with their possessions. *Unnatural* relationships are insecure and therefore amenable to my eventual dismantling of their territories. Could there possibly be unnatural relationships between characters that

46

know each other? No. Their acquaintance legitimizes their relationship. The first rule of my novel would be then: the characters must not know each other. The way to do this is to hide them from each other in ways too ingenious for them to discover. What is the most ingenious thing on earth? Ah, the Cathedrals, of course. They are unsurpassed in ingenuity. I will build my novel like a cathedral and I will place my characters at the intersection points of the naves on elliptical orbits so that no matter how hard they try they cannot intersect. I will then place Monsieur Teste at a corner of a north inner square so that he can look up and see the whole circle of characters above but will not be able to reach them until the circle is squared. And that, I knew, would take a while.

What an insult!

Δ

April 26
The structural design I was looking for was printed in an old *National Geographic*. I was studying it at breakfast this morning when Teste, with uncharacteristic curiosity, peered at it.

"Ha ha ha," he laughed, "I see that you've reached Point Terminus."

I said nothing.

"I will tell you a parable. A rich man had a servant who annoyed him. The rich man could not very well kill his servant because he was a civilized rich man and he abhorred strong-arm methods."

"Hmmm."

"So he decided to take his servant with him for a visit to the Labyrinth in Crete where the minotaur was imprisoned. He planned to lose his servant in the Labyrinth. If the man could not find the exit he would blame his own stupidity."

"Right," I said, guessing the end. "The servant got out, but the rich man was lost."

"Wrong," said Teste. "They were lost together and had to keep each other company until they died."

Ugh! I at once scrapped the idea of losing Monsieur in a novel. I recognized the parable.

THE BIG CHANGE

At this point I will dispense with dates because the subsequent events did not belong to time, *do* not belong to time. Roughly, The Big Change would, if the chroniclers insist, last between April 27 and March 6, making Monsieur Teste's American sojourn exactly twenty-one days long, but I must say to the chroniclers' eternal confusion that not only does time have nothing to do with it but neither do I or Teste for that matter.

I prepared The Big Change with the thoroughness of a fat student preparing for a diet exam. For weeks, just under the skin of my consciousness, my chemistry prepared to flood the outline of the world with a dazzling substance. On April 28, the outline was filled, time evacuated the chamber like hydrogen escaping the balloon and The Big Change reared nervously in readiness.

Since my identification papers were in the disorder proper to a shadowy alien I borrowed a friend's ID and credit card. Under his name I rented a car which I didn't know how to drive. I got behind the wheel and ignoring my ignorance I drove to the house, I packed Monsieur's bag (he was out walking) and I settled to wait for him as an invisible crayon drew black circles under my eyes. He returned at 6:15, stepping, as it were, straight out of a splendid San Francisco sunset pained by Alice C., *circa* 1970.

"Entrez," I said, sliding the car door open like an involuntary wing.

He entered and we were on our way. I turned on the car radio and this song escaped the FM band to complement the sunset, amplify my triumph and underscore Teste's feigned bewilderment:

> *We're on our way*
> *Where to I couldn't say*

We were going, I shouted to Monsieur, to the source of all my problems, to the place where boredom had nearly killed me, we were going to Heaven or, if you prefer, we were returning to the country in the wild depths of which my treehouse stood with the lingering shape of the postmistress still darkening the window. We were going to the place where my cry for help had formed the telegram by means of which humans always telegraph their gods that they are in trouble.

I was taking Monsieur Teste to a place unlike any other: the countryside of northern California, that gothic slumber of prehistoric ferns slowly shaking their scales upward toward trees so tall the clouds had to tear their bellies going over, that place of mysterious murders, bodies floating down the swollen river, sudden red moons, hysterical and ancient inhabitants exchanging gasoline bombs with new but brutal settlers. We were going to the Wild Wild West, AD 1974, ad infinitum, ad nauseam, ad lib.

Up to this point, which was so small no light went through it, I had matched Teste's knowledge of the world bead by bead. I had been born in a city; Teste had, too. I had devised the coarse grains of my wit in coffee houses where Teste had his made into coffee. I had known sex in the shadow of libraries whose shadow Teste was. I had walked to the store at 4:00 AM for cigarettes as Teste had in the hope of being the first one to spot 5:00 AM as it dawned on the clock. Our experience, different as it may have been, had, until this point, sprung from a common landscape like a lion and a man from a formica sphinx. But now I was about to take Monsieur to the place where the crack first appeared on my soul map.

As the first signs of the country began to appear as ruined barns, stray dirigibles, hitchhikers, cows and enormous gold onions, I accelerated and at the speed of 150 miles per hour we effectuated our entry into this world.

A screech of brakes warned me that I had stopped for a hitchhiker.

She threw her gear in and swiftly followed suit.

"Where to?" I said.

"I don't care," said she, "as long as it's out of Sonoma County."

That, it was.

"American geography is bizarre," said Teste. "How can anyone go to a place the roads don't go to?"

"One can't," said I.

"You two," said the hitchhiker, "sound like grapes." I saw no connection but Monsieur did.

"We are grapes," said he.

"Don't get squashed," she said.

"We will," said Teste.

"I wish I was in love," said the hitchhiker. "I want to have a baby."

I care for love. I think that at the core of the universe a glowing lump of love sends its radiance through tremendous obstacles into our hearts.

"Do you have a baby?" Teste asked me, knowing only too well that I had no such thing.

"No."

I didn't have a baby. He didn't have a baby, of course.

"Will you have my baby?" I said to the hitchhiker.

"That depends."

"On whom?"

50

"On your stock," she said. "I will have nothing but the best stock."

"It's good stock," I said. "My ancestors were terribly particular about their stock, they even issued stock certificates on their continuing 99 percent."

"What kind of stock?" she said.

"A rising stock."

"What's your stock?" she said to Monsieur who, throughout this exchange, had fallen asleep.

"I have no stock," replied Monsieur. "I come from nowhere. I'm a clear soup."

"Even clear soup is a stock," the perky vagabond said.

"What kind of stock," said Teste judiciously, "when it didn't even start with water but with ink?"

"Ink soup," she said. "Yeek."

"There you have it," I said, "I'm the sensible stock."

"OK," she said.

I was very happy. Now I would show Teste. I will have a baby in the totally baffling wilderness with an utter stranger. If he finds my reasons unimpeachable he will have to capitulate. And if he capitulates, I will stay in America, get my American citizenship and enlist in the army.

It was not to be.

We arrived, over tortuous roads, assiduous turns, pindrops, cliffhangers, curlicues, mud spirals, and twisted valley bottoms, to the little cabin which I had occupied until I had been seized by boredom. Faithfully, my dark cabin in the deep woods had kept itself for me wrapped for protection in vast networks of spider web. Everything was where it had been, ready to go to where it hadn't.

It hadn't, I am sure, been to the place where the three of us were soon to take it. It had never had more than one inhabitant and an occasional stranger. Its creaking floorboards had never supported the weight of three humans since the day it had been built. Its ceiling had never felt the warmth of three headtops, its walls had never been touched by six hands, its doorknobs had never been turned by thirty fingers, its one bed had never held three full heads of hair and its septic tank had never received an average of nineteen to twenty-seven bowel movements a week. But cabins, like question marks, have infinite patience. We felt at home. At least I did and Ellen, I am sure, did too. Teste had no home.

"Can imaginary characters have real babies?" a peasant once asked Voltaire.

"Of course," the great man said. "It's their way of facing reality."

Δ

First Night   (it is always night)
Monsieur Teste makes a big fire in the woodstove, sits on the floor in front of it, folds in two and goes to sleep.

Ellen takes off her clothes. Her shadow is on the wall.

Her shadow on the wall is pierced by the stars in the window. Her flesh on the bed is pierced by the branch from my body. Flowers fall off and some fruit too.

The fire dies out. We sleep. The wind howls.

Δ

Second Night   (it is always night)
Teste points to the viciously full Scorpionic moon filling our little cabin window to the maximum, and says:

"Reason is an institution of the city like garbage trucks."

"Everything here is done to the maximum, Monsieur."

"*Maximum*," shouts Ellen.

"What?"

"That's the name of our baby!"

"No," I say, "definitely not. He will carry the impossible on his passport."

"First of all it's a 'she,' second it's *my* baby."

"My stock."

"No," says Teste, "it's my baby."

"Huh?" Both Ellen and I stare at him as the stars pour in and we circle Teste considering where to bite.

"Yes," says Monsieur, "one can only have what one understands."

"Are you implying," I say, filling with bloodlust while a savage rhythm emanates from Ellen like a frenzied shaman drum, "that we don't know what we are doing?

"We are human," I whisper viciously.

"We know love!" Ellen and I hiss in unison as the moon, unable to control itself any longer, breaks the window and fills the room with the torn-up cosmic shroud, enveloping Teste in a cold light in the midst of which he stands like a lock of hair in a gold medallion.

Δ

Third Night
Maximum was born. It was an easy birth. I attended Ellen with half-pronounced words, comforting sounds, hisses and animal will. Teste did nothing. He looked into the fire ignoring the extraordinary physical and magical storm that had broken in the cabin. Even the trees outside rustled with the awareness of extraordinary events. A sudden rain fell. Animals pressed their warm bodies against the door. Maximum appeared headfirst so it was a while before we could tell its sex. It was a boy but something indefinite suggested a girl. A violin, its beginning shrouded in mystery, passed its bow through the exact center of my heart. I held the wet child in the moonlight.

"We have created a perfect hermaphrodite," Teste said.

I did not, at first, believe him, but as the night deepened and the exhausted mother fell asleep with Maximum on her chest, it began to dawn on me that, after all, Teste might be right.

Maximum had been born with silky black hair on its head, two oval eyes surveying a tiny yet unmistakably feminine mouth and its tiny nipples suggested already the inevitable blossoming forth of a female's breasts. So strong was the impression that, at once, I was swept off my feet by religious fervor and I thanked the forest for helping us produce our equivalent, as it were, of a unicorn. I knew that it was the wish of forests, of, indeed, the whole world of nature, to bring from its depths constant reaffirmations of its basic unity. These reaffirmations were continually frustrated by the tendency of things to view the world in terms of their dominant characteristics. Thus the obviousness of dominant characteristics carried the ball most of the time and definite pronouns were born into the world. But when dominant characteristics had their will turned off by a deep understanding of nature, the perfect came forth: the unicorn, the hermaphrodite.

It was something worth feeling mystical about, but Monsieur thought that god was a waste of energy. "You get a feeling of gratitude and what do you do with it? You throw it to the winds. Instead, you could be using it to make love."

"To make love with you?"

"No, no ... Not 'make love' like 'fucking' but make love like wine out of grapes. Gratitude is a kind of wine grape. You squash it into your heart instead of wasting it in prayer and, lo and behold, there are thirty gallons of love."

"What other kinds of grapes ... er ... wine ... love are there?"

"There are infinite varieties of love grapes depending on your innocence. There is, par exemple," continued Monsieur, looking into the fire which was now burning out, "the love grape called 'compassion.' This is a hard grape to make love from. It's also a hard grape to come by. This grape is usually found in weak old people who don't have the energy any longer to squeeze it for wine. There are professional grape squeezers who, even though they can't make love themselves, can help you squeeze these grapes. Then there is a kind of love grape called 'The Wonderful' and this makes champagne. The Wonderful is easy to come by but it's hard to see it when you do. The problem is, see, that The Wonderful does not flower in an average mentality"

"This is wonderful, Monsieur Teste," I said.

"Now take that unfinished prayer," he said, "and turn it back into your grateful heart where you have just caught The Wonderful and squeeze!"

I did what he said. I squeezed the love grape The Wonderful with all the might of the not inconsiderable weight of a half unspoken prayer. I don't think the pressure was nearly enough because love grape The Wonderful kept its juices.

"Harder, young fellow, harder!" bellowed Teste.

I threw my weight at the heart of the halfprayer and sank into The Wonderful like an ice-breaker and this time, yes, such a miracle, this time, yes, this time around oh The Wonderful popped its multiskins and exploded in a symphony of juice, leaving the arteries burning. Filled to the inside of my palate and soles with travelling love grape juice I could hear my hemoglobin already beginning to ferment it.

"How long before it's wine?" I asked breathlessly.

"Anywhere from thirty minutes to thirty years."

I sat there drowning in The Wonderful, keeping vigil

over an intensely satisfied and peacefully sleeping female and a marvelous hermaphrodite. I stood vigil all night and, in the morning, when the first rays of the sun touched the face of the mother awakening her, I felt the beginnings of wine or love, if you prefer, stirring in the millions of bottles in my body.

Maximum awoke and stared vaguely at it.

Δ

Fourth Night
We found a fifteen-year-old child in the woods. He wore nothing but a loincloth and from his appearance it was evident that he had been raised by savage animals. The wild child avoided us at first, following us from a safe distance, but when Teste brought forth his box of graham crackers the child leaped in front of him and pulled the box from his hands. At the cabin we washed him and from behind the grime a most beautiful face appeared. The wild child had an oval face surmounted by two brilliant eyes selected by Goya. His mouth had been picked by El Greco and his arms and legs had been ripped from Pericles-era statues and blended into the art-deco flawlessness of a torso molded by Beardsley. He was, in one word, perfect. He was so terribly sensual, the window molding began to melt and, at his slightest gesture, the pots and the plates floated gently from their shelves and landed at an angle on the softest minutes of dust. He exuded harmony. His breasts complemented his male organ with a subtle blending of textures. Merely by touching it I had an indescribable orgasm. An angelic faintness overtook me.

Then the wild child spoke in accents which could have been learned at the court of King Arthur, "My name is Maximum (he pronounced this in Latin, accent on the second syllable). My father is a shiny vegetable who

56

attained, at the moment of my conception, an unbreakable nature and turned into a shiny mineral. My mother is a believer in 'Ask and ye shall receive' and she has made the treachery of the interested ? into the main factor of her life. My uncle Oscar, on the other hand, gives me all the candy I want and takes me up and down in ship cruises across marvelous territories. He makes quite a bit of money in the process because I am a prostitute-saint and in some ports they have built effigies of me and people fight for the right to touch my private parts."

Everything became clear to me now. Teste had taken my child to foreign countries and had pimped him out. I was furious. I turned at once to face Monsieur with a wrench in my hand.

He looked at me through half-open lids. He looked at me abstractly, he looked at my quizzically. I put the wrench down and took refuge in a mean thought. Teste is not important any longer. What with all the responsibility I now have to raise my child and the financial considerations issuing therefrom, I can't possibly have any further use for Teste. He was revoked. An apple wormed through and through. A name on an expired passport. A question mark in a field of daisies. He never did any work! He was a pimp!

It was very late at night. I slept huddled next to the wild child we found in the woods and I had countless orgasms.

Δ

Fifth Night
The natives came. They came softly, almost invisible at first. They surrounded the house quietly like guerrillas. Then some of the more courageous ones came inside. They were, in general, a highly inarticulate bunch with fear written on their faces. They made one think of the distorted mailing

labels that come out of a fouled linotype. Behind them, other natives, armed with pitchforks and grins of such stupidity it was hard to believe one's eyes, gushed forth amidst a geyser of proto-syllables.

They had come to see Maximum. I showed it to them as it lay there sound asleep on the small bed. They didn't see it.

"Is he shitting us?" said the fireman to Teste who was ignoring him.

"Isee eveh!" hissed the postmistress.

"Gentlemen," said Teste, "I think you must be warned that I deal roughly with impolite punks."

"He does," I hastened to affirm, "he really does."

"Yeah," said the fireman, clicking his spurs and disengaging the steel axe from his belt, "let's see, focker!"

Teste extracted a glowing coal from the stove and threw it in the fireman's face who immediately began to roll on the floor, his eyes glowing, a three-alarm fire beginning in his body. Maximum awoke and, seeing what was happening, shouted, *"Uncle O!"* jumping, at the same time, on the auto mechanic's back, pulling, with an expert gesture, a little lid. Gas gushed out of the man's body, felling him.

The rest of the natives suddenly raised their eyes upward and falling on their knees began a heart-rending *Te Deum*. They had seen Maximum.

"The lower organisms," said Teste, "can see only if their sight is awakened by violence."

It was true, of course. Still, I prefer peace to pedagogy.

Δ

Sixth Night
Ellen returned. At midnight. The day after the birth of her child she had gone into space.

I told her how Teste had pimped out our child, how the natives had come, how I felt and what I wanted. I told her, in short, of history.

"No, no," she said, "it was I who, disguised as Uncle Oscar, sold our child for pennies in foreign ports."

"Impossible," I exclaimed. "It would be inconsistent with your character."

"Character, my ass. Men always think that women exist to listen to history. I despise history. I have inconsistencies. I am human."

"There are no inconsistencies," Teste butted in. "Inconsistencies are new characters."

"Which is what we need around here," said Ellen ominously. "Some new characters."

I could not stop what happened next. Ellen rose above Teste like a giant bird. Monsieur withstood the assault with aplomb by making himself entirely malleable like soft tar. Ellen began to mold him. She made crenellated punch craters in his chest, she twisted his nose so that the tip of it ended between his eyes, she put his ears on his nipples, she emptied his eye sockets and put the eyeballs in his scrotum, she split his penis in two and put each portion in one of the eye sockets, she wove his legs and arms in an Inca blanket of vast dimensions, she shuffled his hips and in each of his bones she planted a different flower, she did other minor and major adjustments until the proud figure of the sad European aristocrat looked exactly like the potbellied stove in which the faint fire stirred. The two stoves, the metal and the flesh one, now stood facing each other, hungering for their specific fuels. The wood stove would, naturally, want wood and coal but the flesh stove ... what would the flesh stove burn?

"What should we burn in it?"

"Reason, logic, politeness, irony, silence."

I prevailed on Ellen to wait a bit. I asked her to leave

me alone with my "Teste" stove. (The woodstove was a "Franklin.")

I wanted to commune quietly with what remained, with the new form of my spiritual mentor, with the uninsultable Monsieur Teste. If only he had acceded to my insults it wouldn't have had to end like this. It wouldn't have ended like this if he had gone back to Europe six nights ago. O why did it have to end like this? I was only a normal product of ny environment. Monsieur Teste should have known that I was already an American, that his arrival had been a gamble, that he might lose. Why did he lose? O why?

In the midst of my lamentations Ellen reappeared with a good part of the *Harvard Classics Library* under her arm.

"See if it'll burn this," she said.

She threw the books into the "Teste" stove and dropped a match on it. The light flickered for a moment then it went out.

"We'll have to try something else."

Her eyes surveyed the room faithfully and, suddenly, her gaze fastened on our son and daughter, rolled in one, who was sleeping again. I understood her. I took its legs and she took its arms and we stuffed it into the "Teste." Not even the thought that we were on television would comfort me. I felt heart-broken. Ellen poured a good deal of lighter fluid on Maximum and lit the match. Again, after a brief flare, it went out.

"Goldarn," she said. "Is there anything this blasted intellectual furnace will consume?"

"There is," I said. I crossed my arms on my chest like a soft Christ and with eyelids lowered I pointed at myself with my tongue, "Me."

"Hmmm," said Ellen. "I don't know if I want that child to grow up without a father."

Δ

Seventh Night

This night found us in profound meditation. Ellen was having a technical meditation in which the means and ways of stuffing the "Teste" stove were paramount. In her mind, she had solved the problem. She would feed the immigrant to his old ways of thinking and conquer the geography. The huge seed of the female Hitler in her began to spout technicalities.

I, for my part, was meditating on the failure of intention. I had intended, as my readers know, to inject philogeny into geography for the purpose of owning my new position. I had failed because I had relied on the coded version of my philogeny which had been Monsieur Teste.

At this point I refrained from human affairs and gave up hope in order to concentrate on Ellen's motions as she slid like a suction cup toward the center of my flesh, three fingers above my belly button.

She folded me like a handkerchief and tied knots on each side of my body by tightly pulling long strips of skin slit on the dotted line. Then when I looked sufficiently like a log with bumps on it (she was no artist) she stuffed me on top of my hermaphroditic child and dropped the rest of her Coleman fluid on my shifting eyeballs. I could not see the lit match I knew adorned her fingers.

The flames licked me softly like the tongues of animals and I felt the grip of my "Teste" stove encompass and accept me as the proper fuel for its greedy form.

I burnt curiously. I burnt conversationally. This is how I burnt:

Fuel: "It is almost like going back to Europe in a slow boat full of heretics loose on a burning sea of oil."

Stove: "America has her reasons. She made me hungry, she made you stupid. When I am hungry I will eat anything stupid."

Fuel: "When you've eaten me your walls will be coated with my neural information and you will lose your identity."

Stove: "But what will happen to her?"

Fuel: "Oh, my God, dear stove, but this is the first time I've ever heard you use the '?'. It's incredible."

Stove: "No. What is happening is that your neural neurotic nature is already coating my perceptions. There is something in you that wants to die talking."

Δ

I felt ashamed. Monsieur Teste was returning to Europe without having accomplished his mission. I was in the air, in the form of black smoke, dialoguing endlessly with a silent partner. I had learned the final simple secret of America:

It's a melting pot. It will melt you.

Certainly I had not expected it to melt me in the innards of my spiritual mentor. But it had, it undoubtedly had.

My experienced friend, Monsieur Teste, was returning to his country of origin with the smoke of my mind distributed thickly on the lining of his stomach. I had learned nothing from him and he who knew everything had taught nothing.

Things were as they had been. I took my head between my palms and with a start I came to this realization:

I am bored in Heaven. I really am. I lived to see the day.

SAMBA DE LOS AGENTES

My name is José, I am Catholic and I was not a plain-clothes policeman very long. In Bogotá I wrote poetry and prayed to the Virgin every day for my mother, who was a cancerous balloon grounded in the chicken shack behind the house, and for my two sisters who tap-tapped their way past my window every hour drowned in lipstick and sperm. Here is one of my poems in translation:

> *Every day is a long hallway to death*
> *Every night is an agony of lightning*
> *My heart lies in pieces at your feet*
> *My poor heart is a trampled field*
> *Bring down the rain, Mother of God*

When I first came to New York I was taken under the wing of my uncle Pedro who is a cop. I fell in love with Maria who loved the Virgin as much maybe more than I did because one day, two years after I joined the force, she left me and joined the Virgin. I became a plainclothes cop and roamed the city with two other cops, looking for crime. Because I was the first to spot the nervous, skinny young man playing with a gun in his pocket, I was the first to shove him into one of those doorways which in New York stand for nature, and whisper hotly into his ear: "If you move, I kill you." I have whispered, shouted, mumbled and stammered that line ever since I remember, enough times to get me in trouble. It never did; I think it is a very good line. Skinny didn't move so I slid out his gun like a rubber from a Trojan package and it turned out to be a toy. "What were you doing with this?"

"I was walking thinking up a poem," the man said in an accent as foreign as my own.

"What sort of poem?" I found myself unable not to ask although my next line should have been: "You robbed a liquor store, punk!"

"A poem about the Virgin Mary," he said shyly, beginning to cry. I saw the tear and knew that it was the tear said to perpetually exit from the statue of the Virgin in Fatima. "In it ..." he pushed on, sensing my interest, "I was going to put my heart which is in pieces."

"What da fuck?" said one of the other cops.

Only then did I say my line: "You robbed a liquor store, punk!" I took out the only piece of paper in his pocket, a poem to the Virgin by A. Alien, 54 Avenue C, 2–C, New York City, America.

"Where is your green card, punk?" I remembered my next line.

"At home."

So I dragged him to his home, to the address plainly written on the paper. There, we busted in the door and found ourselves in a room wallpapered with innumerable poems to the Virgin. The refrigerator door, which was open, contained tens maybe hundreds of carefully washed milk bottles, each one containing a rolled-up poem to the Virgin. "What do you do with these?" I asked.

"Launch them to sea," he said.

I arrested him on a charge of possessing a false pistol— a misdemeanor—and took him to jail. There, I visited him every day because A. Alien had no money for bail. When the trial came, I couldn't be found to testify. Reached finally at the Police Academy where I was taking classes, I refused to come to court because I was on my lunch break. The case was dismissed, I was fired from the force and I became a hippie and a filmmaker.

Δ

I wore a bunch of dying violets in my frayed red velvet lapel. My hair is red, my hands are freckled, my eyes are narrow under long maroon lashes and my line was: "I'm from Venus, can you spare a lemon?" I weighed the lemon if I got it, raised it to my ear, rapture and anxiety alternated on my face. Suddenly I dropped to the ground, pitched the lemon high over the skyline of New York and covered my ears. When I had just hit myself with the maximum available quantity of heroin, I entered the sumptuous shower of my otherwise cruddy apartment. Ah, but the shower curtain had blue angels on the clear Hoboken plastic, and the nozzle covered me with gold sparks. One eternity over, I rose to hunt lemons. If the profferer of the lemon was young, twelve to fourteen let's say, and a boy or a girl, I searched his or her smooth body for a place to launch my tongue. "A Cape Canaveral for my rocket!" I declaimed. More often than not, the case was reversed: I was the Cape, they the rocket. The boys or girls, of which there always was one behind the Hoboken angels, bathing in sparks, were movie stars. My camera never rested. The lens protruded from below my neck like the anus of a horny zebra, searching the movements of the world for formal impossibilities, joyful meetings of lay lines at prayer. (My camera was a way of eliminating parenthesis.) When my lens was broken—a furious Hoboken angel stuck a shiv through it—I framed movement with my thumb and my fuck you finger, or simply with my half-shut eyelid. Many stars were born that year as I continually begged for lemons. I went out, in a flurry of cinema and esprit-du-temps, and made the world shower lemons. I could extract a lemon from a policeman. My lemon-extracting line was never just dangling in the water: always taut, it could have made me a millionaire. As it was it merely taught me alliteration.

One day I disappeared. Lemons became irrelevant. Great esthetes speak their lines and go. For them to stay around too long is to risk shrinking of the soul, something everyone but an esthete does flawlessly. "Americans have such smooth faces because they have no soul," Rupert Brooke explained. The soul is an adornment, I was an esthete. Decked in souls, I rose through the eye of my camera and went through the f-stop.

> *Hey man you an alien.*
> *My pleasure.*
> *Holy unclean fun.*
> *The twink of a submarine's insides.*

From the window at Blimpie's, possibilities of magic: the *impossibility* of ever conceiving of a time when the possibilities of magic might stand parodied. The impossibility of old self ensconced in a fiery throne throwing thunderbolts at young self dreaming of magic. The impossibility too of doing it. The availability of magic. Why regret going through the window? Everybody who went out the door is now stuck in the political traffic. I took different ways to avoid the snare of clichés. I confused them but I didn't nip them in the bud. Once I followed a nymph, her skirt barely sufficient for a place-setting at McDonald's, her silver braces and her buttocks followed by squiggly silver script and several pairs of heat buttocks. We marched together along with ten thousand demonstrators to the United Nations. Vietnamese flags were waving. A man was burning in a square. We lay down on the grass. Tear gas cannisters flew over us. She searched my flesh for fruit. I smeared her juices on my lips and eyes.

I became gradually more boring to myself until I stopped writing poems and started writing stories and everyone said you need an agent.

Δ

My first agent, Peggy, picked me up from rumors at a bar because she was new and hungry, and the only way she could be both was to turn each rumor into a person, and eat the pretzels in every bar. It had never—until that drizzly Manhattan day which is no agent—occurred to me that I needed an agent. The sort of people who had agents were the sort of people who wore suits and talked in those excruciating complete sentences I am now talking in, the kind of people who *smell* like offices. A girl I knew who worked in a brokerage house on Wall Street would not let me touch her until she "washed off" the office: still, from her bones, like smoke, the smell and even the *taste* of plastic turf and stock certificates, desk shavings and nylon rayon polyester shirts and socks, wafted violently to twist my nerves; I left her with an empty purse, after I threw up. The needle stuck in a greedy Debussy faun, the only record she had. These sort of folks need agents because they need the universe mediated.

"In America they don't burn books, they boil them," I snarled. She looked decidedly slutty, Peggy did. Miniskirt, tits that "leaped" from the leatherwork of a bondage artist, short, fat limbs which bespoke of a formerly round Jewish girl on a fierce diet, a blinking red cunt I could feel pursed directly at my immediately cognizant cock-eye, lipsticked X-rated red lips, all outlined by phony cheer like a travel poster, and those pretzels, crunch, crunch. We were at a bar which used to be bearable until it filled with literary chatter like a popcorn maker. I can still hear it, a sort of low hum pierced with small press staples. Agents, of course—I didn't know it then—don't fuck. Fucking is terminal, there is nothing to be mediated. Some agents may add fucking to their ten percent but that's highway robbery so see your lawyer if you're fucking your agent. (The newspapers outside: *Agent Orange on Trial* [And don't fuck your lawyer!]).

"At least they don't quick-freeze them," she returned.

The newest in death at the time was quick-freezing, a technique whereby the stiff is frozen and hammered into tiny bits then fitted into a ketchup bottle.

Peggy wanted to read my novel so I said fine why don't we go to this really fine five-dollar hotel I know and discuss it, let's just hope it doesn't rain because last time I was in there we both got soaked, and the time before that my love stiffened under me her eyes pure terror in her head as she beheld a crimson starfish on the ceiling which could only have been the brains of someone who'd put a bullet through them. An agent I figured should be able to take it. After all why would anyone shoot themselves if not for the fact that they had no agent, no one to mediate between them and the cruel cruel world.

"Here is the great work I sure hope you're up for it because it's scandalous ... no one ever ... no one knows ... no one etc., etc. I wrote it in an old Ford doing 80 in the pampas and on the palisades. It's dedicated to the Virgin, the pages are stained with sex of all kinds, even sheep I did not shrink from, even a pheasant and a peacock. I had my friends hold down the neck and the feathers as I upped and outed the aviary. You understand, I'm sure, being from New York and all." I saw it quite clearly at the time. You really had to do all those things to write a novel—how else stand before Cervantes when *that* time comes? I still see it quite clearly, my first agent, a sculptured tube of lipstick, the musical slot machine paying off for all the trouble I'd gone to obtaining a peacock and a Ford and a moonlit night and all the traumas of begging for lemons ... I had to look through Peggy and hope that through the holey fabric of her flesh the light played as always, maybe even generalize a bit, though certainly not as much as to think that words are agents or that I, Sacred Mother help me, might be one too. I know now: words are not agents and I most emphatically am not one. But then, I had to work out a compromise, and in so doing I let in the ugly foot of the beast.

The hotel was out I noticed, so we shifted to a marble table in an Italian cafe, to a dark corner where I hoped to add her juices to my well-travelled prose, and there, under nymphy fountains once attending to Gambino, Gallo and other dark prelates, I spread my wings of hope and begged her to love my work. Only by loving it, I explained, can you begin to fight for it, for fight you must. Above and below all such human signals—as my five fingers slipping on spilled cappuccino in anticipation of riding up your nylons—you must love and understand these words.

I then gauged her thoughts from the vantage point of what I know now, namely that she read only with an eye for signs of decay, which might be turned to profitable ends. Most certainly lost on her were the dizzying wells on whose waters luminous lemons bobbed, the peacock tropes which outshined the peacock I moonbanged, the final formulations of age-old questions on which my genius had stumbled, and the voices, all those voices I can't hear any more. I shall amend that—none of those things were lost on her—they were the very things she meant to stay away from. Like my truly eager hand responding to her falsely eager beaver, my prose responded only to her alert sense of commerce. My hand and my tropes existed only as negative signs, warnings of unsuitability. But, as I say, I didn't know agents—and she took my novel with her.

Here is the story of that novel:

Madam Rosa Alvarez, the widow of a wealthy Bogotá butcher, installs herself as caretaker and mother protectress into a shabby 423-unit apartment building she now owns, and where her late husband once operated the most successful ground floor butcher shop in New York City. With the help of a young tenant—the narrator—she stumbles into a locked apartment where they make love, opening, through their gyrations, a door in the ceiling through which begins pouring the most incredible meat in the world: porterhouse steaks, sirloin tips, filet mignon, prime rib, etc., all cut to frightening perfection, utterly cold and totally fresh. Rosa and Eduardo—who are vegetarians—are buried in the animal wealth and lie there gasping for air until they rise to discover that the door in the ceiling leads into the past, namely to a place in U.S. history called the Gold Rush. The time tunnel through which the meat travels is a converter: it converts dead Indians and murdered goldminers into fresh cuts of meat. The door promptly closes only to reopen when Rosa has her next orgasm. Brilliantly developed over a period of six centuries by the vast Colombian family of butchers—though there are several doctors in the fold—these meat tunnels are adjustable to any bloody period in time likely to jump with corpses. With Rosa's husband the family had begun expanding to the United States where in an incredibly short time they came to control the appetites of the natives, addicted them to the meat and took over the government. The decadent president and choice members of Congress often go visiting—courtesy of the meat tunnels—bloody periods of U.S. history where they are drenched in the spirit of the past, Gettysburg for instance. The meat cartel is firmly in control until Rosa's orgasm throws the operation into chaos. The Trinity which rules the tribe, namely Guzman the Executioner, Alonso the Impregnator and Juan the Guide, converges on the writhing couple covered in meat: all but Guzman the Executioner arrive on time and thus begins Rosa and Eduardo's journey to the Gold Rush where Rosa gives birth to the little girl who is her own grandmother and who will be raised by a tribe of hallucinating Indians. In the circular America described in the novel, the ecology of the world is restored because by eating their own dead ancestors Americans exit history. Very optimistic book. Title: Meat from the Gold Rush. 275 pages.

Δ

A prime specimen of the Nixon-Mitchell architecture of the early 1970s, the Department of Justice, enfolding in its windowless interior the Immigration and Naturalization Bureau like a heart, bakes in the noon heat on the site of a former slum. The edges of the slum, like the extremities of a heart-transplant patient, lie bloated all around it, dotted with idle young blacks lying on piles of rubbish, smoking in the sun. Parts of car bodies, only the useless parts, the unsavory entrails of animals rejected by the white middle-class, rust there too, scooped up from the inside. A child probes carefully the sides of a slice of watermelon, its inside, too, scooped up long ago. The freeway, a black incision still unfinished, stands over the landscape, its wire feelers extended toward the river. The earth too is hollow, hundreds of hardhats are digging below, one day trains will rumble through. Everything hollowed out and the sides rotten—this is the world to which allegiance must be paid by the poor alien disguised in a blue leisure suit like a bad lyric in a barely hummable song—and I go forth to pay it, green card clutched tight, an official shoot within a mannered walk (I almost said manured), my shiny wingtips narrow but properly wingless, my mask in place, the eyes almost fit my glasses which I wear as prophylactics. My eyes, I know, without protection can make reality—or what passes for it—pregnant. A long time has flown—I have had eight watches in that time—since José stood at attention on the chill tar of the police plaza with a shiny badge on his tit. I watch José offering a quick prayer to the Virgin for his Uncle Pedro who watches him proudly, his heart attack ready to claim him in five months. If I consider my twenties as a heart, the motor of my lifespan, I think they have been scooped violently—much in the way of a protracted heart attack—by the understanding—rapid by Colombian standards—that I have become one of the inhabitants of the underworld, a shadow in the land of the dead, i.e., an American with an agent—Peggy's heat widens the circles of sweat under my blue arms—and today I am going to claim citizenship.

The guard runs his outstretched palms alongside my body glancing at the metal detector needle which registers my keys with a slight tremor. With his palms on my hips I chuckle inwardly at the questions on the naturalization form in my breast pocket. Have you ever committed sexual perversities? Have you had any homosexual encounters? Both of these, in the affirmative, are grounds for rejection. Both of these, in the affirmative, are grounds, like coffee grounds, of my American makeup or, more properly, generational lights, beaming in their almost incomprehensible way, from a past epoch. The future, which once proceeded philosophically—which is to say inexorably— from these beams, is already in ruins, an idea junked by developments. Often, on that stretch of magnificent desolation between New York and Washington, D.C., from the window of the train, I saw the paradox of America: the future was in ruins before anyone met with it. The jumbled buildings lining the tracks exposed a complex and charred machinery that had no meaning. No one, if asked, could tell what those machines had made. Those blooms of mid-industrialization had prospered, decayed and died, without anyone's having the slightest inkling of their purpose. The future, which they had once resolutely represented, was past. The only continuity, in human terms, are these hands, resting on my hips, the beefy hands of a well-fed guard, which rest like this on the hips of a million

72

immigrants coming here into the future: a slow dance, samba de los Americanos.

The hands of the guard became the hands, crossed on a metal desk in fluorescent white light, of the immigration officer in charge of my request for citizenship. Hands progress, in institutional neon, from resting on hips to crossing on a desk. In the bureaucracies of hands, these are the hierarchies: the fist, impacting with the face as the immigrant, stumbling off the boat, appears ready to run off into the night past the guards; the index finger curled toward its owner, meaning come here, worm; the index finger pointing to the tubercular youth with two weeks' growth of beard, singling him out of line for shipping back; the vertical fist hitting the metal desk to make a point out of which, rage spent, could come forgiveness; the crossed hands, which I now face, ready to thumb through a greasy, fat file; the palms spread across the face of the man leaning wearily into them after a long day of silent hate and contempt for the Tower of Babel; the hands, finally, of the man, on the Bible, on his way up. All these hands, at no matter what stage in their office life, never lose the gesture of the guard, which they retain like a watermark.

Still crossed, the hands weigh me. Above them is the mustache of a man tensed between the incoming fat of middle age and the veneer of nearly gone muscle. They now uncross, these hands, to alert me that all has come to a point: the file. A mystery to both of us, the file is going to determine my status. My name, José A., is embossed in red ink on it. The file opens. The man's eyes widen from the first page. So they know everything, I think. They know about the Virgin and the man I failed to jail because of Her. They know about the lemons and the Hoboken angels. They know about Peggy. However, I am quite certain, they don't know a thing about me.

"Why have you been driven from the force?"

73

"For the love of the Virgin, by José!"

I replace "by Jove!" with "by José!" to spice up the native parlance. One thing I knew: the man in front of me was my age and he had only recently become a native. I don't mean that he was a foreigner, he was as American as they come, but there had been no natives in my generation until recently. My generation—I can prove this—is the most hated generation in the history of America. Partly to deflect this hate and partly because the prematurely old young are tired of fighting, we have almost all become—over a brief span—natives. Until recently, we were all strangers and exiles, living in a place called "off the wall," which is no place. But like the tide going in, my contemporaries pulled back into the sea, leaving on the beach only the true aliens and their metaphysical brothers, the hunted. However, in beating this hasty retreat astride flying K-Mart lawn chairs, my contemporaries have also left behind the shapes and masks they had worn during the party and—this is serious—inside those shapes and masks they have left their bodies and their hearts. As the shapeless goo engulfed them, some of them noticed and screamed. But it was too late: all that wealth of brain and heart was now property of the straggling aliens, by José!

I regarded my interrogator calmly, assured that I had him. He was not at ease. My file was full of strange, unsettling pieces of his own past. Vague regrets coursed through him like phosphorus through protozoa ... Once he too had, in the dim light of an attic, been bitten by a spiritual lemon which bounced, creating spirals and cones in the air and then came to rest on the Peruvian shawl Her naked body sprawled on. He had seen the Virgin, I was sure of it.

"In 1969, you were arrested for harboring minors. What was the deposition of the case?"

"Fiction."

"We shouldn't let your past stand against you. If you tell me the truth there is no reason …"

"My past doesn't stand against me. It doesn't stand against you, either. My past doesn't stand at all—I am another person now. I write novels. I have an agent. I am an American."

Whatever his doubts, he did not doubt the file. "File is an anagram of life," he sang to himself, almost drowning, though not entirely, something else which sang, "All strains will be played out." But the file, drawn like a primitive imitation of a flower from the innards of computers, field reports, denunciations and informer asides, contained in its body, the truth and the whole truth as accurately as the science of the day was capable of it. We were living in a time when public revulsion, in the form of the Freedom of Information Act, had brought a rain of files on citizens. Files and their subjects were meeting all over America like persons and their lives on the TV show "This Is Your Life!" For an instant, life was reduced to its filable propositions—fallible I should say—and everybody was able to read their obituary. What else is a file or even a biography? A reductio ad absurdum, an obituary. A peace descended over America, a pall, you might say. This peace, this pall, this foretaste of doom, is repeated every time someone opens your file. There you are: your inside equal to your outside. Rigor mortis sets in as facts come to life. No, there is no way my friend here could ever suspect the truth or even that the truth might not be in the file. He had viewed the Virgin but she had not spoken to him.

"There is no reason, if you tell the truth, why you should not, in time, become a citizen." He is generous with reason. After all, it isn't *his* reason he's being generous with. It is the reason of the founding fathers who wanted all the orphans. However, the world is full of orphans and he doesn't think the founding fathers meant *all* of them. Why, a man could come here, display his orphanism, and be allowed to shake down the lemons off the first citizen. We must make sure he is a good orphan. Not orphan enough that is to *cry* for love, for chrissakes, not a pathetic fucking *ultimate* orphan ... A reasonable orphan, a dignified orphan, a calm orphan. José A. here is quite obviously an orphic orphan, even though he's wearing that ridiculous suit. You can smell a new suit an elevator away. Like all high-ranking civil servants, he lived under the building. He rose to work in an elevator and descended home in a paper cone. A cardboard vase filled with paper roses awaited him: his wife. She bobbed her many heads, and hamburgers came out. The evenly spaced skis along the wall invited his feet to strap in and go: his children.

"Your file raises questions."

I too raise questions, darling little things, on the window sill of my cruddy apartment smoothly run by Madam Rosa Alvarez.

"We will look into them. I see no reason, etc., if one day, etc., if the truth, etc., you may not, etc., one day, etc."

Δ

You can go quite far on a word. The word "go" for instance. An insight like that can go a long way—possibly the whole way—toward making an agent. Agents are born from aphorisms the way other people come from mothers and fathers. That insight has nothing to do with the agent— it is an insight about writers. Properly, a writer can go quite far on a word, the word "go" for instance. An agent is the creation of a random aphorism about writers, then, and think how far a writer can go on *two* words: "go, man," for instance. "Man" is an addition of genius—it is the agent's coming of age. The aphorism slanged. The insight humanized. The inserted concern. The bridge. Go, girl.

76

When I hadn't heard from Peggy in a year I got tired of leaving words on her tape machine and staked out her building. She came home with a young businessman with a bushy mustache in which cocaine flakes were embedded—I could see them from the fire escape. Under a low-cut glass table on artificial turf was my manuscript scattered, open, and I could see the page where the narrator discovered that he didn't remember anything he wrote, and that by rereading what he wrote he could predict the future. His writing, he decided, was oracular and on that page he revealed his methodology.

"What do you do?" the businessman demanded of Peggy, now that a slight burning sensation seemed to attend his still-tingling nub. He could well imagine his wife receiving penicillin.

"I am a masseuse," Peggy confirmed. "I just wrote a book." She pointed to my manuscript. "I describe my life in there for a million dollars which I am going to get as soon as Xaviera Hollander writes the blurb."

When he left, my agent chuckled to herself and still in bra and no panties began to play with herself right in front of my face in the window which she suddenly saw. I pulled up the window and went in.

"Don't move or I'll kill you," I quoted myself.

I killed her.

I did it as I had been taught in the police academy, two squeezes and a chop to the back of the neck. No mess. I then fed her half-dead cat and watered the totally dead cactus and then turned on the tape machine with her messages.

"Hi, I hate to talk to machines. This is George, the author of *The Vatican Follies*. My parish priest says he knows a publisher."

"Hi, this is Dr. Lupus. I have a superb idea. It seems to me that people have been turning into rocks. Over the past ten years we have been slowly petrifying. 'Petrification," the O.E.D. tells us, is the gradual numbing and hardening of the cells. At the rate of present-day petrification, it takes ten days to turn into a boulder. The eyes become shiny, reflective pebbles turned inward, rolling in their sockets like marbles. Just take a walk, see for yourself. We could turn this into a slab of a book, with examples from contemporary poetry and pictures of rocks. That will do it. Damn it—denying me tenure after fifteen fucking years ...'"

"Hi, baby. I'm a gambler on the big time gambol. I have a system now that's one hundred percent. If you can get me ten Gs I can make you, your mother, the publisher and all the suckers who read, real rich. Do you think a gambler's desire is money? Wrong. It isn't. A gambler's a mystic—all he wants is total attention, total presence. At that table there is no one between his concentration and himself. Money's nothing. Beats yoga any day. We could sell it as a spiritual sort of book for people with money who can't sit still. A gambler don't need an agent, baby. I just need money."

"Peggy darling, where have you been? I'm worried sick about this business you're in: your father got it into his head to move onto a barge on the Hudson ... you've got to talk to him, dear, I get seasick so easily ...'"

Peggy had been the consummate agent. All this had interested her, all the unfocused fantasy of America had channelled through her like toxic wastes through the Love Canal. She had seen herself as a purifier, an air filter, a meter gauge on her country's demented psyche and that's why she had been horny all the time.

Δ

When I came home Madam Rosa Alvarez had a surprise for me: she flung open the door to my crusty rooms and there, in a circle reminiscent of a village dance, all embroidery, high-heeled shoes and black and red hair, were my mother and two sisters. The result of a miracle still much discussed in Bogotá, my mother had deflated and her cancers had been sucked out of her. The renowned psychic surgeon Xavier Urmuz had had his picture in many papers as a result, particularly the dramatic one which shows him stepping on wriggling brown spots pouring out of mama's body like hailstones through a grass roof.

My mama became a rapid American. So rapid I took her to Atlantic City, and for a moment there I panicked, I thought I'd lost her. Looking over the dazzling rows of madly whirring bright slot machines, each one facing a wrinkled middle-aged woman in electric green pants, I couldn't tell which one she was. It was a movement that gave her away, a jerky spasmodic upward twitch of greed, which made it seem as if she were pulling the machine off its black stem. Cherries and apples whirled past, and out of the tumbling fruit, something of mother appeared. Getting closer I noticed the fierce and familiar pursing of her lips in what was her unique and ancient quarrel with fate, or luck as she sometimes called it. Luck, luck ran through her lips in a flow of mixed syllables in various dialects. Some have luck, some have all the rotten luck. She had already forgotten her miraculous cure when faced with the evidence of her machine-neighbor, her identical image, her fellow bus passenger, pulling showers of silver out of the air. Before the coin she proffered to the secret quarrel with her destiny had even reached the insides of the machine, she pulled it hard and stalled it. She had to duplicate her movement every time, as the arm of the one-armed-bandit would not comply the first time around. This double movement, notwithstanding the miracle, running as it did through her whole life, divided her days and nights. Her days were now dedicated to achieving the semblance of an

American woman. She competed for blandness in endless shopping sprees, which were fast draining my sisters' hard-earned whoring money, and which yielded the same plastic colors as the stuck slot machine. Her nights were occupied by the dead. Useless to resist, unresponsive to medication, contemptuous of doctors, the dead came to her every night to converse, ask and answer questions, as much at home in her dreams as they had ever been. Her years in the chicken shack had been crowded with dead people, her shack had been the coffee house of the necropolis. They had all come to her to America now, happy like all new immigrants, a dream come true. For the past two weeks, I had been sleeping elsewhere, unable to listen to the wild cacophony of my mother's dreams. My sisters, who were used to it, said that it was this constant dead talk which had driven them from home at night in Bogotá. By the time they had had her removed to the chicken shack it was too late: they liked what they did. For the past two weeks, my mother had been teaching her dead English until dawn. When the last of her quarters brought forth a mixed bag of grapes and cherries, she turned to me and sighed with the satisfaction that I, at least, looked exactly like everyone else, an investment which she had made earlier and which had, unlike the *pure* operations of luck, paid off. She had no way of knowing that the blue suit of which she was so proud— she had sent it to me by boat—had only been worn once before, when I had gone in to ask for citizenship. In her mind I was always clad in the blue suit, and when I wasn't she didn't see me. Invisible in my childhood, I was still partly invisible. Unfortunately, I *was* partly visible. This is the part that writes prose.

Δ

I made small talk with the man ahead of me, Number 15, on the bench at the Immigration and Naturalization Bureau. He was Romanian. He told me that, contrary to popular belief, Dracula was a man of the people. He was man enough to impale them. He boiled people. He stuck a lid with holes for heads over the cauldron people were boiling in. He ate in front of the boiling cauldron with relatives of the boiled. He nailed people's hats to their heads if they didn't remove them fast enough. He made dishonest merchants swallow their money. He nailed thieves to one another and impaled them horizontally on the dotted line. He poured poison into people's ears. He saved Christianity from the Turks. He invented nationalism. His portrait hangs in classrooms all over the country. He has been maligned. Then his number, Number 15, was called, and I was next.

"We have perused your file, José. We have half-looked into your soul and found some good things. We know that you are a writer. What have you written, José?"

"A Guide to Fucking in the Great Cathedrals. A Guide to Gargoyles in Ten Great Cities. A Spiritual Guide to Gambling. A Transylvanian in Disneyland."

"How do you make a living?"

"I am a philosophical fashion arbiter. I decide what colors the ideas should wear."

"Do you make enough to eat?"

"Enough for Shrimp Imbecile for two. Sizzling flied lice too. Flied polk! Oystels! Egglolls! Watel! Evelything! I am a well-fed American who doesn't even moan in his sleep ... though the silence was terrifying at first."

"I sense a bit of resentment. An old wound, perhaps?"

"Yes. The wound winds all the way around my body, through the air. My aura is unzipped. A kind of spare lyricism attends my movements. Sometimes I am Spartan and hemophiliac at the same time."

"That sounds like a paradox."

"To find a true paradox you must dig at least six feet. I sense nothing of the sort. True, I have had many serious, late-night discussions with people in the know. The world is dying."

Getting up from his desk, the immigration agent looked furtively around, then closed the door. He winked. I understood from his automatically lowered voice that his inner police ear had been activated. He implored me to listen to his position. He spoke cautiously, as if behind every word someone or something waited for him with a slingshot. He tested each word in his mouth, prodding each letter with his tongue. Even to himself he appeared as a conscientious consumer, making sure of each tomato before buying. But his words, when finally released, turned over and bought, came out tired, boring and insipid, settling on me in their reasoned predictability like flies on the summer sweat of a bald pate. I have no idea what he said.

"What do you mean?" I asked.

"I can't tell you that. Suffice it to say that under the circumstances, we will have to keep working on your file until every shadow of doubt is erased. The whole world comes through this door: Vietnamese peasants, Cambodian spies, Cuban killers, and writers. You know ... I have here something a writer once wrote, I flushed it out ..." He handed me a dog-eared mimeograph pamphlet entitled *Dialectic of Terrorism, or The Pleasures of Exile.* Leafing through it I saw underlined: "Rely on your basic transparencies." On the margin, a hand had scrawled: "Pictorial key to terrorism." I saw also, "Happiness is a loss of integrity," and on the margin: "Psychological milieu." On the back cover was a picture which looked like random meat after a TNT blast; the caption said: "Fragments of a Comrade." "Needless to say, we had the author deported ..."

"Why?"

82

"Anarchism. Subversive milieu."

"I have arthritis of the milieu," I confessed.

"On the other hand," he continued without hearing me, "we have a writer who deserves to stay, it is a pleasure to keep him." He handed me a poem.

Counterrevolutionary Song Sung by the White Guards in the Ukraine 1921 in Praise of the United States—A New Translation by (name deleted)

At the small arms seminar
Vera and I whispered about Lenin's bananski
There isn't any said Vera
He left it behind in Indianski

The mountains are covered with manna
We have only just begun to fight
Like the corn in far away Indiana
We will conquer the Bolshevik blight

At the small arms seminar
Aliosha inserted the firing clip for Anna
A snow drift came from the mountains
As beautiful as the hair of Fata Morgana

We will stomp each Bolshevik with our book
Like a wriggling scarlet piranha
The mountains will be free forsooth
And we will be famous in far away Indiana

I handed it back.

"You know," said the agent, carefully folding it in four and putting it back in his suit pocket, "to this day the Cossacks are very famous in Indiana. In my little town we have the Cossack Inn, a White Tower and we have a corn ritual where we sing Cossack songs."

"How long, then?"

"No one knows. Form's just benign content, as the

doctors say ..." he said, waving my application, "but content may well be malignant form ..." He pounded my file.

Δ

I have a new agent now. He wants me to be a ghost. He's on to something; if he can turn America's hungry writers into ghosts he can turn the ghosts into cash. And when you see the creations of ghosts on television, conjuring their ghosted memoirs amid the show and the ghosts, you think, why not a ghost, everybody's dead.

Things knot though when the ghost I am to be is ghost to the first lady of forensic pathology. "In his lifetime," she says of her late, beloved husband, "he has carved up 37,000 corpses." All those ghosts, I am sure, are all eyes and ears as the marvelous scientist incises their former eyes and ears. "Ah," they say, "What wonderful fingers! What a splendid wife! What charming children! What parties! What friends! What fire! What a life!" They should know, they are all his ghosts, part of the doc's own TV show: *All My Ghosts*. In his life, the famous pathologist caught criminals like flies. It was his splendid embalming which brought to light the heinous murder of an acrobat by his lover, a circus clown: exhumed two years later, a trace of the poison was still preserved in a needle track in the creature's left buttock. So masterful was his analysis that years later, pathologists all over the world are still asking for slices of the acrobat's buttock in order to make independent studies. Such textbook cases!

The doc himself has now been a ghost for two years. His greatest accomplishment, a seventeen-story institute of forensic pathology, dazzles the casual viewer with the gleam of its endless stainless steel drawers, each one containing a cold corpse ready for science. In the scintillating formaldehyde chill, white-coated young doctors in the

84

bloom of first youth move softly on pink slippers, with tinkling chrome trays or, at festive times, cocktail glasses. The institute is known for its parties—forensic specialists the world over gather here to thrill to new autopsy techniques. But the place hasn't been the same since the great man left us. This is why his beloved wife has called the ghost agent.

The ghost agent is young—he has, of course, a bushy mustache—and he hasn't been an agent for very long, only since the unfortunate and untimely demise of an older ghost agent who is now a bona fide ghost. The charmingly titled manuscript entitled *Housekeeper at the Morgue, or Living and Loving in the Shadow of Death* is on his desk the day he takes over the office. He pays it scant attention, he barely has time to breathe, what with all the hoopla attendant to the funeral of the older agent, and the thousands of funeral invitations, some of which haven't been sent, and the telephone ringing every few minutes with people wanting to know *who* was going to be at the funeral, and him having to explain over and over that, yes, it was well worth the party's time to attend because anybody who is anybody was going to be there … But the manuscript keeps bothering him, lying there on the desk right next to the telephone, imploring mutely to be ghosted. Might as well take care of business now, he tells his girlfriend who is lying on the vinyl sofa with her feet in the air, smoking a joint and regarding him with amusement. So he calls me.

I am sitting quietly on the stairs of my building when my mother drops the telephone receiver out the window on me. I have been sleeping on the stairs at night, watching my sisters transform the neighborhood into a little corner of Bogotá, and I get all my calls here. "Do you want to be the ghost of the morgue?" he inquires. Well, I'm surprised the place has no resident ghost. It is a little like a shoe factory where none of the workers have any feet, but I'm hungry and pondering as usual my citizenship, and the only

85

superstitions I harbor have to do with life not death. So I say, "Yeah, well, lemme mull this over, lemme think about ghosts, read up on 'em, maybe look at some pictures, watch some TV, study steam, listen for creaks—there's one ... it's my mother stepping on the raisin bran—sniff this out, I'll be in touch later." Formaldehyde has a rather wonderful smell ... I remember all sorts of horrible things in pukey old museums. What the fuck, the offer doesn't sound all that bad. So I call back and say yes, and then just like that, I'm the ghost of the morgue.

Great, my ghost agent tells his girl, he's taken the job, now I can get on with the funeral and my career.

My first ghostly duty is meeting the forensic widow, and for that purpose I shout the number to my mother who dials it three floors above my head, a telephone number you would do well to note because it is possibly the only direct line to Hades: 201-665-2341.

"I only want to know one thing, madam: was your late husband for or against ghosts? I wouldn't want to have him on my back."

"To a certain extent," replies the spirited old woman, "he must have been for them or he wouldn't have spent his life trying to vindicate them by nailing their killers. On the other hand, if you and his ghost become involved in some sort of astral skirmish, I'm on his side no matter what, do you follow me, young man? This is why I'm paying you. Has your agent discussed the contract?"

"He has not."

"Well, you're not a ghost until there is a contract. Contract ... ghost! Get it? Ha ha ha!"

At the morgue where we meet, the silver grey couloirs are blazing with light. Neon lights are sending down beams so powerful that they develop the memories of employees like photographic plates, causing them to remember things they had never experienced. Everyone wears dark glasses and I, who do not, see halos over every head. Erect but mushy like an overgrown banana, my yellow-clad host takes my arm and we visit her hero's empire.

Floor upon floor of cadavers unfold before my rapt gaze, dancing to the measured cadence of the widow's tales. It was in this room, for instance, in tray number 625, that the good doctor extracted the sliver of the silver bullet which killed the richest heiress of the 1950s. In these four trays once lay the bodies of the four Kent State students killed by the National Guard. In this drawer was the shrivelled body of a kidnapped steel magnate. And it was here that bits and pieces from Richard Speck's Chicago nurses came to meet the eyes of the formidable doctor. "This, you might guess," she said pointing to an oversized niche in the wall, "was especially built for the five men who self-immolated in the United Nations Plaza. In there we had Jimi Hendrix and in there Malcolm X." We then arrived at the top, a recently finished room where the temperature was an eternal 16 degrees Fahrenheit. "Here," she said, "are all the unsolved crimes of recent fame. For instance," she smiled, as a tray slid silently from the wall, revealing the beautified remains of my old acquaintance, Peggy... "No one knows who did it or why anyone would."

"Yes, Madam," I said.

Δ

My sister Tabita's boyfriend gave her the crabs and now she can't work. She's been told by everyone, myself included, to get rid of them, but she demurs. "Crabs," she says, "are jewels from Venus." She clings to them as if they were ideas. She says that at Lourdes, Christ's tears fall on his toes and turn to gelatin and then his greenish fungoid feet, soft and wobbly, walk over the minds of his worshippers. "Would you remove his tires?" she screams. "I am no less attached to the ancient rottenness of my whimsy!" she hollers. I try to talk sense into her. "If Christ would think of us as fondly as you think of your crabs, Tabita, we would all be in Heaven!"

But there is no talking to Tabita and now there are crabs everywhere: in my hair, in my eyelids, under my arms. I didn't even sleep there—I got them just by sitting down. And as I get up, I can't make up my mind if the little beasts have colonized or inhabited me. Likewise, our earth must at times ponder this question. I know it is not an appropriate moment, at the very beginning, nay, before the second chapter of *The Queen of the Morgue* (as I retitled my ghost job), to ponder this, but nevertheless: when writing, am I colonizing or inhabiting the language? Until Peggy, I would have laughed this question off as utterly stupid. Until then I had been sure that words came to inhabit me, little astral spores in search of a mouth. Shortly after I thought, well, perhaps I am inhabiting them, though Lord knows *what* inhabits them if that's the case. As bad as that proposition was, it can't compare to the criminal magnitude of colonization. And yet, as a still honest—though barely— ghost, I must ask. That this sort of inquiry is utterly inappropriate for a ghost, was made abundantly clear to me by my ghost agent, who having just read the first chapter of *The Queen of the Morgue,* tells me that my "love affair" with the American language is somewhat one-sided, as if I'd persuaded her to give me an unreluctant hand-job and then lost her phone number. There are true ways of writing a story, you little prick, even if I have to—as you never tire of pointing out—make the old bag look like Mary Queen of Scots and her ghoulish departed hubby like Sir Galahad. Ways of making it believable at the very least. Truth is like rooms one looks for in strange cities. You don't know the neighborhood, but you have to trust your idea of a room, even if it's only the fact that it's got to have walls. But try fighting conformity with your feet in the goo; the material is like a rubber tree. No one is ready for the slightest bit of truth. But don't worry, it isn't you who points the gun at my head. The hand that types is the hand that squeezes the trigger, and rocks the boat that rocks the cradle, as Tabita says when her boyfriend implores her to be normal. I must remember, in whatever twisted fashion, to allow language to breathe, ah, ah, scratch scratch.

Tabita's crabs and mama's poltergeist have turned my habitat into *Luna 4,* I can't even eat lunch there without drama. The poltergeist, a recent escapee from her nightly cafe for the dead, turns chairs over. If I look away from my bowl it turns the soup into my lap. On a mild day, it's only Tabita's feather hat floating around the room and the dead flies in mother's Inca Cola swaying from side to side and the glasses in the cupboard toasting each other in an intimate sub-tinkle. I can live with that, but on bad days it breaks windows, snaps legs off chairs, breaks mirrors, twists doorknobs, lifts up the couch, aims knives and forks at the flesh. On days like that, interpretation wears thin, the severe diet of faulty premises begins to show itself as ribs, I see the skull under the peachy skin, I feel like Little Red Riding Hood and the Wolf all rolled in one, my face half in shadow.

Tabita's boyfriend, who plays the guitar, plants his mournful physique and his untuned instrument a few steps over my sleepy head and lets go fortissimo all night of such classics as *Don't Wait for the Shrimp Boats, Honey, I'm Coming Home with the Crabs* or *The Albino Sexpot Blues* which, when added to the amplified gravel of Mama's soccer-crowd-sized company and the poltergeist crashing the furniture, and the wailing of New York City in heat, seriously put language on the block. And they say America is running out of energy! Bring on the Colombians! I'm having so much fun I can't remember my name. And Madam Rosa Alvarez threatens to evict us.

By contrast, the morgue is an oasis of calm. I have been given a room to write in there, a carpeted broom closet with the brooms still in it, but I can't sleep there because they fly around at night: the brooms are brand new and there is little to sweep anyway. The uniformed negroes who flit like luna moths around at night have nothing to do. The little dust balls, the wisps of etherized fluff escaping the dead disappear into thin air before anyone can lay a broom on them.

I stay until midnight, ghosting thus: "The good doctor was jogging around the fountain of alienated youth in Central Park when the future queen of the morgue spotted him." Which becomes: "I was giving my pooch Diamond his daily dose of freedom, hoping that someone might kindly relieve me of mine—I had been a widow for over five years—when I spotted the distinguished, middle-aged jogger whose perfect body might have descended from one of my reveries." Which becomes: "I had been a widow for five years but I felt no freer than Diamond, my faithful pooch, when I spotted the youthful jogger with the distinguished white hair, circling effortlessly the fountain in Central Park." Three stages: language in an increasing state of bondage. Three stages: José in an increasing state of citizenship. Three stages from which a pharmacology of subtlety and health may be devised by you, people of the future.

I rise to salute the custodian who is making his ten o'clock rounds to make sure that the dead are alone. In his mind, the janitors and I are part of the dead. He speaks to no one since the night when the great doctor, who was working late, summoned him to one of the drawers. "See this," he said, allowing his hand to float over the flowering

90

body of a bloated form fished from the sewers, "this is the spirit of our times, the *esprit-du-temps,* waiting for a chance to come into power. He once wore shoes and had a mind full of concepts. Often, his mind, like most people's, was full of shoes and his feet had a mind of their own. It was a mechanical and harmless operation: man is a wheel. The feet fit nicely in the head and the wheel turns. For a brief time, he made a profit: his concepts sold shoes and his shoes were a concept. His shoes, for that brief time, were beyond good and evil, merely a commercial passage between concept and concept.

"Usefulness is a restroom between concepts, a rest plaza between spins of the wheel which never stops. The concrete is illusory. Matter is a suggestion of rest, the hallucination of mind unaware of its own spin. Things are rest homes, health clinics, green spas. They are also words and bodies. The body and the word are the two things created by the mind—one outside, the other inside—in order to imagine itself at rest. The earth, which also spins, is perfectly still when we walk. It has invented gravity in order to imagine itself at rest. As the mind which invented self. The spin exists solely to create the illusion of standing still. The entire energy of the universe is spent on creating its opposite. The self labors to produce not-self. But for those of us ..." and here, his hand floated off the body to include the night custodian as well as himself, "... who are figments of a certain detachment, due to the nature of our jobs, who won't put up with either shoes words or bodies, the mind has a special treat: itself. In it we cease to become fragments. Death is a commercial passage like shoes. Shoes are death. We traffic entirely in death. Objects are particularized fragments of death. We trade in order to maintain the product of consciousness: unconsciousness. Money too is abstracted death." From that hour on, the custodian refused to be paid as well as to speak.

Which becomes: "Late at night, the great doctor often had long talks with the night custodian. A democrat, he loved and respected all people."

But if the truth be known, the doctor never spoke to the man. The man was deaf-mute and only doing his job. And the doctor, he was a snob and a power-monger: he wanted his picture in the newspapers. Which is probably what he meant by "the *esprit-du-temps* waiting to come into power," because although he'd never spoken to the custodian he had nevertheless made that speech many times, many a late night, over many a bloated and incomprehensible shape. His picture had been in the newspapers more often than not: shown firmly grasping a bullet fragment between thumb and index, or a broken arrowhead, or a vial of brown viscera, or an empty clock of sleeping pills, face unsmiling, eyebrows knitted. He had been the dailies' *éminence grise,* the agent of justice, the man who made the dead talk.

Then I go home, to sleep on the stairs, waking only to see my sister Raquel, a fat shadow in tow, climbing the stairs to the abandoned hallway where she works. Whenever the end of the world seems near, Raquel brings up a john. There is, in her relentless ascent and descent, sufficient evidence that the world, after being destroyed, repeats itself. A whore is the eschatologist's point of support on which, cried Archimedes, he could make the world turn. My dreams are dotted with the dance of psychopathia sexualis in the graveyard of the planet. I do the maggot frug in Manhattan.

Δ

The turn-of-the-century Park Avenue building where my agent makes his office twangs a nostalgic chord in me—give me that optimistic gargoyled façade over trees any day. The mask of end-of-the-century America fits over my face tightly: its energy is my energy, its ruthless capitalists with bright ideas live in my head, ruthless and bright as ever. Jews in passage from pushcarts to steam engines race through my veins. My agent is an idiot but he works in a great building. I did not know why the two women standing in front if it were speaking Spanish in my mother's voice. My mother's voice has a pitch both below and above all other voices: it is high and low like a poker game, and like it you never know which she will be going for. To hear it coming from *two* mouths at the same time was wholly astonishing: they both must have been from our street in Bogotá. With this in mind I smiled broadly and said the name of our streets and the name of my mother and the name of my sisters and the name of the seltzer man and that of the butcher and of the knife sharpener and of the corner cafe and of its owner and two waitresses and the name—the secret name—of the killer of the policeman in 1963, who was known to all and denied by everyone. The two women stopped briefly, no longer than any New Yorker will stop for anything, and continued to talk to each other in my mother's voice without taking further notice of me. Unable to understand, I reeled back from the building. I couldn't face my agent now, I had to figure out what happened. I walked into a cafe and sat at the soda fountain. The waitress asked me what I wanted in our Spanish dialect with my mother's voice. Leaving her, pad in air, I leaped back into the street and climbed aboard a bus. It was filled to the brim with thousands of voices speaking Spanish with my mother's voice. Since I couldn't get out I posed myself the healing question: "If they are all speaking Spanish, why don't I understand what they are saying?" Because, in fact, I had no idea what anyone was saying. The tiny Catholic girls in green and black uniforms hanging in the aisle from the rails may have all been my mothers but I didn't know what they were saying. With this discovery, my audio-vision began to recede. While the majority of women on the bus spoke with my mother's voice, some of them spoke in barely audible but perfectly clear Bronx. Before the stop, more than half were talking the native tongue, while only a handful continued to speak in madre. That was good enough for me, I was ready to face my agent.

I slipped past the doorman—there isn't a doorman in New York City who can claim that he has seen me except the doorman at the morgue—and took the wire-cage elevator to the fourth floor. My agent was speaking on the telephone. A $10,000 stereo system blared the only record on the premises: the latest sales figures of the ghosted memoirs of Casanova put to music by John Cage. (I am always ready to rescue a fallen style, said someone.) I fell to my knees in front of the candle and said a prayer.

> Emotion, communion, desire,
> Natural right, connection, fire,
> Communality, interior, paradise,
> Completion, brown mud, hot spice,
> Oneness, vastness, calm.
> Your shade is on me like a palm.

I signed the contract carefully, with an eye on eternity where all the Mephistopheles rejoiced. How much neater than a soul, which no one understood, was this agreement to become a ghost! Bypassing the soul entirely, the contract defined only the duties of the signers. Instead of the encumbrance of wealth, love and youth which the devil had hitherto had to deliver, I was promised only money, and not a lot of it. In exchange I became a ghost. True, my ghostliness was only for the duration of the contract, but what a refinement duration is, over eternity. Eternity is the unsophisticated imagining of the paradisaically inclined but duration is the refined machine of the demonic. Duration succeeded eternity like the devil succeeded god like petroleum succeeded coal.

The office, which was wallpapered with the successes of the deceased, smoked with the heady perfume of sex. I removed my little suede grammar thinking all the while that continuous perception is hard work, and contamination by ancestors makes the work even harder. I leafed through my sleep library in search of an orgasm suitable for an agent. But, sotto voce and for your eyes only, I must say that I have never been either a fan or an apologist for orgasm. The only orgasm I inhabited completely is the one I had in the lap of the Virgin in my parish church when I was fourteen. I didn't know what it was which made it so much sweeter, and as it flooded me I was so rapt in prayer I thought my angel had urinated on me.

Δ

The Red Square in Moscow is full of people looking up expectantly to Gorbachev as he is about to speak. Suddenly, a sound, like that of a field full of grasshoppers in August, breaks the silence: a million men are pulling down their zippers at once! And another time, when the lack of meat drove everybody crazy in Russia, the crazed Russians poured across the borders into Romania and ate all the cows grazing there. And those are just some of the things that go on behind the Iron Curtain, Number 15 told me.

Number 15 was ensconced in my former bed in the middle of my apartment, tended to by my mother with wine, and by Raquel who rhythmically brushed her breasts across his chest.

"What about Dracula? And did you ever become a citizen?" I asked him.

"Dracula," he said, "was Gutenberg's son. After Gutenberg printed his Bibles he printed a book on Dracula's atrocities. This was the first mass-produced book in the world and the world's first taste of literacy. Dracula made print successful, and the vogue it has enjoyed ever since was rooted in him. The ink of that early tale about the blood he spilled is indelible. The content of cultural democracy is a horror tale. The blood he spilled issues forth from the source of the modern mind like sperm from a bull.

"I am not a citizen yet," he concludes.

Raquel had broken the house rule. Even Tabita was not allowed to bring men in, she had to work wherever the light was dim and the place deserted. Tabita is obsessive and therefore certain things are forgiven her, like her fondness for dwarves and her passion for crabs, but even she does not work in front of mother. Raquel, on the other hand, is a murderous fury clad in outward calm who glows like a brilliant panther when aroused. She has been known to murder and mutilate and will no doubt do it again when the moon is full. I am afraid of her because she is full of intricate canals through which flows a crimson substance which isn't blood. So instead of throwing her on her ass out the window followed by her john, which everyone tells me I must do if I hope to assert my authority, I prefer to make conversation. Authority to me is like sleep linguistics. Words in dreams, awkward flights over rooftops.

"But you must ghost Dracula's autobiography," I tell Number 15. "If direct violence is unadvisable, you would do well to sell the object of your distaste to the devil." But he is not stupid, this foreigner. He sips his wine like a fox, intent on citizenship. Dracula, who was the father of the modern state and the inventor of nationalism, stands firmly behind him, with one hand on his skull and the other on the book.

"Justice," he says, "cannot be established without terror. Ivan the Great copied Dracula. As did Machiavelli. The fatal flaw of Western democracies, the United States

96

chief among them, was to transform Dracula from a voice of the State, which he has always been, into a private citizen with a taste for blood. You can stake an individual through the heart, bury him at the crossroads, lop his head off with an axe, transfix him with a hawthorn bough and quarter him, but there will always be another individual ready to rise and take his place, or another movie. No wonder he's bigger than Christ! Where Christ merely offers his blood like a wimpy liberal, Dracula takes it!" Number 15 became so excited he stood in bed and lifted his wine glass high over his head. My mother took her pulse compulsively and I saw large drops of blood on the ceiling. In the tiny film of light winding through the blood drops, history marched in rags, endless waves of men covered with wolf hair.

Yes, his tale had to be written, and I said so again, but mainly to recover my body which has a tendency, when excited, to rise up on a flood of adrenaline and leave me stranded among dictionaries. But Number 15 was drunk and making doleful sounds of wooden instruments. His hands—he had dropped the glass and crashed it to the floor—were drumming on the ceiling, from which protruded two boars' heads covered at the neck by tight skins; his feet were pumping two wolves' clawed feet which operated an accordion-like contraption formed partly by Raquel's bosom; and his cock was solemnly banging my sister's echoing skull.

This is when Madam Rosa Alvarez burst into the room, her flat yellow mug streaked by orange tears, her hands in the air. "Tabita is dead!" she screamed.

"She is not dead!" Number 15 screamed back at her. "She has gone to marry the sun! The moon and the stars will be her bridesmaids and the heavens will look on her wedding! The moon will wear a red velvet dress, and the angels of God will hold their gold mirrors to her face so she can see how beautiful she is! The angels of God are blind but their mirrors see for them! She will marry the sun, and the sun will shine on earth to tell people how happy he is with his bride! On beautiful summer days you will be able to see her sitting beside her husband, the sun, greeting you!"

"She is dead, I tell you! She has been positively identified!" shrieked Madam Rosa. But at that moment the room was flooded with light, and the sun, which had been in the clouds for the past few days, came through the crepe curtains and put roses on everybody, so we all knew that the old landlady had been lying. Tabita herself came in a few minutes later to say that she had been stretched naked on the roof hoping the sun would come out because she was "white as milk and freckled as a general's map," when Madam Rosa had burst into tears over her and ran off screaming, "I knew it! I knew it! The bugs have killed her!" Madam Rosa shook her head adamantly and declared, "You were dead! I saw it with my own eyes! If my husband was still alive, God bless his soul, he would throw you all out like rabbit bones from the stew!" She shook her head violently from right to left, Tabita shook hers from left to right, mama began to shake hers, Raquel shook hers and Number 15 shook his up and down—only I, in the midst of the storm that shook the tree, kept mine still because I needed it to think with.

Δ

The flaming buoyant defense lawyer circles the ear—which is the accused's most pleasing feature, often nibbled by the acrobat he murdered—with a finger so long it sends a 200-volt charge through the jury, and sums up the case: "This man is guilty of no more than trying to put a little charge and zip into his life. Is *that* a crime?" Fighting that fresh voltage are only the quickly fading shocks—about 100 volts—of the doctor on the witness stand gripping the wooden drawer containing a slice of the victim's buttock. The slice prevails over the finger and, shortly after, the accused fries in the Ohio chair at some 10,000 volts, the sum total of the shocks experienced by the ladies and gentlemen of the jury, which is about to become "Another famous case, involving the well-known lawyer F. P. Pearley, consumed much of the doctor's time that year …" When into my broom closet, limber and jaunty, pill-boxed, mink-furred, pulling a panther on a long gold chain, bursts the morgue widow, younger than her wedding pictures.

"How?" I gasp.

"Lamb fetuses! Gerovital! Virgin blood!"

Fresh from Transylvania where she just spent two weeks, the widow beams from a new body. "Dracula's castle has been turned by the Romanian government into a youth clinic," she explains, green lightning in her eyes. "I lay on a terrace looking up at the Carpathians as young Gypsies shot me full of unborn baby lamb juice. The only noise was the whirring of the huge fetus blender where five hundred lambs fresh cut from their mothers turned into youth paste. In the afternoon the Gypsies carried me on their shoulders to Countess Bathory's castle over the hill. The Countess, you may recall, was arrested in 1611 by the Lord Palatine of Hungary and charged with the murder of 650 virgins in whose blood she bathed daily. She so depleted the region of virgins (not to speak of the fact that she gave virginity such a bad name, that even to this day little girls in that region beg strangers to deflower them) that her cousin, the Lord Palatine, had to do something. He had the Countess walled into her bath where she lived ten years on caked blood. It is a lovely old castle, also restored by that shrewd little government, and there we took our afternoon bath—some sixty of us—in blood as fresh and virginal as the Countess could ever hope for. In addition, five Gerovital injections every evening ... I'm going out of my mind, I tell you!"

The widow made as if to bite me. Her panther snarled and I ducked. She laughed heartily. "You're too old for me, dear. How is my hubby's courtroom career coming along?" I read her a few passages and she approved full steam ahead. "That's just how it was," she sighed. I sighed too because I'd made it all up.

The widow's rejuvenation threw the morgue staff into utter confusion. They had been expecting her to die any day, hoping, alas, because she was always underfoot, pulling out drawers, criticizing procedure and offering opinions. But her Transylvanian vacation continued to work: every day, instead of dying, she kept getting younger. Old friends she had become suddenly younger than, often did not recognize her.

"Is that you, darling?" they asked, every time she appeared. At last they quit asking and simply accepted the fact that an increasingly younger woman was prowling the morgue at all hours of the day and night.

She looked about twenty-five that Friday night. I'd worked past my midnight deadline and was preparing to go down the stairs when I heard a soft noise outside. It sounded like someone slipping a razor back and forth between two pieces of felt. I went out to look and the noise moved ahead of me, up the stairs. I followed it. There was no sign of the custodian who at this time took a nap in the supply room on a pile of fresh white shrouds. I followed the noise six stories where it stopped. The sixth floor, like the rest of them, was an empty hall with drawers in the walls climbing like ladders to the ceiling in the eternal 17 degrees Fahrenheit. In the dark I heard a drawer slide out of the wall and then a muffled sound like that of a body throwing itself on a wrestling mat came from there. There was rapid breathing, an *ah!* then an *oh!* and when I turned on my

100

penlight I saw the widow bite the face of a cadaver in what was apparently an effort to suck out the eyeball.

"Don't move or I kill you!" I quoted myself.

I killed her. My penlight was also a knife and I stabbed her in the heart with it. I found an empty drawer and laid her in there.

"Oh, God, why me?" she asked when she saw Him.

"Is that you, dear? I didn't recognize you!" He said.

The scene had somewhat awakened me so I went back to my closet and worked some more. It seems that Winston Churchill, Somerset Maugham, and the Duke and the Duchess of Windsor, had all been converts to the lamb fetus therapy. The good doctor himself had, just before he died, recommended it to his wife. He had had a harrowing day on the stand and the lawyer's continuous efforts to discredit him had worn him out. But now as he looked fondly at his wife as she lay sprawled on a woven map of the moon, her buttocks on Mare Somniorum and Mare Tranquilitas and her left breast on Mare Nectaris, he knew that the mind was elitist—it refused sleep fully earned by the body. But sleep did finally come, and in it he realized, and then saw, that the unconscious was the unidentified caller who had left her telephone number earlier with the ambiguous message that "the dark horse" was still on sale. At the door of the pantry leading to the attic where he went to inquire after the horse, he was met by a maid who spoke with a heavy Baltic accent. "My name is Reciprocal," she said. "Your horse is in the kitchen." Which becomes: "Often, when the doctor came home tired from a particularly trying day in court, I lay on the couch telling him fairy tales (which he liked enormously, particularly German ones) in a soft tone of voice, until he fell asleep."

Δ

It is a cliché, I know but within the confines of a police-man's uniform there often beats a huge, trapped moth, the tips of its wings brushing frantically against the sides of the ribcage. In my old police soul this butterfly beat so furiously it burst its cage, and that's how I came to beg for lemons and film. It's an old story, made complicated by the fact of police love, which is that the euphoric sadism of power can never have enough to feed itself. Policemen, like the rest of us, want boundless love, and they die for lack of it. They want to bind, be bound, beat, be beaten, piss on and be pissed on, and more than anything they want the butterfly to stop the agony of its thrashing. And like the rest of us, they eat to still the ache, and eat, and eat, spaghetti, sau-sages, egg foo yung, cheese, meat, pies, candy and bacon. The more they eat the more insatiable they become ... the spirit is a bottomless hole. Cops have been known to aim their service revolvers at their chest, where they imagine the head of the moth is, and then fire deliriously. Often this wild firing does no more than enlarge the hole into which they then pour redoubled portions of pasta, tomato sauce and leftover casserole, until they become so large they have to be given an official reprimand and ordered to trim down. The fat cop is a tragic creature, the victim both of a furious desire for the world and of a crazed butterfly in his chest.

I am telling you this so that you may understand the spirit in which I am teasing my immigration agent who, frozen with terror and suffering in his chair, faces me, his butterfly wild and out of control, fluttering visibly and ruffling the hair on his chest. My butterfly, freed long ago, calls and sings to his butterfly, trying to lure him out to mate. I am being cruel, nay, sinister as I improvise the prettiest canzones ever hummed and ever woven, as I dive and circle and pirouette and shoot golden pollen. Come my darling, I sing, let's make a four-winged being, enter each other until no one can feel the seam, let's be utterly crazy and demonically deliberate, let's give the space horse a whack with our wings until it shoots through time, obscurity is hateful, let's proclaim the approximate clarity of feeling, let's whip out of the sordid history of the police body into the coolness of the night, let's create en route the solid delights we can't imagine!

"Level with me, José! I have no time any longer for shots in the dark!" he pleads.

"Yes," I agree. "The dark is bigger than all the rifles."

"Once, I too ... considered being an artist ..."

"Oh ... what happened? Did she leave you?"

"How did you know?" He is surprised, but in pain.

How did I know? Because she is written all over him, just the way she sprawled that afternoon on the Peruvian blanket with cones and spirals everywhere, ready to make him into an artist, a devotee and an ecstatic until, later that evening, she left for the jungles of the Americas with two men she found sleeping in a bus station with their heads on motel Bibles and chains around their necks. Yes, my judge of citizenship, you still reek of her, her smell is indelible, she was the only one who knew the secret of stilling the butterfly. And your idea of the kind of art you were going to make wasn't bad either. You had noticed—thanks to the vision she lent you for one week—that people made all sorts of involuntary gestures: a pat on the hair, a fingernail in the crotch, a wink, a grimace, a gentle tug at a stray hair, a knee jerk, an opening or closing of hands or buttocks, raising one shoulder or another, a tip of tongue darting out. And you conceived, in a reverie, the possibility of having these involuntary mannerisms replicated in stained glass. You saw a church rising out of the floor, composed entirely of representations of coincidental movement arranged by you in classical religious scenes: the Wedding at Cana, the Stations of the Cross. After the vision you saw, for the week she gave you, that people's willed and ordinary beings were framed entirely by their unconscious gestures. You even saw, though too briefly for understanding, that a great deal of devotional faith inspired people to move in ways which they knew not.

"What sort of artist?" I asked.

"Oh ... stained glass ... nothing much. More of a crafts thing really."

"That makes you a foreigner. If you would like to emigrate to art I will be happy to look into what I can do to get citizenship for you," I said. "Artland has stricter entry requirements than the United States of America. To come to the U.S. you need merely a clear anti-communist conscience, proof that you always screw on top if a man and on the bottom if a woman, no aristocratic titles, not even Discount, no hidden hate of taxes and no authorship of even minor crimes like drinking hootch at fourteen, am I right? But to gain admittance to Artland, ah! You must, first of all, remain vague while the circumstances are attacking or circumstantial when vagueness does. Then you must be nobody, you must divest yourself of your person, your class and your property not to speak of your so-called mind and your opinions, you must allow yourself to lapse unexpectedly into metaphorical Corinthian, let no one take you for granted, you must make sure that everyone knows, including yourself, that you are capable of perpetrating any enormity at any given time, and never under any circumstances must you finish your sentences, you must never know how a sentence will end, you must escape confinement continuously. That is, you must never serve your sentence, you must brutally uneducate yourself, the world is a speech malfunction, the simplest things must be a complete mystery to you and you must approach them with the eternal idiot questions like a child bearing flowers to the enormous tractor leveling the old cemetery. You must live verifiably in the huge emptiness between possibilities and decisions, loving the former, amusing yourself with the latter, and, above all, you must always be amused. You must destroy agents, editors, censors and representatives of the state as often as possible, all dirty tricks permitted, and you must approach the universe in a militant fashion because you make it up as you breathe. Also you will allow yourself to be kidnapped by all and sundry forms of whimsy and will refuse to follow plans. You will not set foot where anybody wants you to but you must visit Plato's Republic as often as you can so that you can be thrown out of it. You must not above all believe in art or any other form of confinement, you must inspire madness, impossibility and confusion. And on the ladder of discarded negations, with a mouth full of grass, holding a lit bomb, you must climb at all times into the movies which you must trust are being shown in their entirety, any questions?"

"No," he says, "only one. Can I visit your place of residence? It is routine."

"Sure. Put your coat on, man, and let's go. My mother and sisters will be delighted. They love doctors, lawyers, engineers and the rest of the middle class. In fact, there may be some already there so you won't have to feel out of place ..."

"No, not now. How about tomorrow?"

"Fine, but I don't think you'll get into Artland with an attitude like that. But who knows, maybe the moth will bust out ... if properly coaxed, goodbye, goodbye."

Δ

When I say that Mama cleaned up ... well, maybe you know what happened to the two girls who every morning swept up dust into the eyes of the sun. The sun turned them into the stars with the broom, up there by the Southern Cross. Well, if the sky had been in the mood he could have

105

turned Mama and my two sisters into meteorites, moon vapor and echoes, because the three of them swept all day and all night, and when they were done sweeping they tore open Mama's collection of liquid, gaseous and solid cleansers, everything advertised on TV since they had come to America, boxes and boxes and bottles and bottles which until then had been piling up in pyramids behind the bed, dresser and in front of the full-color poster of the Virgin, covered up in her robes and by the left foot of the Holy Infant. Simultaneously, grainy blue powders foamed on the walls and liquid plumbers burrowed through the pipes. Bombs exploded causing roaches to migrate, long sorrowful lines of refugees leaving under the door crack for the neighboring apartments. The windows became transparent for the first time in memory, letting in a view of dirty windows across the street behind which startled fat nudes watched early morning television. The mattresses were beaten savagely, stains cracked and springs moaned. The floors vied with the boots of old-fashioned sergeants in reflecting our faces. The ceiling could be read like a coloring book through hundreds of exposed layers of ancient paint. "Now if I could," Mama said, "I would like to clean up the street of all these dirty houses, this one first of all, get rid of all these people, wash the sidewalks, suck all the dirt out of the air and move New York out of New York."

"Ugh, look at this!" Tabita exclaimed, pointing to the screen of the old TV she had just finished scrubbing and sponging, "Now you can see what people are wearing!" Indeed, the game show host and his guests shone with new-found details. Ties and shoes stood out distinctly. Tabita touched one of her breasts fondly but exclaimed mournfully: "All these freckles ..." We were all naked because our clothes were boiling in the kitchen, spewing clouds of steam. Our bodies, dissimilar only in the distribution of skin, loose like a crumpled wino bag on Mama, taut and

106

stretched over breasts and hips on Raquel and Tabita, and pinned niggardly to my pointed bones, were otherwise and for all theoretical purposes, the same body, particularly in the pubic area which was stamped by four identical pyramids of red hair. Known as "the Amazonian forests of First Avenue," my sisters' bushes were legendary where such legends circulate. It would have been inhuman and unnatural for these lush growths to contain no life and here was the rub ... they teemed with it.... Mama had tried to pour a bottle of A-200 on Tabita while she slept but she'd awakened screaming genocide and hadn't calmed down yet. "You might as well kill me too ..." she repeated every five minutes. Raquel tried to talk sense into her: "They are just like roaches, only smaller ... you don't seem to speak up for roaches, do you ... No one else is either ..." "That's tough!" screamed Tabita. "I can't champion all the bugs in the world!" I saw her point: the roaches had no apologist, no house critic, but they could take care of themselves. The crabs needed Tabita the way corporate publishing needs *The New York Times Book Review*. The only concession we were able to extract from her was a solemn promise that she would not scratch herself during the immigration agent's visit. I don't think a visit by the Pope would have caused such a promise from her. Only Immigration had such power and I never understood why until later events revealed that Raquel was in love with Number 15 and Number 15 had twice attempted suicide when denied citizenship, and Tabita loved Raquel more than anyone else in the world. Our household was a household of love and one person's beloved crabs were the others' beloved crabs no matter what we happened to think of them. And that is how it came to pass that amid the shining cleanliness, an oasis of purity in the heart of New York, only a few crabs, the more visible for being the sole survivors of a truly American cleaning binge, made their accustomed rounds in the forests of our beings.

But just when it appeared that all was in order and in pristine readiness for the visit, tragedy struck. The lush use of Lysol, bleaches, Clorox, detergents and soaps in the water, destroyed our clothes. Every last piece of cloth had boiled irretrievably away and there wasn't another garment in the apartment. The water in the cauldron had turned into purple paste. My blue suit had merged with my sisters' lingerie and my mother's polyesters had merged with our Colombian flannels.

Only four hours remained until the visit, a time Mother had deemed sufficient for the clothes to dry, but now we were in trouble. Raquel picked up the telephone to call Number 15 to ask him to purchase anything he could find but the telephone was dead. It seems that in scrubbing the walls Tabita had dislodged the connections. Either that or one of the powerful detergents had corroded the apparatus. There was only one thing to do and that was for me to wrap myself in the plastic shower curtain with the Hoboken angels on it and go to the store, and this I did.

Roaming the streets in transparent plastic, o bards, is no big deal in our city. I noticed many hundreds of people in similar attire. I had never seen them before which confirms my law of New York, which is that you only see your own sort of humans in our great city, depending on the speed of your walking and the demands of your eyes. Rapid businessmen with swinging briefcases see only their own kind. Parallel to them but slower is another world and parallel to that is a yet slower one until you arrive at the motionless bums who see only the motionless. And parallel to the worlds of speed are the worlds of tweed, cotton and plastic—likewise aware only of each other. So it was no surprise really to see thousands of Hoboken angels dancing on frayed plastic around the bodies of an entire social subclass. But when I got to Orchard Street where all the

108

affordable clothes are, I saw that I had no money. In our haste to boil our clothes we had boiled away our wallets and purses also.

One thing to do then. I walked into the crowded offices of the Manhattan Chemical Bank and stood in line. When my turn came I advanced on the teller, a spry Puerto Rican blonde standing on twenty-inch platforms, and said, "Lean over the counter as far as you can and look down. You will see a weapon pointed at you! Take all the money in the drawers and put it in a blue deposit bag or these are the last words you hear!" To make my weapon as visible as possible I filled my mind with the curves and buttocks of my filming days. I bent in memory over the deliciously spread body of the adrenaline-filled love of my Buddhist burning days, and then lowered myself into the ghost agent's girlfriend while Peggy studied us playing in the window, and helped these images with my hand, up and down. The teller leaned far over the counter and looked down and saw the weapon grinning at her and pointing straight at her ruby-lipsticked heart-shaped mouth. "All right," she mumbled, and filled a bag with cash.

Loaded with clothes and feeling not a little crinkly and quite a bit squeaky in my brand new striped green suit and tight wingtips I flew up the stairs of our apartment, convinced that a rush of bank robberies by penis awaited our mimetic city in the next few days as soon as the *Daily News* hit the stands. I had purchased lush silks and expensive shoes and exotic perfumes and Persian rugs. I opened the door, dropped the huge parcels and saw that I was too late.

Sitting stiffly in the better of my two wooden chairs, was the immigration agent, his eyes riveted to the square tips of his shoes, which slipped on the waxed floor back and forth, while facing him, on our other chair, was my naked mama, making conversation. On the bed, with their legs crossed, and their arms around each other, my two little nude sisters smiled large fixed smiles like birds about to attack a ripe plum tree.

"Yes, you should have seen my little son in Bogotá. Always praying to the Virgin, always reading ... Reading and praying, he was an angel he really was ... Would you like to see some pictures?" Mother got up and removed from a trunk the carefully dusted photo album, exposing, as she bent over, her ancient wobbly buttocks atop her jiggling old thighs.

"If he becomes a citizen," Raquel explained, "then he can get far more work as a ghost because no one trusts a foreign ghost, they think a foreign ghost pulls back to the place where he was born."

"And maybe then we can be citizens too!" shouted Tabita, who had a problem adjusting her voice controls.

"Would you ... like that?" coughed the agent, avoiding but seeing nevertheless the immense brown aureolas of Tabita's breasts.

"Here he is at ten, in our parish church ..." Mother moved her chair closer to him so he could look. She put part of the album on his knees while another part rested on hers. "Here he is with the statue of the Mountain Virgin of the Eight Miracles when she came through our town. Little Joselito didn't sleep for many nights before she came. He prayed and cried until his eyes were red ..." Page by page, the devoted little boy went on his knees from icon to icon and statue to statue, crying rivers of tears.

"I brought you some clothes," I offered, directing their attention to my bundles. "I hope I got the right sizes ..."

"Ah!" said the agent, "I'm glad to see *you!* Your mother and sisters were kind enough to entertain me but it is you I have business with. Could we go into another room?"

"I am sorry, there is no other room. We could sit outside on the steps ..."

110

"No, that's fine. We can sit here I suppose, if your family doesn't mind ..."

"No, no," they all hastened to reassure him, moving off the chair and beds to examine my purchases. They tore open the packages and a storm of underwear, skirts and blouses broke over the room as they lifted their legs and their arms to slip them on, and bent and shook to adjust them. There was a rush to the mirror and Raquel and Tabita had their usual mirror fight. "There is only room in the mirror for one of us!" "Mirror, mirror on the wall, who's the biggest slut of them all?" "I'm surprised you don't keep your mirror in your pussy! Then you could see yourself from the inside!" "I've got a mirror in my ass, why don't you look at yourself in here!" "Every time you look in there you grow warts on your lip!" and so on, but just before they were about to let fly at each other they smiled and embraced and, amazingly, they both fit in the mirror and there was even room for Mother.

"You have an understanding family," said the agent. "We place great value on harmonious family life. The family is the base of our way of life!"

"Yes, I have been blessed that way. I am lucky, I really am."

"I like your mother very much. She is a fine lady," he said, but what he meant was he liked Tabita very much because his eyes were glued to her.

At this point, the door burst open and Number 15 rushed in, one of his arms in a sling and the wrist bandaged. "You!" he exclaimed, when he saw the agent. "I almost died because of you! Where is my citizenship?" He took a menacing step, holding up his wounded arm.

"Regulations ... Forms ... It isn't up to me ... Procedure ..." He was visibly alarmed. "We never determined how you came to this country ... Where is your green card?"

"I told you how I came. I flew, that's how. I lost my green card in a parking lot in Hollywood! What more do you want from me?"

"There was no record of your flight!"

"Of all the nerve! Every bird between here and the Black Sea can vouch for me! I even smiled at the stewardesses on a transatlantic Pan Am jet and they waved at me! Jerk!"

The agent stood as if to leave.

"No you don't," grinned Number 15, a large blackened and calloused paw on the official's shoulder. "Not until I tell you what we do to tax collectors in Transylvania."

In Transylvania a tax collector was lacerated bit by bit, until his reason was destroyed. Often, he was attached to a chair or a bed hung from a horizontal arm attached to a pillar in the middle of a damp dungeon or cave: by means of a system of gears the machine was set for any degree of speed. The rotatory machine gained speed slowly until it looked hell-driven and the sufferer's pockets shook loose all the pillaged taxes while his reason fell away in spasmodic chunks. The inventor of the rack, a Transylvanian nobleman named Baron von Bruckenthal, refined this machine to such heights of perfectability that in 1731 an imperial tax collector was completely dismembered by the centrifugal force and pieces of him were found as far as Vienna sticking in the weather vanes of some of the finer houses on Elisabethstrasse. Later, it seems, new techniques came into use, including the infamous "tax collector music machine" which was inserted into the body through what was called "a rigorous system of organic and moral penetration." It consisted of tiny disks resembling roll music for the player piano which were put inside the intestines, the brain and the spine. Seven strong fellows with wooden hammers hit the wooden keys of the machine a little distance from the tax collector who then

112

began to fill up with music and to hum and reverberate louder and louder until all his internal organs started dancing. The music eventually attained such strength that all the whirling and waltzing organs exploded, merging inside the man in a furious and indistinct sea which rose in a single wave and lifted the body into the clouds, pulling him off the disks.

"And that!" shrieked Number 15, "is only part of the story!"

There was only one way to anesthetize Number 15 so he wouldn't harm my fragile link to citizenship, and Raquel took it. She dropped one of her large breasts into her palms where it fell with a heavy plop and she introduced the nipple into Number 15's angry mouth which closed immediately and began to make baby noises. "There, there," she said, patting him on the rough black Brillo pad most Romanians seem to wear on their heads, "There, there," and he closed his eyes and fell asleep.

When the agent saw he was out of danger he became indignant: "That man!" he grunted. "To every simple question I asked him he replied with riddles! Fairy tales! Vampire bats! I said 'Have you ever been arrested?' and he gave me this history of his twelve cousins' cardiac arrests! He probably doesn't have any cousins! He doesn't even have a mother, I'm sure of that! He's a down-and-out orphan with a big mouth!" The agent half stood, shaking his finger, while Tabita nodded gravely, agreeing with every word. He now addressed himself entirely to her: "Some people think we are robots! They have no respect at all for what we represent! And then they want to be citizens! Sometimes I think I'm being punished with this job for sins from another life but of course I don't believe in that nonsense! Believe me, after a day of the strangest gibberish in one thousand different accents, I'm ready to hang my hat!"

113

"Hang it! Hang it!" cried Tabita, falling into his arms, "Hang it on me!"

He had no hat to hang but he held on to her as they both fell on the floor and wriggled there utterly penetrated, he by red-haired Colombian heat and she by compassion and a big man. I prayed Number 15 wouldn't wake up and he didn't. Mama got up to fix some snacks because she knew they would be mighty hungry when they got up off the floor. I was rather hungry myself—emotions render me famished—and I rocked back and forth on my heels, abandoning myself to the familiar and lovely sounds of my now wordless household, Number 15's snores alternating with the content suckling sounds of his lips, the agent's and Tabita's *ahs, ohs, madres, dios, god, oh my gods, oh fucks,* and the sizzling heavenly aromas of frying hot peppers, thin slices of marinated beef, bubbling beef bones and fresh bread coming out of Mama's pans and oven. Ah, yes, even everloud New York appeared to have been stilled outside the window in hot afternoon sun. All was peaceful, quiet and safe. Sometimes, not often enough, the world is like this, gently immobile in an eternal Sunday afternoon. We stop our banging and clanging for long enough to taste the sweetness of things at ease, their hard edges softened, harshness gone or out of focus, something dimly remembered flows sluggishly through the body. A gaucho, asleep on his horse, stands still in the Sierras. There is no wind, the animals sleep. On the half-eaten head of a cow the flies stop buzzing. The maggots too take time off for a nap, stretched lazily in dark tunnels of food. Sudden peace illuminates the eyes of the man dying in the house next door. He falls into it like a fat snowflake on a white field. I am six years old and I am watching him, not moving. Later, when the adults come back, I tell them how the Virgin came in softly and took his soul with her. They too can feel the peace. This peace is a gift—you cannot buy it and nowadays to people my age it comes only rarely. Only violence can at times bring it up, often with death in tow. And there are many to whom it never comes. It never comes to dreamers who have become cops. To writers who have become agents. To lemon lovers who now sell houses. The price for re-entry into the society which hated them is half the hate, which they must take into themselves to lighten society's burden. A true Sunday afternoon comes only to those able to make their experience public and this they are forbidden to do by the self-hate with which they bought their way back in. The prodigal son is an anomaly, he fits nowhere, he has denied his past but has no taste for the present. His parents do not want him now, they want him then. The labor market will only take him grudgingly and then at a substandard wage, he suffers all the agonies of a turncoat and none of the pleasures of forgiveness except money and money is garbage so the only place short of death which he has also forsaken in favor of old age is Tabita's pussy and in it he goes, up and around, up and up, up and out, unaware that myriad-legged swarms of Venusian jewels are migrating onto his body, riders of the storm awakened by heat. The content of his revelation, the fleeting beginning of his abandoned art return briefly in orgasm without the mushy edges of political hysteria and they are public for the first time in his life because I am watching carefully and Mama too, her pan full of sizzling red peppers held in suspension briefly, because this is one of the few moments that bear watching, being both incomprehensible and totally true. But we aren't newspapers, of course.

Number 15 woke up feeling mythological, throwing his startled body out of sleep with a stream of curses invoking fabulous beasts. He was about to strangle the agent, who was struggling to his feet, when Mama served the food. We ate it and with each dish we became sadder. Number 15 remembered the food of his country and began in low monotone to recite the names of all the dishes of yore. It was a litany of the dishes of Transylvania, as beautiful as a funeral dirge. And it seems that indeed, at funerals, the people of that country recite the names of all their best dishes over the body of the departed, in order to remind the angel of death that the deceased is on a special diet and will not have anything below par in the next world. Mama became sad because the peppers and tomatoes were not the way she remembered them—they tasted limp and airless, not at all like the robust vegetables of Colombia. Raquel was sad because every time she ate she got a little fatter and one day would come when she would be too fat for love. Tabita was sad because in reaching inside the agent she had found only a terrifying and whistling emptiness and now she wasn't hungry. And I was sad because the world is sad and my loved ones were very sad but my sadness was happy like rain in the fall. I was sweetly sad and not at all unhappy. The agent, of course, was sad because he didn't know what he wanted from these people, and worse he didn't know who he was anymore, and the food was foreign and it didn't warm him.

The agent left with his report unwritten—the first time it had ever happened. He strolled aimlessly through the riverfront park. At one point he felt what he took to be a prick of his conscience but it was only an itch in his chest hair. Soon came another false prick of conscience which again was only an itch below his abdomen. As the pricks began to multiply, he thought, well, maybe it is my conscience. After all, I was derelict of duty. Soon his entire hairy body seemed to be on fire and the passersby slowed down to take a long look at the madly scratching bureaucrat set on fire by his conscience. By this time he had almost ceased looking human as he leaped and jumped like a shaman deer dancer trying to pull off his skin. He ripped his shirt and drew long bloody lines with his nails. They went

116

up and down his body, deep and crimson like railroad tracks. Trains of maddened guilt ran on them at great speeds. His pants and shoes and socks came off next as he contorted and rolled into balls of pain attempting to tear open parts of his body he had never touched before. It was not much later that the moth in his chest, temporarily stilled by Tabita and by the hot peppers, began to flutter frantically inside him. This itching from the inside awoke in him what can only be described as the collective guilt of world bureaucracies. The unfulfilled nationalisms and sadistic racisms of all the buried strains in the dream of the uniform attacked him with the fury of their incompletion. Every new itch said, "We counted on you!" and every letter of that reproach was a line of red ants berserk in his body. I could barely keep up with him from the distance I was following but I knew he couldn't recognize me any more, so I came closer.

"Don't move or I kill you," I again quoted myself.

I killed him. I pushed him into the river, but instead of swimming he continued to roll and tear at his insides until a long rubber object, the likes of which float only on the East River and nowhere else, wrapped itself around his neck and squeezed the air out of his lungs. He sank rapidly and I knew that it had been a mercy killing.

Δ

Rolling Stone magazine, the magazine for rock lovers, surveyed its readers, the rocks, demanding to know where they had been the night of the day President Kennedy was assassinated and all of them all the readers had been losing their virginity at that precise point in time being deflowered in cars and motels so many of them that if you lit up the map of the United States with little red fires for all the cherries popped, it would have looked like the country was on fire that night and the magazine concluded that the "You Ess of A" had therefore in a single night lost its innocence.

I would have liked to continue *Living and Loving in the Shadow of the Morgue* but the widow's widowed panther ate the manuscript. Left alone in the apartment where I delivered all the fresh pages, the animal clawed its way through everything: Steuben glass, ceramic ballerinas, gold forensic instruments, love letters, Biedermeyer furniture, Victorian fainting sofa, butcher block counter tops, several Impressionists, books, manuscripts and finally walls, emerging into the neighboring apartment, famished, wounded and streaked with blood. And there it found and fell upon the heir of Substandard Oil whom it ate in two large clean bites. The evening papers published grisly photos of the panther as it looked finally shot down by the police with dumdum bullets, and one final picture that shows a policeman pulling the head of the heir from the mouth of the beast which lay supine on the Turkestan rug. The newspapers then dealt at length with the relations of the deceased to power including a curious episode concerning the Kennedy assassination. Jim Garrison, the New Orleans district attorney who hunted conspirators in the Kennedy case, had once served the heir with a subpoena. But the heir never testified. He obtained postponements until the panther ate him.

The widow's death made my ghost agent very happy at first, with the pure happiness of agents whose clients die with all their papers in order. "If we now play our cards right we can get the whole loot...We split her fifty-percenter right down the middle." Her only heir was the dead panther. The agent was so tickled by the prospect he patted the lion paw of the couch. He had made the office couch into his home. The floor surrounding its pillowed hollow was littered with the wrappers of a year of meals from McDonald's. When he went dancing he went with his couch, which was carried to the dance hall by two unemployed ghosts. There, they put wheels on it, and the couch careened over the floor scattering dancers in its wake. The couch was a hit in New York where it replaced roller skates. Couch dancing spread across the land. But in the office, in its original habitat, the couch looked rather ordinary. Under Big Mac boxes were his clothes.

It gladdened me to pour cold water on the swindle. "The panther ate the manuscript and I have no intention of redoing it. What a panther eats is withdrawn from circulation. That is the ultimate review."

The wounded agent might have torn his hair but decided instead to pull the taffy of an interminably silly argument out of his body, namely that I should rewrite the story as rapidly as possible—he would feed me steak and bennies the whole time—because all that mattered now was cash. There was no widow to placate. Words are only means to an end, he proclaimed. The idea is to create a semblance of chill glamour. He was at the forefront of the movement which seeks to devalue our currency.

"Would you hurl yourself into her absence until you took shape?" I asked him.

Waxing most definitely philosophic, he said, "A means to an end is a curious proposition. The end of man is at the tip of his penis but the end of a woman is never in sight, therefore the woman is always the means. Words as means are words as woman ..."

Ergo, I would have had to sacrifice my sisters in order to rewrite the story. I stared murderously at the man who would kill Raquel and Tabita for a fifty-percenter split down the middle. Devaluing my currency, killing my sisters, the agent took on the light by which I need to see whom I am killing. But he was a slippery bastard and possibly psychic as well because he smelled danger and dropped the

119

subject. He thus prolonged his life momentarily.

"I have something that might interest you ..." He said this in a hushed voice. He lowered the window although it was hot and the air conditioner was broken. He opened the door abruptly and satisfied himself that no one was listening on the other side. "Something so ... staggering only a true artist would be interested., In fact, the job might be suicidal ... I don't know if I should tell you this."

I urged him on. My interest in him was proportional to the things he had to tell me. His life depended on keeping my interest. A single minute of silence could be the end of him and he knew it. So he talked on and this is what he said: "Never in my entire career as a literary agent or even before as a young apprentice to the Gutenberg Conversion Principle have I come across anything as potentially profitable or dangerous as this ... Are you familiar with congressman Uberstein?"

The Gutenberg Conversion Principle is the process of turning words into cash through print. Money is printed and words are printed so it stands to reason that printed words can in a maximum mimetic state, become money. The laws regarding this procedure are put forth in a pamphlet distributed exclusively to agents. It seems that the congressman had barely put down the freshly debugged —weekly—Princess phone when in came a starving man from early radical days and shot him fifty times in the head. "You are taking over my dreams," he said before he fired.

That morning Congressman Uberstein had delivered 250 pages of a manuscript to the former partner of my ghost agent, the former ghost agent, now ghost. The manuscript contained a brand new conspiracy theory on the assassination of the Kennedy brothers. The manuscript was barely in the safe and the congressman barely dead two hours when the ghost agent suffered a violent heart attack whose lack of symptoms would have delighted the chief pathologist if *he* had been alive.

"Now here is the thing," the agent went on in a voice no louder now than the murmur of a top floor water faucet. "If any similarities exist between the Kennedy and the Uberstein assassins we may be on our way to the source ... a Manchurian candidate factory ..."

"And what would my job be?" I asked, pretending not to know. I knew what my job would be. I know what my job is. My job would be what my job is which is to make a beeline for the heart of American evil. I had no doubt that sooner or later, in order to become a citizen, I would have to bathe in black waters. Now that my job was about to be revealed to me in all its technical splendor, I wasn't sure I wanted it. There was still time to pack mother and sisters and go back to a dark corner of the Cathedral in Bogotá and weep at the feet of the Virgin. I could spend the rest of my life praying for the undoing of her generosity, which brought me this close to citizenship. Like everybody else, however, I am helpless before fate. I am just an average Joe really, I should have been a citizen a long time ago. I didn't have to take the *ultimate* road to belonging for chrissakes.

"Your job would be to co-author the congressman's book, using alternate chapters. One chapter of Uberstein assassin tales followed by one chapter by you on Uberstein's assassin. One Kennedy story by him, one Uberstein story by you. I have the contract here ... you will be rich."

He handed me my death warrant, and lo and behold, it was filled with small print. The agent reached for a statuette-sized black vibrator on the desk. "Don't mind me," he said, "I'll just buzz off for a while" He buzzed as I studied the document. Dentist music or humming vibrators are the only true music for the signing of pacts with the devil. Many times on the street, listening to power drills forcing their way through New York City cement, I had the inkling of shadowy presences. The devil's favorite listening music is industrial serialism.

Δ

THE AGENT'S NOTE:
This manuscript was delivered to me by José one hour before he was shot on the stairs of his house by an unknown assailant. It is obvious that together with the Uberstein manuscript this makes a most intriguing story. Should you decide to take the job and sign the contract you could write it using alternate chapters, one Kennedy death tale followed by an Uberstein death tale followed by a José death tale. He never did, by the way, get his citizenship.

Sincerely, Your Agent

THREE SIMPLE HEARTS
a youthful farce

I

Gossamer is my wife's name. She is a pothead. I love her. She pretends to sleep and then she masturbates. She has fabulous dreams. In one of these, a well-wisher gives her a horrible, cruel and fascinating head. It is a shrunken African head for her to draw from. Repelled but fascinated, she puts the head on a shelf and contemplates it. It is horrendous, nauseating, inexplicable. She looks at the other objects on the shelf: they are normal, quiet and unobtrusive. God, my God, she thinks, what am I going to do with this head? I can't very well bury it in the garden because a foul murder may happen there. And I can't very well bury it anywhere else for the same reason ditto. So she wraps it up instead. She wraps it in cloth and then she wraps it in paper and then she puts it in a cardboard box and she sends it to the Museum of Modern Art, New York City, New York 10012.

Sometimes, when I lie there knocked unconscious by a superb fuck, I look up at her and all I can see is the night sky full of stars and then a shiver goes through me and my body in which my life is, slips off me like a glove. Gossamer is a witch and when she doesn't make herself into a sky full of stars she flies out of her body, mashes jimson weed into mashed potatoes and rubs it on her temples, paints enormous canvases filled with borderline colors or, simply, throws seeds into the ground in random patterns so that, where we live, radishes grow next to tulips and peas climb the gladiolas.

123

Gossamer exudes sex and it is for her sake that I underline passages like this in biology books:

> *It has been soberly calculated that if a single female cell were to release all the bombykol in her sac in a single spray at once, she could, theoretically, attract a trillion males in the instant. This is, of course, not done ...*

This isn't, perhaps, done. But there is enough bombykol leakage from Gossamer's cells to attract a few hundred at the very least.

Ah, Gossamer!

II

Juana is the daughter of a well-known composer. She is our friend. She has the most beautiful way of looking up inquisitively without saying anything and Gossamer thinks that this comes from lying for hours under her father's piano while he made his music. Juana does not exist in her father's music except as an afterthought during a lull in the romantic malaise by which his music is characterized.

Juana is very silent. The few times she speaks she is mostly concerned about the obvious which she doesn't understand and probably never will. I would say: "I will close the door," and Juana would look up in utter astonishment and say, "The door?" And in her case, this isn't stupidity. She is simply overwhelmed by the thing called "door." It knocks her out. It amazes her. She and Gossamer will talk for hours about such subtle things as the effect of various people's vibrations on driftwood or about esoteric qualities of astral projections.

Juana is also very sexy. Her sexuality is very insistent, it is like a constant knock at the door. She continually bares her breasts at the slightest pretext and she loves to fondle them in public with a mischievous and self-involved smile.

124

Gossamer and Juana constantly pose for each other and, the few times I came upon the scene, chills ran up and down my back. It was a snake dance. Unbearable.

III

I am Jess or Cress or something. I often think that I am a woman. I am a lesbian. I can't imagine a world without women and the very few times I've been in male company for longer than two hours I got very sick, very nauseous and I got a cold.

I have harem memories. There is Turkish blood in me and for as long as I remember I keep hearing a faint cara-vanserai music in my inner ear.

I have a horror of work and, in order to support Gossamer and me, I juggle. I go to children's parties, weddings, parks and bars with my juggling bag. They all love it.

Often I feel as though I'm juggling with three lives: Gossamer's, Juana's and mine. We all go up and down together, fall but go up immediately again.

Because I am a man, my task is to lend weight to the fantasies of the girls. I explain Gossamer's dreams in as much of a prosaic manner as I can muster, and I enforce Juana's silence by talking myself to death.

IV

We are, all three of us, going to see our mothers who live on the East Coast. Gossamer is driving. We have just picked up Juana and her child, Zuni, from the small town north of ours. Our child, Willow, is the same age as Zuni. The children are in the back of the car pulling a small wooden Indian away from each other, Juana is sitting up front with Gossamer and I sit in the back machine-gunning Mafia staff

125

cars with my water pistol through the open window of the convertible. YooHoo! Life is fine! We're on your way!

"That's charming," says Gossamer and I know that she means the Frank Lloyd Wright Building in Marin County past which we are driving. She also means that ironically because it's in that building Judge Haley was killed and Angela Davis went to trial.

"The wonderful thing about this gas crisis," she continues, "is the fact of people now getting stuck in strange places."

And without a transition she adds, "We sure changed the world."

"The world?" says Juana.

We had long gone past San Francisco and we were now going, down 101, toward Los Angeles. The California coast skipped gently upward like a sleeping animal. The sea was bright, the sun was shining, the beaches were beautiful and our AM radio was drunk, positively drunk.

We drove all day. At sunset we checked into a motel in Monterey.

V

The room had one double bed and one single and the double bed faced the TV set. So Gossamer and I lay for a few minutes on the double bed and then Gossamer got up and went into the bathroom and took a shower.

I said to Juana, who was sitting on the single bed looking at me, "Come here."

She laughed pleasantly and said, "Just a minute," and kept looking at me in a sort of puzzled, childish way.

Gossamer came out of the bathroom without a stitch of clothing on and Juana looked at her and said, "Jesus."

I could tell by the temperature in the room that very soon we would be locked forever in a tremendous orgy and

126

that we might not go East at all. In anticipation of that delicious moment I got up and went into the bathroom myself. I stared at the mirror in there and at the towels and at the two glasses wrapped in paper and then I took my clothes off and opened the door, fully expecting Juana and Gossamer in each other's arms.

But this wasn't so. Juana was still sitting on her bed looking at Gossamer who was fiddling with the channel changer on TV. When she saw me, Juana said "Jesus" again. She also laughed.

I lay on the big double bed for a minute and I began to fondle Gossamer's breasts and caress her public hairs, conscious all the while that Juana was looking straight at us and sending waves of white heat our way.

"Come and join us," said Gossamer.

"In a minute," said Juana and began, very slowly to take her clothes off. She had taken everything off except her panties which she unrolled slowly, slowly downward. She then sat back on her own bed, on the edge of it, with her legs spread wide apart and shot her puzzling looks across.

This time Gossamer stuck her tongue out, licked her lips, and said to her, "Come here, Juana."

Instead of doing that, Juana shot wildly upward and did a headstand. We waited for her to come down for a full five minutes but when she showed no signs of doing so, Gossamer and I began making love, slowly, with great abandon, leaving wide spaces for Juana to jump in whenever she felt like it. But she stood there watching us fuck upside down, and when we both expired noisily and melodramatically, she came down, pulled the covers over her head and went to sleep.

Gossamer did too and I must have also because the night passed.

VI

Early in the morning Gossamer went out to take a walk, taking the kids with her, and I woke up to see Juana standing in the middle of the room, naked, staring at me. I was very hard and I too stood up and went up to her and embraced her and as I did so I noticed these amazing circular red lines that looked like scars all around her breasts.

"Are those fresh scars?" I said, and Juana laughed. I looked closer and I saw that they were drawn with a magic marker.

"Did Zuni do those?"

"Yes."

Zuni is 3 years old but he still gets the full benefit of his mother's breasts every night before he goes to bed.

My arms were around her and I was kissing her nipples and rubbing her pussy which felt incredibly tight and then we both stared at ourselves in the motel mirror and we looked beautiful, my hard cock planted at the apex of her triangle and then she said:

"What if Gossamer comes back?"

"She wants you just as much as I do," I said but I saw that she didn't believe me and then Gossamer walked in and a delighted smirk appeared on her face when she saw us standing there.

"Juana thinks I engineered this whole thing," I said to Gossamer who was already taking her clothes off. "She doesn't think you want her as much as I do."

"I do," said Gossamer but she stopped taking off her clothes.

So Juana and I sat back on her bed and I licked her nipples and her cunt and she responded but her eyes kept going to Gossamer who watched us smiling.

"Take off your clothes," I told Gossamer. She did and she came over to the single bed and lay next to Juana and

128

when I saw their beautiful naked bodies next to each other I thought I would go mad and I leaned back, away from them, and I almost fell off the bed seeing how, very slowly, they entwined their arms around each other, looked each other straight in the eyes and began to kiss lazily.

Their legs were also intertwined so there was no room for me to dive in, really, so I contented myself with licking random parts of their combined bodies and stroking available extremities.

Just as I thought everything was going according to fantasy, Gossamer leapt abruptly out of the bed and ran into the bathroom.

I stared at Juana for a baffled moment, then I said, uselessly, "Where did she go?"

"Go?" replied Juana absentmindedly.

I was kissing her when she too sprinted out of the bed and ran into the bathroom where I distinctly heard her lock the door. I heard the water running.

Feeling perfectly ridiculous (good thing the children were outside!) I looked at my rapidly shrinking hardon and concluded that life was strange.

Seeing how they weren't coming out of there, I put on my clothes and, gathering the kids, I took a walk on the seashore which was very bright and sunny that morning and I saw frogmen in black suits diving after abalone.

VII

I have always tried to teach Willow, ever since he started making sounds, that the world isn't really here. To this purpose I taught him all the wrong words. When he pointed to the door and tried to name it I supplied him with the word "sky." When he pointed to the sky, I said, "sheep." It didn't take him long to become a poet.

Gossamer, as a rule, frustrated these efforts. She taught

him the right words almost as fast as I taught him the wrong ones. He didn't hold grudges. On the contrary, this knowledge of two languages gave him a great sense of authority with other kids when he began practicing his secret language on them. I had merely tried to teach him that life and language were at odds with each other even though many of our friends disapproved and thought I was being cruel. It is my belief, however, dear friends, that our mission on this planet is to free the world from words. In any case, misdirected or not, Willow could take care of himself. He had his mother's beautiful blond hair and graceful dreaminess while he had my stubbornness and practicality. He also, very likely, had his mother's temper which was short, erratic and generous. But anyway, dear friends, it occurs to me that if one has a secret language one has an immediate access to a metaphorical view of the world. And metaphors are little doors leading to other worlds. They are automatic religion and, if there is one thing I can't stand, it's the way our society destroys the marvelous.

Willow would stare at the cowboys in the motel's TV and say, "There come the crabmen." Or he would say, "I want some soda meat" whenever we passed the millions of gas stations America is made of.

He was addicted to soda meat and to the delightful click of the coin falling and of the bottle being released.

But this time he was mistaken. What he had taken for a gas station was actually the outline of the city of Los Angeles as seen from the Ventura Freeway. It was a correct misunderstanding. Millions of people lived in a gas station.

VIII

Zuni, same age as Willow, 3 years old, was different. He had dark, dark hair like his mother and he was equally silent and intense. He had sudden, ferocious flares of jealousy and fought over a toy for hours. His mother was his slave. She gave him anything he wanted. He would point at three ice-cream cones at once and Juana would get them for him knowing only too well that they would end up uneaten, dripping over everything. He was a tiny king and he knew it.

He agreed, generally, with Willow's odd verbalizations of the world but he did not participate in words. He merely looked quietly and when he wanted something he spoke his mind at once in a complete sentence.

Willow defined their common needs and Zuni agreed or not.

Willow would say, "Toy soldiers in balloons fall from the sky," and Zuni would think this over and exclaim, seconds later, "I want a balloon."

IX

The desert was, at first, unobtrusive. It did not scream itself like the sea or hide like the mountains. It was suddenly there, implacable, inevitable, self-contained. It was neither accessible nor impenetrable, it was somewhat obvious. It baffled Juana. It fascinated Gossamer.

After a while, with the sun burning high, it began to insinuate itself into my consciousness. I didn't know how it happened. It just did. Time passed. I found myself staring at things that changed too fast for a definite perception. I looked behind me. The cities we had left shrank in importance. We were surrounded by desert. It was the end of winter and new shoots of ocotillo, yucca, palo verde, agave and joshua trees pushed up. The desert mountains had the light of ghost islands in ancient illustrated books. We were at the bottom of a sea. Everything was well outlined but sudden.

"I know," said Gossamer, "why saints go to the desert."

"Yeah," said Juana.

"To have learned conversations with the devil," I said.

Neither one of them replied. But Willow said, "Look at the water monsters!"

"Good thing they don't have nuthouses in the desert," I said.

I had a short vision of saints sitting naked under the burning stars, juggling with question marks.

"A snake," said Zuni.

A long, lazy rattlesnake was climbing a mud embankment. Gossamer stopped the car to watch him disappear.

"Let's camp here," said Juana.

X

The poptent was in pretty good shape and we had three sleeping bags. It was decided to lay all our blankets down and put the sleeping bags on top of us. The children had one blanket and a sleeping bag all to themselves and the three of us took the other blanket and the two remaining bags.

Without much planning I ended up between the girls.

It was warm there and my hands rested comfortably on the breasts of both girls. But we were very tired and sleepy. I felt, for a brief moment, Gossamer's hand on my cock and Juana's on my neck.

Something very sweet passed between us, a sort of shiver, and with it came sleep.

I must not have slept very long. I woke in a kind of terror. I remembered the rattlesnake and it felt almost as if it had curled under the sleeping bag. I was out of my mind with fear. I opened my eyes as wide as I could and I saw that Gossamer was awake too.

"I had a dream," she whispered, "that there is some *thing* in here who is imitating us."

Without going into details I knew what she meant. I had the same feeling. A thing which changed voices as fast as lightning was in the tent. It spoke with Juana's voice, then with mine, then with Gossamer's. And yet it wasn't us.

"Me too," said Juana softly.

The children were quietly sleeping, their small breaths coming regularly.

I got up, unzipped the tent and peeked outside. It was very cold and nothing stirred. The stars were enormous and rare cactus threw intricate shadows. I got out of the tent completely and ignored the cold. There was a full moon out. But the *thing* persisted.

... back in the tent, Gossamer said: "Is anything out there?"

"No."

I felt, somehow, that now, since we were all awake, it was time to make love and ward off with our heat, whatever was there.

We did, in fact, get started in this direction when I felt a fourth person with us. The girls stopped moving almost instantly.

"Sleep," said Gossamer. "Attack with your dreams!"

She turned over. Juana did also. I lay on my back and, strangely, I fell asleep immediately.

I dreamt that a caravan of Gypsies had invited us into their wagon. An older Gypsy man with a tambourine smiled as we walked in. The wagon tilted when we stepped inside and the maddest change took place. Inside, the seasons of the year were changing quickly into one another. Winter, during which powdered snow fell thickly, was followed rapidly by Spring, Summer and Fall. The Gypsies danced. The walls of the wagon were covered with instruments. Gossamer picked up a tambourine. Juana took up a silver flute. The children grabbed finger cymbals. I looked about and I lit upon a drum. We made music, madly, for hours, the seasons changed without appeal and a great happiness spread through me. "You are a juggler," a voice said.

The realization that I indeed was a juggler, gave me enormous strength. I woke up.

Gossamer, also awake, was smiling. I could tell she felt good. The *thing* had passed. Juana, who was still sleeping, felt warm and peaceful. Her body was soft and friendly. The children slept on.

In the morning, we ran around naked. It was going to be a beautiful day.

XI

The horizon, possessed suddenly by a pink glow, erupted and Las Vegas burst on the landscape like a mad woman in a Hollywood bible.

"What's that? What's that?" said Willow and even Zuni let escape a gasp of disbelief.

We had driven all day, feeling fine, saying nothing, and the evening gave us Las Vegas.

"That's where people go to play with their money," said Gossamer.

"It's a monument to capitalist morality," said I.

"Monument money," synthesized Willow.

"I want money," said Zuni.

The Tahiti Motel was lit from across the street by the Tower of Pizza so we didn't immediately turn the lights on. Our room, similar to the one in Monterey, had two double beds this time and both of them faced the TV set. We watched, from the window, a well-lit casino crammed with people and slot machines.

I had few fond memories of the place since not long

134

before I had been what you might call "Juggler-in-Residence" for the State of Nevada, a position like "King of Beggars" or April's Fool.

The Nevada Arts Council had decided, two years before, to bring jugglers into Las Vegas schools. They had tried poets and it hadn't worked out. This brilliant idea was, though the local government didn't know it, the equivalent of importing prostitutes to jail. It was a revolutionary idea.

Juana now reminded me of it, as we sat silently watching the Strip, because she had read my letters to Gossamer during the week I'd spent here.

"You taught them good juggling," she said, and we all laughed because the Strip seemed to, indeed, be juggling neon balls.

Willow turned the television on.

"I'll take a bath," said Gossamer. "Why don't you two go out and get a pizza."

I slipped my arm around Juana and we walked out into the cold desert night, the wind was blowing a newspaper around, and I fancied coyotes howling but it was just the casino, ceaselessly whirring.

XII

The pizza would take fifteen minutes so we walked across the vast parking lot to a casino. I had six quarters in my pocket and Juana had three so we decided to give it a try.

A strange thing happened when we walked into the bright lights of the place. Juana became very pale and she grasped my arm tightly. I had an inkling that it had something to do with the frantic nature of the place. She must think she's not suitably dressed, I thought for some reason, but then I looked around and it was like a circus; women in nightgowns and fat men in Hawaiian shirts sweated merrily in front of machines. Juana had this thing about clothes: she had an idea that she was going to dress very "straight" so that no one could identify her as a hippie. Sadly for her though, Juana had no idea what straight was. She was wearing blue jeans (faded), red sneakers, an ancient silk blouse with ruffles and a diamond brooch in which her long black hair was caught. She looked incongruous.

"Look at everybody else," I whispered, thinking to comfort her.

"We must leave," she said.

But something was pulling me forward and it wasn't greed, certainly, but curiosity.

"Let's just play these quarters," I said and, despite her will (which wasn't very strong) I placed her on the other side of a two-armed bandit that takes two people to play it. I inserted a quarter and I said, "Now," and we both pulled on it and there was an insane screech and the lights started flashing and piles of quarters began spilling at us. Everyone stared. Juana was very pale. I gathered the quarters in the small paper cups they have by the side of the machines and put another one in.

"Let's go," Juana said, more insistently, and I knew that she might faint. I hastily filled my pockets with quarters and, leaving the quarter in the machine, I took her arm and we pushed our way through the curious crowd.

We had it almost made but just before we got to the door, a fake Gypsy with a red bandana accosted us and thrust three flowers at us. Why three I'll never know. Did she know there were three of us?

I bought the flowers and by the time we reached the cool night outside, Juana looked as if she were being shaken by waves of nausea.

And then I heard it. The music. It was faintly coming out of the casino lounge and it was a popular tune her father had written in the '50s.

Her reaction unsettled me but the pizza was ready so I

136

didn't ask a thing and when we got back, Gossamer was stretched out on one of the beds in all her glorious nudity and I put the flower right in between her legs where it looked as if it had freshly sprouted.

Juana went to the bathroom and I sat on the edge of Gossamer's bed thinking, "Strange."

Suddenly, Gossamer was all over me and she tore savagely at my clothes. I had my shoes and pants off and I was trying to get off my shirt as her mouth devoured me.

Juana was coming out of the bathroom when Gossamer turned me over like a big fish, mounted me and began to fuck me. This was something new. This was rape because she was using every juice in her body to attach me to her and suck through every pore of her skin. I was a powerful and beautiful beast and a helpless victim at the same time. Gossamer made me fully aware of her command of the situation. I had no free will and I was brought outside of myself.

I forgot about Juana, her father, the music, the pizza, the money and everything else.

When I came too I was lying on the floor staring at the starry, sparkling ceiling. Juana sat in a chair looking at us, her mouth slightly open, her hands folded in her lap, like an old Indian woman.

I was mad at Gossamer. I felt as though she had laid an irrevocable claim to me and, while I gladly granted it to her, I did not feel that it had been necessary to accent it so.

I crawled, naked and ridiculous, toward Juana and I put my head on her lap where her hands were but she did not move, and when I looked up at her I realized that the flower in her lap was glued with sweat to my temple.

Gossamer went to sleep and I watched television. Juana did not stir. Then I too drifted off and I don't know what happened because when I woke in the morning the pizza was still there, on the table, not a slice taken out of it.

137

XIII

We had the pizza, cold, for breakfast.

When Juana went out for a few minutes, I said to Gossamer, "You wanted to show her that I am really yours."

"Maybe," she said.

She dressed slowly, looked in the mirror and went out with the kids to look for Juana.

XIV

She found her, crouching alone by the side of the swimming pool, facing the casino we'd been in last night. She was crying.

"My kid doesn't listen to me," she told Gossamer.

It was true. Suddenly, Zuni had become very defiant. He refused to put his clothes on, did not let her kiss him and spilled everything on purpose.

Willow had, for a time, tried to do the same but I made it clear to him that it wasn't going to work.

"Let Jess handle him for a while," Gossamer said.

So I tried. I spoke to both kids in the same even-handed and what I thought to be calm manner.

Things settled down enough so that by the time we got back in the car we seemed to be good friends again and the cloud passed.

XV

Route 15 out of Las Vegas winds insanely through the demonic land of southern Utah. The builders of Route 15 could not have been human. If they had been human I fear that they all met with a sorry fate. As in some legends, the

138

masons of certain churches had to be buried alive in them in order for the churches to stand.

"We are not on earth any longer," announced Gossamer.

The children became so quiet staring out the window that for a moment I felt that I was completely alone in the car. And then, this feeling of being alone permeated me to the extent that I could not *see* anybody in the car. I looked for Gossamer and she wasn't there. Juana was gone and where the kids had been I could hardly make out fast disappearing cinders.

This was compounded by the fact that I could, instead, see millions of other things. These things were carved in the cliff faces on both sides of the road but there were some that stood in mid-air, not moving. The figures on the cliffs were all religious. I did not recognize most of the gods carved there because most of them were alien gods, belonging not so much to other earth cultures as to alien ones. The kind of thinking that went into most of the carvings did not belong to the imagination of this planet.

I longed to be back with my four car companions. Now more than ever, I wanted to touch them, hold them and make sure, somehow, that there were a few of *us* around, too.

But I did not see them and I began to feel afraid. No, I was terrified. I was insanely afraid. I felt like shouting something but I was afraid of the echo. The echo must have been tremendous between these cliffs.

The eeriness came also from the sun. It was a perfectly sunny, clear day with no cars anywhere from here to Flagstaff.

I shouted, "Children!" and the whole giant landscape echoed with thousands of tiny "CHIIIILLLDREEEN!"

This is when Gossamer reappeared and I saw that she was scared too and that she looked desperately for everyone else. She had found me. Then the two of us combined forces and we found Juana. She sat rigidly, in a shamanic trance with her heavy mass of hair fallen forward on her face. The three of us found the children.

But the fear hadn't subsided. And because I could still hear "Children" in the air all around us, it occurred to me that we were all children and, because we were all children, somebody was going to eat us. I was sure of it. We were in a dark tunnel now, blasted out of sheer granite, and I knew that this tunnel would not end, that instead of driving out of it we were forever driving to the core of it.

A children's defense came to me. When children are afraid they tell each other scary stories until they are so scared that everything is OK.

"I fell into a grave once," I began.

There was no protest and everybody wanted to play the game.

"It was putrid in there. They were taking apart this old cemetery in my hometown and I went there at night with a flashlight and I fell into an open grave on top of something rotten and muddy. It took me four hours or a thousand years to get out of there.

"And one time, when I taught juggling at Folsom Prison because they had this program called 'Jugglers-in-Prison,' I thought that I would be kidnapped. But instead of that I saw the horrendous *fear* of people living in there.

"Those men's techniques for survival were incredible. Well, mainly their technique was their personality, every one of them had a kind of carved-out personality like those figures."

I pointed to the figures but that was a mistake because my fear returned.

"Bullshit," said Gossamer. "This medicine is too strong, that's all."

Juana looked up.

140

"Everything on earth," said Gossamer, "is a medicine. Mountains are certain types of medicine. Certain rocks are too. It all depends on what ails you. If you eat the wrong rock you get sick."

"Sounds like a huge pharmacy," I said.

"It is. Our consciousness is always sick. We always look for medicines so nature is a giant infirmary.

"The flirtation between consciousness and death goes on, at all times, on all levels of infinite space."

"You sound like you're quoting some goddamn book. I'm really *afraid now!*" I said.

"Fear is a constant interruption, a natural defense. Without fear we'd all be in heaven with the rain below us."

It was exasperating. I could have cared less for the definition of fear. I felt like screaming, frankly. Again. I did want to. But I didn't, I sort of swallowed it halfway.

The brutal, bloody words. I hated them.

XVI

There was so much fear in America that you think we would have drawn our first quarrel from a less abundant source material.

Why had we quarrelled about fear? It would seem that this was a subject everyone could agree on. If you're scared you're scared, that's all.

Something else came to me. Since Juana rarely talked, I'd never know if she was scared or not. I asked her:

"Juana, were you scared?"

"There were a lot of things in that tunnel ..."

"What kind of things?"

"Well, this and that. Globs ..."

"Globs?!"

"You know ..."

I didn't. Goddam. I didn't. I felt furious. And imagine

now that furious as I felt, I began feeling six times as furious when I saw Gossamer and Juana exchange some kind of smug, self-satisfied smile, that told everybody I was a fool. Which I must be.

XVII

I thought about my fear some more. I felt a generalized fear. I loved it, practically. It exalted me. I don't think this is masochism. It is more like, er, research. I felt *noblesse oblige* that I know that state fully. I did not want to be afraid. But when I was, I savored it like a piece of rare candy, I flirted with it. I felt, I suppose, that fear ran, somehow, a whole sector of the evolution game and, as such, it was rooted in the center of the universe.

Gossamer, I knew, could identify fear by its images. Whether she caught the glimpse of a ghost by the kitchen door or had felt that a chicken sat on her chest all night, she knew where to find the culprits.

While she had this basic trust in the solidity of the world, I had none. I thought of light as just another phenomenon on the move along with the seasons, etc. Everything that could be seen, felt or explained was to me on the move like juggling balls and the only reality was my skill at maintaining the balance. Reality was my effort to adapt.

The difference between us was in the materials. She worked with mud, earth, clay. I worked with movement.

Also, Gossamer was a thorough American WASP whose unlimited faith in her possibilities, her judgment and her beauty never wavered. There was that suffragette irony in her. Her reply to Dadaism was Mamaism.

I was a Turk. It is written but you have to try.

Juana was half-Indian. To her, this landscape was, no doubt, a lot more familiar. She did not have to fear the

142

ghosts of Indians with which these mountains were thick. She was ritualistic and non-verbal. She fit in the world by taking certain positions with her body. If she was afraid, she crouched like a native woman and wrapped herself in her hair. Harmony to her must have been the right hand gesture, the correct body posture.

We were certainly different.

XVIII

For a moment, I felt that I could not possibly get close, physically, to either one of them. I felt completely impotent. And I was still scared.

I knew that somewhere in me there was enough nerve to make things right again. In a way. I knew that if in some other place, away from here, someone would accuse me of loving pain, I could have said, flippantly: I am only practicing, with abandon, the ancient art of suffering.

But not while we were still here.

To prolong the agony, Gossamer stopped the car and got out to draw a pastel picture of the mountain.

I didn't get out of the car. I leaned on the back seat, closed my eyes and decided not to move until we were back on the road again.

A minute later though, everything started to spin and I got dizzy and opened my eyes. I looked outside.

Something miraculous had happened. The landscape, so threatening a few minutes before, looked benevolent. The evil power seemed to be gone from it.

And then I looked at Gossamer, who sat on the hood of the car, smiling and looking at the mountain, and I had the crazy impression that the place was *posing* for her.

I looked back at the cliff. It was true. Things had softened as if the place was contingent upon a favorable

143

impression. It was posing for her. Incredible. Even the Devil was a prima donna. Especially the Devil.

XIX

That night, at the only godforsaken motel in a thousand miles (I refused to camp out!!) I felt awkward.

Juana and Gossamer, however, were on best terms. The kids too had mysteriously resolved their differences.

They all smiled at each other.

I lay down on the only bed there and pretended to go to sleep. I didn't feel like talking. I was drained. There was a horrible wind outside, rattling the window panes and the room was freezing cold. There was a Gothic murder lurking somewhere.

I expected Gossamer to get in bed first. But that didn't happen. The kids were already asleep on the floor in their sleeping bags. Juana didn't come to bed either. After what seemed like a reasonably long time I opened my eyes and I found, to my surprise, that the room was dark. I raised myself slightly and looked around. The girls were sleeping together on the floor in a sleeping bag.

Of all the nerve!

I boiled with indignation for a while. But, obviously, there was nothing I could do. I lay back down listening for sounds of lovemaking. There were none. The girls were sleeping.

So, so, I thought. I slept badly.

XX

Next day we drove through something that was not consoling: lone buttes dotting an immense horizon, dry reddish mud, and sky, enormous, blue, implacable sky.

144

I kept sending out waves and waves of hurt from the back seat to the girls up front. But they seemed oblivious to my plight or pretended to be anyway.

I lapsed into a sullen silence trying to shut out their merry chatter. They sounded like two crows on a fence. They were gossiping about people I couldn't remember.

After a while, I spoke in monosyllables to the children.

Finally, bored, I took out the little pillbox and took five desoxyn capsules.

Ten minutes later I didn't care any more. I felt great. Let them play their games, I thought. I'll play mine.

I took out my juggling bag and I entertained the kids by losing all the balls under the seats. They dived for them and I was feeling better and better and the car became a carnival. We were going to the rodeo.

We were in luck. No sooner had I thought up the rodeo-carnival than we drove into a little town where a raggedy-ass circus was in progress.

XXI

Banners with the word CIRCUS hung over the main street and there were six or seven brightly colored tents on the common.

We paid the dollar fifty a head plus one dollar for both kids and went in.

The clowns were funny. In a country-poke, slow way, the two clowns did their best to figure out where things went wrong and they tripped and fell so much that the whole tent was full of dust and Willow was hanging on the edge of his seat with his eyes glued in disbelief and, all around us, the folk were laughing a kind of up-and-down uneven laughter pierced by shrieks.

We were having a grand time. I was curious about the locals in their cowboy hats and their mostly fat wives who

145

cheered on. I wanted to live here. With the kids. Without the women.

And then the main juggler came up to us. He had a great weariness about him as if he juggled despite himself and, since he was a bit middle-aged, fat bulges showed through his tights in uneven places. He juggled in a resigned sort of way as if he had no choice. I thought that he wanted to tell me something about our profession, its incredible conditioning quality. I saw myself, ten or fifteen years hence, dressed in those ridiculous greenish tights, throwing balls in the air for a small crowd and constantly identifying the balls with the women and children.

Gossamer—up. Juana—down. Ball #1.

Mother—down. Mother —up. Ball #2.

Head—down. Body—up. Ball #3.

One kid down. Another on his/her way. Ball #4.

And then the same thing vice versa, add or subtract a few balls.

The juggler was followed by three women riding one horse and I thought, "Thank God. Only two ride me."

The circus went on for a whole hour. It ended with a tired-looking lion jumping through a tired fire.

The kids were playing clown, juggler and lion with each other, and Gossamer sort of walked up front twisting her hips and arms and then turning her head and giggling girlishly and for a long time.

The local tavern was crowded with the folks from the circus—we squeezed in and found a table right in the middle.

I ordered a steak and a Coors and everybody else did too. Our backs were sort of leaning on other people's backs and they were leaning on us.

We were drinking our beers and waiting for the steaks when I noticed that we were leaning against two cowboys. And, at about this time, they too noticed us. The one

146

cowboy I was now trying not to lean on, turned around, lifted his mug of beer and said to me:

"It's a Christian country. Let's drink to it."

"Yeah," said Juana, looking up. She lifted her mug.

The man looked friendly, so I lifted my glass too and said, "Lachaim!"

The buddy on his right looked me up and down and said:

"You liked the circus, lady?"

Now it's funny to think that in the city, among my friends, I would sometimes declare: "I am a woman." Being accused of it, though, and claiming to be it are two different fishes. I said:

"You're looking at me the wrong way, Mister."

I didn't actually mean to sound like John Wayne but I must have.

With an effort that must have cost him a thousand tiny muscles, the man half-stood and leaned toward me.

Gossamer squeezed me under the table.

It was too late.

"You're a queer, that's what you are," he said.

This too was funny. It's chic, in my town, to be queer. But, again, this wasn't my town.

Juana looked scared. She looked almost entirely Indian now and the whole scene took on more Wild West features every second.

"I ain't gonna fight over a word," I said.

"I don't fight," he said, and pushed my head with the heel of his palm. Then he half-threw a punch to my chin but I was leaning too far back so he barely clipped me.

I still held my glass mug in my right from toasting the country so I leaned forward and brought it down on his head except that it was his face and the mug broke just a little below his left eye and blood came out.

The jagged remains of the mug were in my hand so

when he threw his left forward he aimed straight at the glass and his fist started bleeding too.

Curiously enough, the others weren't doing anything except watching. The place was quiet and everyone looked at us.

Suddenly, I was lifted out of the seat and dragged outside. I saw, as I went through the door, that the waitress was sitting there with a tray full of steaks and milk, and both Gossamer and Juana got up and followed me.

Willow screamed: "Leave Daddy alone, you fucker!"

Outside, I scrambled to my feet and faced, again, the old bleeding pardner while the others had let go of my arms.

This time, his first punch threw me right into the ground. He hit me in the jaw. But instead of stomping on me as would have been his chance, he stepped back and waited.

I got up, clenched my fists and walked toward him. He could hardly see from the cut. There was blood all over his face. He threw again and missed and then I ran toward him and hit him in the stomach with my head. He staggered.

The Sheriff, who must have watched until he was satisfied, turned on the siren at the top of his car. I turned around to look at him as he got out of the car he'd been sitting in for the past ten minutes.

"Identification," he said to me.

I looked for Gossamer. My head was beginning to swell. She nodded and went up to where we'd parked.

"She'll bring it right over," I said.

"She your wife?"

"Yes."

"Who's she?" said the Sheriff, pointing to Juana who had Zuni in her arms.

"My friend."

148

The crowd laughed.

"I better take you in," he said and snapped the cuffs on me.

In the back of his car, first thing he said to me was "I've got a glass eye."

I nodded respectfully.

"I used to be in the circus myself," he said.

"Oh yes?" I said. "In what capacity?"

"I was a private guard," he said.

"Oh."

"What do you do for a living?"

"I juggle."

"You tryin' to be funny?"

"No, sir."

"You with the circus?"

"I've been in a circus," I said. "I was with them for two years. Good references. They'll vouch for me. Except that they're in Siberia right now."

He didn't say anything for a while, then he sighed and said slowly, "I guess life is a circus."

I could hardly contradict him.

At the station, in the back of the hardware store, he made me coffee.

Gossamer came in, breathless, with my wallet.

"Sit down, Ma'am, and we'll be done in no time."

He wrote down a number of facts on a piece of paper while my head began to feel like a wilting eggplant.

"Can I bring him some water?" said Gossamer.

"Sure, Ma'am, right there in front of you."

I was afraid he'd be searching our car any minute now for contraband, of which we had plenty, so I motioned Gossamer to go outside and tell Juana to clean up.

Before she could do that, however, the Sheriff looked up and said, "That'll be fifty dollars fine for disturbing the peace." He paused. "We got no jail."

"How about the other guy?" said Gossamer. "He started it all."

"He'll get his, Ma'am. I've known his pa for twenty years."

After the ceremony of turning over one-third of our cash was over, we said our goodbyes rather fondly.

He watched the three of us get in the car. The kids waved at him.

"He's got a gun," said Willow.

"I want a gun," said Zuni.

XXII

On the road, as I lit a joint, I felt good. I didn't even have to look at the girls to know that they loved me. I was a hero. I felt it in every fiber. Both Gossamer and Juana sat up front listening to every sound I made. I am a real caballero, I thought. I got the girls out of trouble. Prince Valiant. I've defended their virtue.

Up front, Gossamer laughed. It was a light-hearted, beautiful, loving laughter. I felt warm towards her.

Juana turned around and caressed my swollen face. Ah, yes. I was a Pasha. I was crossing the continent with two beautiful women who loved me.

Willow and Zuni were playing Cowboy & Daddy in the back of the car. Wam! Pow! I shoot you! Boom!

I felt so good that despite the little shoots of pain I was able to go to sleep easily.

XXIII

It was a sort of sleep. It was deep reverie. I was dreaming of the motel we would stop in that night and of the fact that now, I was sure of it, I would get to sleep with both girls

150

and that we will make love with one another. Things had been made right again.

Then my reverie became a real dream and I dreamt that it was night and I was sitting, all alone, at an adobe restaurant in the desert. I was warned not to go out the back door because it opened into the sky.

A waiter dressed in blue like a Chinese worker shoved a Bible-sized menu into my hand. There were thousands and thousands of items to choose from and I chose something called *pinoles,* which were these small cars that ran on injections of dog blood. I ate three of these tiny *pinoles* and then, against better advice, I stepped out the back door into the sky where I floated happily for hours.

I woke up long enough to recount the whole dream and the deliciousness of it all. In the process, I remembered that, like mountains, important dreams showed up at every juncture of my life.

Before I moved to San Francisco, I dreamt that a train full of convicts whistled to a stop in the arroyo to welcome me to Mexico. At the time I had decided to love two women, a palm-tree full of apes sprung out of the ground to shake my hand (I was being congratulated by Darwin!). At another time, when I got a job (the one and only job I held for longer than six months) I dreamt that two terminal cancer patients were trying to sell me a valise full of fake gold watches.

"What did you dream about?" asked Juana.

I told her.

Gossamer said, "Wow."

Juana laughed in her sorrowful, quiet way. She was very happy. We all, as I've said, were.

XXIV

At the motel, after the children fell asleep, we sat on the bed, all three of us. I leaned against two pillows and the girls faced me. I made jokes through my swollen face, laughing in pain, as the words got lost in my tender gums.

Gossamer mimicked our eventful day four or five times and Juana kept hugging herself and repeating, "Oh, please don't make me laugh so hard!" She had tears in her eyes.

Then we lapsed into a little silence punctuated by *The Untouchables,* who were breaking up a giant still.

Gossamer lowered her head on my lap with a little smile and Juana stretched full length alongside me on the bed. She gingerly turned my blood balloon around and began licking my purple fat lips.

And then, as my desire waned, I thought: Last night you did it to me. Tonight I'll do it to you.

I raised myself up abruptly and I said, "Every bone hurts. Do you think you could leave me this whole bed tonight?"

I had struck home. Harder than I thought. I had really hurt their feelings. But they had hurt mine. Well, hell, I was feeling terrible.

I wanted to retract what I'd just said.

It was too late.

They both got off the bed, laid the sleeping bag on the floor without looking at me, turned off the light and the TV and got in together.

I listened in the darkness for a while waiting for sounds of lovemaking. There were none. What a fool I was. I really wanted them. I really did. How could I be so stupid?

No clue came and I slept, dreamlessly.

XXV

Arizona was a bluish-green sheet dotted with Venusian architecture. All my bones ached, I had a giant hangover. The girls were quiet.

But the sun was shining and it started to snow. We were high, high up on the First Hopi Mesa. The place of emergence for the Hopis, people of peace. They had migrated across the continent in a swastika pattern and had then settled exactly in the center of it. Which was here.

We stopped in the Hopi village for coffee.

We had chili and coffee, looking at Indian faces. Then Juana came into view, simply, and I nearly let out a gasp. She had changed. She looked completely Indian. The snow covered the window and the light was dim, it was a sort of church light. The calm faces around us transported me. Gossamer, with her long blond hair, looked like the long lost white sister. Juana was our guide. I had been brought along for the record. We could have been celebrating Easter.

When we walked outside, the car had snow on it and more snow was coming, in drifts, in bushels, in allegories.

We drove silently. From the mesa, I could see the snow falling into the valley below, falling, falling but never filling it and we were going higher and higher into the mountain where it came from.

We made a short detour to go to Old Oraibi, the oldest city on the continent, the Hopi Mecca.

We were already five miles out of our way and it looked like we were driving into pure white nothingness. Then there it was. Old Oraibi.

There was a sign at the entrance to the village. We made it out through little bursts of snow. It said:

THIS VILLAGE IS HEREBY CLOSED
TO WHITE VISITORS FOR NOT OBEYING
THE LAWS OF OUR TRIBE
AS WELL AS YOUR OWN.

It was a moving rejection. The snow was white, I was white. I received it in blissful humility. It didn't mean, however, that I felt good about it. I looked at Gossamer, our eyes locked, and I felt very, very close to her.

Juana wasn't looking at us. She wasn't smiling. It occurred to me that it wasn't Oraibi that I wasn't supposed to enter, but Juana. Juana was my Oraibi.

XXVI

Willow's favorite story was *Jack and the Beanstalk*. Zuni liked it too but he got bored around the middle. I read this story to them over and over on long empty stretches of road.

After listening to it for the nth time, Gossamer said, "That story's an allegory of the primal battle between father and son. Jack trades in his mother's cow for a bunch of seeds or sperms so that he can grow to be a man. The beanstalk is the umbilical cord by which he is still attached to the womb. The cord is what keeps him from taking his father's place. So he asks mother for a hatchet and cuts off the cord and Dad's cock at the same time. He's a man."

Willow listened to Gossamer's explanation with some concentration, then turned to me and said, "Read some more!"

Zuni, however, grabbed his little prick and said, "Cock, cock, peepee, peepee!"

Juana, who was driving, stopped the car and Zuni went out in the snow and peed.

I read other stories too. I watched them all disappear

154

in the devouring passion that children have for impossible situations.

XXVII

It was late when we arrived at the Hopi Cultural Center on the Second Mesa. The place was dark, it was cold, the stars were bright blue. I fumbled in the dark for the motel buzzer. It sounded shrill.

After a few moments, a face appeared at a window above. It was the face of an old woman. "Old woman, old woman, old woman, says I, whither, ah whither so high?"

"What do you want?" she said.

"A room."

"Wake up my son below," says she.

I knocked at a door. A man woke up. He fumbled for some keys and then handed me one. It was perfectly dark because the falling snow covered up the quarter moon.

We found our room with some difficulty. It smelled like clover and it looked like all the motel rooms that preceded it with one difference: there was no TV.

Before finding the light switch I felt that I had wandered into a dark kiva during a ceremony. The place was alive with presence.

Juana read to Zuni in one bed, Gossamer read to Willow on the other, and I went into the bathroom and took a long, hot bath.

I thought, during this penetration of my aching bones with warmth, that many things had happened between us on this trip.

Last night I had been very close to both girls. I had been the conqueror, the hero, the superman.

During today's drive I had been drawn close to Gossamer and there was a certain distance between me and Juana.

Gossamer and I understood each other well on the road. I was familiar with her moods and the one mood of hers I hated the most, boredom, was conspicuously absent.

I daydreamed some about healing Juana's wounds and I saw the three of us travelling forever, inseparable, a perfect *ménage à trois*. Gossamer would explain, I would juggle, and Juana would dance. The children would grow up.

I got out of the tub and dried myself. I brushed my teeth, I shaved, and I decided to make love to Juana.

The room was dark, both girls were sleeping with the children on separate beds.

I got in bed with Juana.

But as soon as I started kissing her left breast, Zuni woke up and said, "Scoot away from Mommy!" a chilling expression to say the least. I looked up at Juana and said, "What now?"

The child plopped himself right between us, grabbing both breasts in one swoop.

"I want to sleep," she said.

"Do you really, or are you just saying that?"

I lay there some more, feeling my blood pound.

I removed Zuni, who had fallen asleep after cloistering his mother's breasts, and I mounted Juana. She pushed me off and turned her back to me.

I got up, went to the other bed. I was pissed and humiliated. Never, I thought, never. Never, never, never.

Gossamer was awake.

"Did you?" she whispered.

"No," I said and stuck my thumb into my sore cheek, making it hurt.

XXVIII

In the morning, it was still snowing. We had coffee in the coffeeshop downstairs. There was no one else there. The

156

museum was open and we looked at Hopi crafts, katchina dolls, paintings, drawings and ancient tribal agreements, as well as an exchange of letters between the Hopis and the government. The Hopi document was drawn with all the careful poetry of a people who respected the foreign language they were using. They offered, literally and beautifully, to exchange the knowledge of growing corn in the desert for whatever knowledge the white man had to offer. The letter from Washington, D.C., on the other hand, had numbers and letters at the top and it bore the scribblings of hundreds of bureaucrats as it had been referred from one bureau to another.

"It makes me sick," I said.

What the fuck was the matter with the world? I didn't know. But I would have liked, for a bit, to be something else. Not a human. A bird or a pea. Not out of embarrassment, certainly. But out of weariness.

I didn't feel like being myself.

Zuni and Willow attacked the katchina dolls, so we had to leave.

When we squeezed back in the car, Willow wanted me to read him *Jack and the Beanstalk*. But I didn't want to.

I would have liked to tell him a totally made-up story that had nothing to do with anything, a story that was perfectly simple and yet contained everything in the world.

A story that was mindless and went on forever.

XXIX

A young Indian stood hitchhiking under a billboard that said **GET US OUT OF THE U.N.** Indeed. We picked him up. No one said anything the whole way and he sort of kept staring at Gossamer in a way that gave me a hardon.

He got out in Gallup, New Mexico.

"He was cute," said Gossamer.

"Yum," said Juana.

"I didn't mind him myself."

We all smiled. We all realized how incredibly horny we were and the smiles, no doubt, made fun of our silliness.

Caught in the criss-cross between Gossamer's and Juana's smiles, I thought of the millions of understandings Gossamer and I had come to in these matters.

In the beginning, this smile of hers had been a frown. I have, since the dawn of time, considered it my privilege to fuck any girl I wanted. At the same time I felt as jealous as a Tartar about Gossamer. This classical double standard put a cloud over us. I never told her about my adventures until they were at least three months old.

My adventures weren't all that great, really (oh, some of them were!), but I liked to be in love at least once a week.

I picked up girls at laundromats, on the street and on the bus. I didn't much care for class or appearance. I preferred, in fact, ugly horny girls who did their best to look as hungry as hell, with their mouths slightly open, carelessly dressed.

Later, as I began juggling professionally, I met a lot of actresses and dancers, but these girls weren't the same thing. They usually dealt with me on the strength of their professional camaraderie. When we had sex it was as "artists" or something. And they had the bad habit of falling in love with me. Gossamer said nothing when scented letters and dried flowers began to arrive and, yes, scented letters and dried flowers kept coming.

I felt no guilt, in general, if I could contain my affairs to a few afternoons or mornings, but I felt terrible if things dragged on.

One night I was waiting, at 3 AM, for the Mission bus. It was very cold, so I decided to hitchhike. A little red sportscar stopped. The driver was a blond boy in his

158

twenties. As soon as we took off, he put a gentle hand between my legs and said, "Can I do this?" My impulse was to tell him that he couldn't because I belonged to Gossamer, but I couldn't do it. The hand felt good. At stoplights, the stranger would take his hand away and I found myself waiting impatiently for it to return.

"Can I suck you off?" he said.

"Yes."

He drove off into a dark street and parked. He bent over me and proceeded to suck it exquisitely, gently and slowly.

I couldn't, at that point, bring myself to do the same to him but I gave him a nice hand job.

Gossamer had affairs too, but she covered for them a lot more expertly than I did because I knew nothing about them.

I found this out after my hitchhiking adventure, when we both sat down and talked about everything, and our adventures surfaced and, with each detail, things got more exciting between us.

It seemed so easy to be free.

We began, mildly put, to fuck around.

Together and separately.

We did it with abandon, regardless of sex or place. We fucked boys, men, women and girls, together and separately, and we authored, as a sort of manifesto, this poem:

SEXUAL POLITICS

The things that made me come in 1966
are now as different as
America is in 1974

In 1966 I liked to fuck straight on top
Or bottom

mostly women
mostly men
and America was an active country
with men at the top

In 1974 the government is collapsing on TV
while the country watches from the bottom
as I fuck boys, women, men and girls

and a new lyrical dimension opens
in both of us

My sweet juices, where are you leading the world?

We saw this matter of our liberation as something concerning the whole world. Sex, we decided, was the crucial communication and we were in an ecstatic state. My juggling got so good at this time that I could perform extraordinarily complex movements on stage.

Gossamer became frighteningly beautiful at this time. She had demonic power in addition to her usual grace. We could fuck people easier than we could talk to them and *that*, I thought, was a great thing.

Human communication at its best was, I felt, a frequency. Paying attention to words was a mistake. Verbal meanings messed up the original frequency. The appearance of meaning marked the end of Paradise. Conventional meaning was a jamming device. I didn't care what people *said*. I just wanted to lie with them.

In essence, the facts of a life were not needed. Only the warmth of presence was necessary.

Lovers came and went, with the exception of Juana whom we loved so much we were sure that, sooner or later, we would become eternal mates.

XXX

Juana liked very few people.

I have no idea how Juana saw us. Juana was to me a perfect mystery.

I couldn't really explain what attracted me to her. But I will say this: I was madly in love with her. I loved the way she carved the air to fit herself in it. I loved her apparent or imagined vulnerability and I wanted to fuck her so badly I could have screamed.

XXXI

The wind kept brutalizing it and the poor car swayed. The skies narrowed and the roads got populated. We were getting close to Oklahoma City where Juana's mother was and where we would have to part.

I couldn't stand the idea and there was no other motel between here and O City, no more nights, that was all.

I wanted to create a diversion. I couldn't think of anything. We stopped someplace to eat and I kept hinting at some far off parks and places that we could visit for a day and night.

It didn't work.

The first signs of the city appeared. Juana was driving and I leaned over, from the back seat, and cupped her breasts with my hands and we rode like that all the way to her mother's house.

Mother was waiting.

XXXII

Juana's mother's house looked a lot like a motel, the kids turned on the giant color TV, and mother sat us all to dinner immediately.

I could tell mother had great authority and that everything had been planned for days.

I certainly wished, for Juana's sake, that the visit (3 weeks!) with her mother was better planned, in terms of success, than our journey.

And yet, it had been successful. It made me realize that I wanted both Juana and Gossamer more than anything else in the world.

And I wanted them together. My balance depended on it. I knew that I would never give up until the three of us lived together happily ever after in the South Pacific.

Mother talked and Juana was silent. Zuni and Willow played with a large number of toys. We ate.

"You can stay here," Juana's mother said to Gossamer.

But our minds were made up. We would get on our way.

I kissed Juana goodbye fully on the mouth.

Gossamer did the same. Later, she said, "That kiss was sad."

"I'm really glad it's over," I thought for a few seconds but I knew that I didn't mean it, on the contrary, I hoped it was not.

As we drove off we were all sad. Willow's friend was gone. Ours was too. We were terribly sad.

I looked at Gossamer.

"I have a lump in my throat. I want to cry," she said.

And then we rolled on, in silence, nuclear again.

Tenderness

Fresh water can make it seem like next day." She poured it on his ear. His ear was vast, a conch-shell in the desert, forgotten by the sea. The water cut through it, a thin blade buried to the hilt in his listening. A radio musical played the water, she kept on pouring.

"Let's face it, no woman's sexual fantasy includes cerebral palsy," he murmured, and then switched to, "ET looks like Menachem Begin, don't you think?"

"They imagine they think," quoth she, and kept on pouring. "They imagine that they stand, as in childhood on a makeshift stage, and they imagine that they are saying, 'A Reply to Mr. Brain,' and that everyone waits, on the edge of their seats but there is only silence, they have forgotten their lines. Mr. Brain laughs." She laughs.

He laughs. "I know who's listening inside my ear. A sprout. A listening sprout listening for someone else who is listening to a sphere." The water falls drop by enormous drop on the profound listening of a musical sprout. Adjectives rise from the sprout like mist. Metallic praises evaporating.

"This is what you can tell yourself when I go: 'She came. She came too soon. Not yet. She came not too soon yet. She came she poured water on my ear because there is someone in it listening for her to come. So she came too soon not yet.' "

He stands. German literature falls around his uneven shoulders like a mantle. "Ah, mein Herr, we are human, all too human. Last year, ah, you should have been here last

163

year—we had fine wine here. Only Herr Nietzsche knew how and where to get it. Since he has gone mad, we all suffer very much. When reason has had a good sleep, he might find Goya's monsters perfectly appropriate."

The pitcher is empty. She goes. He goes. There is a little zoo full of shadows in the middle of the room, waiting for dawn.

Perfume
a tale of felicity

Il y a des gens bizarres
Dans les trains et dans les gares ...

—*Edith Piaf*
Paris-Mediteranée

On my way home, I stopped to see Enough. Enough is a beautiful girl who lives with a man named Much. Their house is a hovel with half a roof through which fall wounded birds and acorns. When I opened the door, a large pig walked in too.

Much was on the porch trying to birth something. He squatted weirdly on the ground, his body was strained, he was in pain, his hair stood on end, his fingers were distended. My greeting went through him like a feather through a keyhole.

Inside, Enough sat naked on a faded star-and-flower sheet proffering her two breasts to four infants. Two were happy and two were furious. Ahhhahhh! Aaaahhhahh! Mmmmaaamm! Mhahmmm! The furious pulled her hair, the happy stuck fingers in her eyes.

"Remove your clothes, Rafael, and make love to me. Making love is enough. You make love to Enough and you'll be OK," she said when she saw me.

The furious quieted down when I embraced their mother. The happy began howling. The quiet (formerly unhappy) were thus able to attach themselves to the nipples

165

(thrown overboard, over the sides) while the howlers (formerly happy) increased their laments.

I moaned in her ear: the conch-shell echoed. Unthawed omniscience, old laughter. She gave me something then that I was poised to take or not to take. What was there to take? What was the object offered and what did possession entail? A heartless man plunging forth into a nameless woman. Maybe she offered me "heart" in exchange for "name." Maybe it was a gift. In any case, I took "it." I could have escaped from her womb. We connected clumsily like astronauts in space, floating first through the vaulted hollow that had formerly housed my heart, then through an infinite cave dotted with glittering female shapes in states of substellar translation, powdery, indefinite, sparkling, and then I took "it." My blood roared. *Come!* boomed Enough. Come where? Not waiting for an answer, the canoe twisted furiously and plunged headfirst on the rushing river to the end of history where, like a high basalt wall, I glimpsed the beginning of biology (Life is a High School). The lovers, curled up in the hot iron seat of biology, rushed toward each other with the stern will of Fascists applauding an execution (inwardly, soundlessly). Sperm is a metal. Attila the Hun came from one (henceforth he slept on the wet spot). Swimming counter-current in sperm it was easy to fall into hyperbole, which is apparently what I did, after I took "it." In fact, hyperbole accompanies each sperm like a winged creature, a prenatal obituary. And there are millions, with specific memories.

Enough walked me to the door. The infants looked up from the manger, four pairs of eyes in which shined the star. Jesus had undoubtedly a multiple personality. Pointing at Much she told me that the day before he had given birth to enough barbed wire for the chicken coop and that the day before he had aborted a threshing machine. Alternating successes and failures on Much's part read like a history of

166

technology. It still only seemed like yesterday when Much —with an agonized scream—brought forth the Printing Press. Alas.

Much must have birthed something: ecstatic sweat lit up his rotundas. He was smoking from the top of his head *comme une pipe.* Lying on the straw at his feet, rocking back and forth, was a perfectly round, white chicken egg.

"That's not bad," I said.

"Not bad at all," agreed Enough.

Δ

On my way home, I greeted the populace. There was Syrius, in the torn flag, Many Jokes, New, Phallus, Electric, Evolution, Contrast, Selectric (the four-year-old daughter of Electric), Retrospective and Future Past, *tout le monde.* They were on their way to an Identity Festival, a wild show patterned in part after the Circus and the Grand Opera, which took place every six months and during which the natives changed their names while trying to remember their original ones. These shows had, in their brief history, utterly convinced everyone that roots (which, like wings, are revered) cannot be grown overnight.

> *Roots dangle from our feet*
> *Roots sprout from our noses*
> *Roots of light and roots of sound*
> *But the door of birth closes*
> *And the earth stands its ground,*

they sang as they filed past, jumping up or twirling. I would have liked to join them but I was, as I still am, on my way home.

Here in Wits End (Pop. 450), dogs, cars, hills, hovels full of salt (of the earth), chickens, a few stereos, dog-eared records, a number of gardening magazines, naked brats and

167

giant onions, intertwine in macramé with the haphazard geography through which the river of America's future flows toward an awesome Kilowatt, a "power nexus" which glows in the future. The inconceivable Kilowatt, part of Whom is hid in clouds, lures the masses toward him, singing, as they are doing. Over it all falls the shadow of the dinosaurs who have once lived and died here, and are now forever laid flat on the narrow couch of land on the edge of the Pacific plate—above our heads—where they are being simultaneously cooked, psychoanalyzed and made to throw their shadow, in a vast mythical retrospective which goes on hourly, *sans but*. All around us the volcanoes snore thousands of fumaroles. These wisps of white smoke attach themselves to the tourist's heel and the native's nightmare. Fog and clouds roll in and out, bringing the news and managing opinion. All the people are brand new and the only sound of any significance is the suppressed (not all the time) mammal moan of an imitative quasi-primal Paleolithic Fuck (not the garden variety however). Elements and humans have the rosy freshness of a beginning drama class. They are pretending to belong (first exercise) and have high hopes of one day actually belonging (gesticulating from the top of a redwood stump to a horde of descendants dressed as toasters, blenders, irons, corers, grinders and other homey symbols of victory over nature). The audience of dinosaur ghosts throws shadows. Crusty goldrushers with bullet holes in their foreheads stand on their toes to catch a glimpse of the future. Relax, there isn't any.

I could show them some though. I could give them a show. I have a blood full of futures. A million dead guys running away from home to the future boil and seethe in my blood. One drop, a thousand hours of film. For instance:

A giant man wrapped in rawhide, his face hidden by a wide felt hat, stands looking into the window of the

168

General Store at the liquor. Between a bottle of Johnny Walker and one of Old Crow stands a ceramic ballerina on one toe. The cowboy feels his balls. Very heavy! Very heavy!

A young woman, wrapped in the remains of a sarape through which the pink flesh of a breast and a dash of pubic hair make eyes at the public, drags four screaming infants into the Store. *Enough!* she tells all, which is her name. When she pushes open the door, one of her darlings pulls off her vestment.

From the Bridge, a teen girl appears, rolling a pizza-fed ass like a roulette wheel and Enough is taken by the tight bulge in the crotch of her faded blue jeans, a bulge she imagines in the hand of a young AWOL soldier who removes trembling his white shorts: his hand is plunging through the hairy snatch in search of the meaty labias which can be heard making kissy kissy noises. Enough stands, perfectly naked, watching the girl approach.

Planted between them, the cowboy spits out the gum, and puts his paws in his back pockets. The sun stretches one leg over the withered town, the fat cloud streams lazily between his legs, and as I round the corner all this is well in progress.

This is all that happens.

There is no future.

My eyes are a window—I watch the street behind it. I am a master of watching from the window—as I walk—I am a perpetual voyeur with a single image in my mind: Felicity. I watch for signs of Felicity. Sometimes I fall asleep. But through the closed eyelids I still see the street. I know everything except when Felicity is going to return. This I would pay good money to know.

A succession of days, a procession of people in front of the window ... when and if I choose to move them. There is nothing to distinguish one from another. A lump of time, a cowboy, a naked woman in the door. But subtly my growing unease and impatience are taking the world apart. Enough slaps the child. Pulls her garment back up to her waist. The teenager creates a huge white bubble of gum. The cowboy takes a step forward. Where is Felicity? Every second (the lump atomizes) her absence adds itself to the absence in my chest, and I give off just a little more florid putrescence like the bottom of a pickle barrel.

Here is a picture of Felicity. Her nose is a curved bridge in the Flemish countryside (Vermeer). Peasants cross it. Her blue eye is atop her green one in the yellow fire the stained-glass dragon breathes upon the red saint (Chartres, Vespers). The fluted base of this Minoan column, her hand, I think. The other hand is only a hand—though beautiful—resting on the buttocks of an angel, plump and in the choir (Donatello). The red fox in the autumn forest (Turner) makes me reach for Enough. But she's gone into the store already, children howling ahead and behind. Felicity looks to her side as if watching an arrow head for a place below her breast.

Take a bow, Felicity. You must not fade into time.

For instance: after dinner (modest: dew drop, starshine and datura smoke) we took out the huge map. Rolled up like a rug, it leaned against the bedroom wall. Our considerable bedroom measured five acres. The bed was one square acre. The rest were armchairs, chaise-longues, brooks, swimming holes, nooks, the homes of friendly animals. We unrolled the map and tacked it to the entire wall behind the bed. On it, traced with colored inks, was the human universe of Wits End. All over it the populace moved, leaving colored jets of green, purple, black, orange, red, gold, blue. We followed every move. If a couple were to split up, let's say, we would pounce on the two luminous dots blowing up as soon as we lit eyes on them. Felicity would ride one, I the other. Similarly, we attended every birth and rode every new child (gold and blue ball) to wherever it eventually settled. All was visible. If this cowboy, seized by an epic horniness, would step forward another step, for instance, intending to carry off the teenager, we would see it and be with them in the truck before he even floored it. Most of the luminous dots on the map stuck to groupings of similar color most of the time. Before any one of them became ready to move, a pink concupiscence flared around its coordinates, marking the place. A blush, a balloon, a red tantrum suddenly surrounded the activist. We always interfered with the map. I reluctantly, Felicity fully. If there was any way to influence a decision, to prolong a ride, to cause action, we would do it. Naturally, we had no interest in stability. It wasn't beautiful when nothing moved. This, perhaps, is the reason why Felicity left. One day nothing moved.

We had been lying there for some time watching a still human world. Humanity was dead, we were bored. The red flare lay untouched between us. This flare is what we used to put ourselves on the map with. Red was what we chose to express a state somewhere between wealth and sex, a state we concurred was ideal for us. Thus a red line going from me to Enough could mean (depending on thickness, speed, etc.): I intend to give my gold to Enough; Enough means to enrich me; I fuck(ed, will) Enough; Enough fuck me (now, later, yesterday). Every day we used our red flare to insert ourselves in the life of the community. But the flare only worked when things were happening. There was nothing doing with a still map. There was nothing doing. We were at the mercy of luck, the twin moons of sex and wealth, stuck in a forgotten train station. Luck was wind. No wind, no luck. No wind, no ruffling the still pool.

Can't keep her from fading. Sorry. This is an old photograph. The map is covered with spider finery, still on the wall. They have altered the lines, created new ones. The spiders are now in control. They amuse themselves. They lower a paw behind the eyes. A different style. I don't care. She is far lovelier than I say. The paper crumbles. She used to insist on sex between monologues. All monologues, she decreed, must have their visible ends in sex. She held the invisible ends, tightly, in her hand, and whipped the dogs. The troika moved rapidly. Without her, my monologue is an endlessly revolving penis striking a glacier. Its invisible end is in my mouth, its visible end freezes. This sexual-intellectual fiasco can then be added to the hollow in my chest (which words will never fill) where my heart used to be, and you have Rafael Papiri, a heartless creature plunging with his binoculars into the abyss.

Δ

The cowboy listened to his heart before he took that step. He heard nothing. His heart was gone, like mine, and he didn't know it. There was a muffled beat which reminded him of a phony watch an Italian had sold him (I am that Italian) on the street in Naples. Next morning, when the watch stopped ticking, the young soldier threw it to the floor. A spring jumped out. This was all it had inside. He knew that beat well. And it was now in him. His heart was gone. He stepped forward.

Between the soldier and the cowboy, he had been a student. He had worked days, studied nights and strived to be an average man. What is an average man? he asked himself. He is, most of all, the master of common sense, a man who, standing with both feet in the murk or the rainbow of his life, will not allow any ideology to sway him. Common sense is the gift of experience, racial and personal. No truly average man, no matter how tired, will allow ideology to expunge him from the network of things. What is ideology? Other people's ideas. Without his common sense he would have been offed by the easy grace of nature a long time ago. He studied the ceramic ballerina. Poised there on a toe, ready to pivot, she made a lot of sense. His common sense had not deserted him in Italy and it was not going to desert him now just because he had lost his heart. He had always had and needed his common sense, especially now when he can hear the hollow gourd of ideas rattling across the buttons. And the muffled beat. And the desire for the naked woman. And the menacing approach of his younger sister. As a student he had often thought: my common sense is all I have. It has taught me a unique personal iconography. It is the only weapon I have in an ideological world and I must clutch it like a peasant clutching his cross in Hell (lithograph). Hell begins at birth for people like us (workers, soldiers, students). We are born in a hospital: the architecturalized ideology of sickness. We spend our lives trying to stay clean in a sewer pipe through which flows the drowned innocence of our ancestors, only to be killed by ventriloquists, long distance. The average man is a heroic man. He erected himself a monument momentarily. He is certainly not the fantasy one hears echoed, in which an average man is a man who never quit dreaming of a uniform, or a man who strives toward the hepatic mentality of a goose. If such exist, they ought to be whipped, certainly. Order is the art of enduring, and such order as a man salvages through common sense is, ultimately, the weight of his existence, the twelve grams of his soul. He dropped out and became a ranch hand, in charge of the bulls. His foot was in the air.

His foot is in the air.

Δ

The Aztecs took mine. Telling the truth involves severe penalties: that limbless, organless trunk is me. I have been

173

mutilated beyond belief for telling what I am about to tell. But they did. They took my heart just as they are about to ... I have resolved to get along without the help of poesy or of common sense. I will speak the factual truth, I will be a child no longer, I will be a father. There is nothing I can do about it, it has been decided by internal vote. What matters is that the factual truth be a lie, that the child is not dead, that the father be mother. For instance:

I was walking between two rows of kneeling people. The sky was blue and empty. The people formed a V. The two branches began as far behind me as I could see when I looked. The V closed at the foot of a large flat stone. On the stone was an empty black chair made from onyx or jade. My hands were thrust forward and I saw that I was holding, between the cupped palms, the living hunk of my heart. It pulsed there with unbearable sadness. At the foot of the rock I turned around to see if I really had to. I showed everyone the pathetic red meat: a chill rippled across the backs of the worshippers (I couldn't see their faces) like wind over wheat, like parentheses rolling away from official texts ... I shouted: *All right! I cannot accept this wonderful award! Give it to my heart!* I then put my warm heart on the jade or onyx chair. It stood there bleating like a lost sheep, lowing like a cow with bursting udders, howling like a loon, blinking like a traffic light, lost, juicy and urgent.

After I came home, I spied on myself. To no avail. My heart was gone without a trace, like an arrow shot by Dacians into blue sky. I took a compass and traced the circumference of the absence. Nothing moved in the whole four centimeters of it. Well, I said, one can live without a heart. But not without you, Felicity.

These heart sacrificers (Aztec mostly) have not disappeared. They are still here as plain as you or I. As plain as maize and tobacco. Where could they have gone? Their ghosts stand in groups, and fly about. They took my heart to feed to one of their gods: a terribly hungry, primeval god who sits in his azure grotto dreaming of reigning again, of being fat with belief and sacrifice. In terms of a meal, my heart couldn't have been much. Like my contemporaries, I had killed so many of its natural impulses, it barely hung in my chest by a rayon cord, crucified to the externals of life like a jaguar to a car (hood ornament) ... a sorry snack, to be sure. The god must have mumbled to itself: *I need stronger food*, sending his ghost patrols in a panic all over the country looking for juicier hearts. But where in North America would they find an unbroken heart that did not, at the same time, belong to a moron in a precambrian state of slumber? These patrols, lost in the thick fog of weak and broken hearts that go along with being conscious, could do nothing to restore visibility. They are blind these ghosts and as runty as the divine runt they serve. So every time the bell rings they load up on broken tickers and pray for the best but their god keeps getting skinnier and more nervous, causing earthquakes and countless disasters.

Well, go get it back, said Felicity.

From whom when where what? I asked.

Make a scandal, create an astral hubbub, go after him, make battle, be mad, kick ass, rip, shove, smash, dance. (At times she sounds like the sports page, my Felicity.)

I imagined my heart in the god's stomach: layered rows of refrigerators with their doors open; inside each refrigerator there are four stainless steel cold chambers; inside each chamber are sixty frozen hearts piled on top of one another to form a lump of olive-purple meat. The mountain of refrigerators looks like a cross-section from an enormous honeycomb. And then, as if to extinguish the view, thousands of refrigerator doors slam noiselessly shut (Fascist applause renewed) and a solid wall of frigid white rises in front of my eyes. I am dazzled. All I can think is: the

Aztec god has swallowed the White Goddess. She is in his stomach and my heart is in *her*.

Now you know where it is, Felicity said.

Yes, I knew where it was. But I was no detective, no surgeon and no mystic. I was all the no-things I needed to get my heart back undigested.

A digested heart is irrecoverable. (Embroidered sampler)

Δ

Enough would have been surprised to know (as would have been everyone who knew him) that Much wasn't terribly interested in birthing at the time under consideration. (Focus, please.) His attention was wholly taken by the creation (the attempt) of a black hole by means of which he would recover his own heart. Yes, him too. You would be hard put to find three humans in Wits End who had a heart. Squatting there like a marionette struck by lightning, Much gathered tightly (in a ball) all the instances of his life when he had done things like everyone else. There were very few. Ever since he remembered he had been hatching, planning, designing and expunging. But by concentrating very hard, he soon had a handful of banal memories. These he rolled and rolled around and around his skull until he extracted their juice: a philosophy that denied him. This philosophy (juice) made him obsolete. The philosophy he so laboriously extracted is given to most people gratis. It is called common sense. For instance:

A shirt, yes. A pair of pants, shoes, yes, of course. But how obtain a "no-shirt," "no-pants," "no-shoes"? Would he go to the extraordinary trouble of visiting thousands of shoe stores with the express purpose of obtaining "no-shoes"? These new things he would be craving, these "no-things," what was their use? Were they the intellectual

176

wealth of the nouveau poor, flying through time and space to find their pilfered hearts? A kind of possession by denial? Or were these "no-things" an advertisement for a "no-being," a being so dressed in absence he would not need a heart, he would be busy haunting stores in search of things he would not have, a man convinced, possibly *engagé*? And what would this being's life be like with his "no-things"? Would he be receiving, perpetually, a traffic ticket for crossing lanes between life and literature at the hands of a meter maid or a "no-meter maid," depending on the direction of the street? From constantly putting his hand out for the ticket, and cringing from the insult, he would be an ode to weathervanes everywhere, a perpetual *cri-de-guerre*. A life with "no-things" after birthing so many things was the ultimate denial of Much.

Of such stuff are black holes made.

As to the success of this black hole in recovering his heart, he couldn't say. He didn't know how a double negative operated in a black hole. But one thing was certain: if he didn't succeed he would beg a cop to stop him from his folly. The DNA (The Race Cop) received its instructions for the possible cancellation of Much in silence. (Tanguy Edison)

Δ

She was now close enough to smell. So he smells her. Raw young animal, soft armpits, plump musk. This is his sister, his childhood is upon him. Summer. One time ... But Enough snips his reminiscences when she exits the General Store dragging the four infants right through the middle of a romp under the cherry tree. She looks at Sis, the cowboy looks at the kids. They are his children. How could he have forgotten? For a moment he spins: he desires his sister and he has forgotten his children. What

177

kind of man is he? Where is his common sense?

He finds himself in an immense Playground. The children, and their mothers, are all done in signs like freshly painted balustrades with tiny palm prints. He is too far away to hear them so he watches the signs, which reproduce.

At times, the children are hidden behind walls of numbers, counting their mothers right out of the world. Their lips move as they count, their bodies mimic the symbols. Everyone, it seems, holds high hopes for these children, that they will be the first to reach Infinity (if the hamburgers they eat don't get there first). Everyone holding these high hopes lines up at the (invisible) gates of the Playground with ready jobs. Without having to prove it, the cowboy knows that he is the father of these precocious transcendentalists. The question of proof doesn't exist. A father does not need a heart, only a profile on a coin or a foot on a ball in an old photograph. Also, there are no other fathers on the Playground. Only mothers and children. So they are all his, and, if it is true (he knows it is) that this situation prevails all over America, he is the father of trillions of children (looked over by billions of mothers). Where are the fathers? In cities, they've seeped through bad sidewalks (corrupt municipalities), flowed through sewer grates, vanished in pool hall smoke, industrial waste, radioactive steam, chemical fog. Busy. An endless rain of lit sulphur pellets ignites the electrical wires. The walls buzz. They are aiming (when not transported out of themselves) to become a unified noise (buzz, slap) with enough force to provide the world with energy until Doomsday. Boomsday. Anyway, something to be remembered by. Occasionally, a father emerges from the collective and sees his children. Suddenly. The shock is too much. He passes away. Why is Daddy white, Mom? He is a miller, son. Truth is he's white from rage. Rage at not being listened to. What did he die from, Mom? He drowned in noise, child. Traffic, washing machines, power tools, TVs, firecrackers, they all drowned him. Birds too? Birds too. Briefly, father rises from the dead to add to the record: "I was being hurt in a cement cell. It is a difficult century for a man to talk. I imagine myself born into the silence and verticalized tremor of the Fifteenth Century, occupying the basement of my palace with an *absolute* right to the *entire* fury of my consciousness ... and I swoon ..." He swoons! Jesus! Ecstasy at the center of the fleur-de-lys and the shamrock! Meanwhile, here is the bill. But Daddy is still. He only rises once more (in memory) to claim that everyone is deaf, especially these children, in the Playground, who have been made deaf in the womb by their mothers leaning on their backs with vibrators activated by rock-'n'-roll music and wind.

The cowboy cocks his ears. No, they aren't deaf, he's just too far to hear them. He peels off the rawhide and puts on the Santa Claus suit. Takes off.

The child is surprised to see Santa standing there, in the middle of the kitchen, pointing a gun at Mom. Then Santa sits and screws the child into his bony knee and says (without lowering the muzzle): You wanna hear the truth, kid?

What's da matter mister doncha know any stories? replies the cheeky bit.

All right, he says, here is a story: At midnight, the music stopped in the hospital. All the patients were dead, no use wasting the electricity. Only the TV in the lounge still worked because of radiation coming out of the corpses ...

Outraged, the mother jumps up: What kind of story is that to tell a child?

Santa smiles and tells another one: There are vast masses of people thriving on pure sentiment; their tears ring telephones everywhere. We must turn away in disgust! Really! Where is dignity? God sold us out!

The veins stand out in his forehead, he stands, waving the gun.

179

That's enough out of you, asshole! Where are the presents? mother and child demand simultaneously. Hand over that gun!

He does and is an unarmed crying Santa, flooding the modest home with shlock. As it is, I can barely hold on to both the gun and my type of fiction, so he aims to leave now. Mother and child rage like a storm on television, their arms flailing.

Back in rawhide, he raises his arms to embrace his children and his sister. But he is still only halfway between the General Store and the Playground.

In a eucalyptus grove, for instance.

He studies the aimless erections in the sunset: reaching up and coming short, reaching down and coming up empty-handed, these trees are possessed by misery. There is eerie unease at the core of these constantly peeling clusters of sadness: brought here from Australia to replace the redwoods, they emit the guilty aura of strike-breakers, fast growing pretenders shunned by the local weeds. They stand alone these eucalyptuses, basing their beings on their failure as ship decks and house walls. Their leaves kill fleas.

Only now can he return to the General Store, to see just how alone he stands. His sister walks right by him, brushing his elbow with her loosely confined tit. And the infants all howl at Enough, their eyes intent on the ill-concealed food depots. They do not recognize him.

Take another step, cowboy.

Δ

On my way home, I pass the Postmistress. I do every morning.

"The heart attack rate in America is staggering," she says.

"And what is a heart really," to keep up an ancient

dialogue, "but the love of a place, a love denied to me who loves only Felicity. I care nothing for place, country and the picturesque. And neither does anyone else, partly because they too love only Felicity, and partly on account of a curse left here by the murdered Indian nations. The white man is not at home in America: town, cities, hills, mountains move ... the landscape moves from in front of his eyes ... a moving target. We've taken a long breath of burning air, Madam, and are not allowed to exhale for fear the world will be blown away. The unease dangles like a straight razor over our heads ..."

She looks up. She sees it. "Haircut or lobotomy?"

But I am, apparently, too far gone. I foam: "Let the earth shake, the revolutions start, the blade come down, my Marat streak show, the veins glow ..."

"Well, that's for a surgeon to tell," she says. "I'm only a Postmistress. I think our town is a fine place. In the old days it used to be called Reality Junction, then they changed it to Realty Junction and sold everything. Now it's Wits End. Thank God for zipcode. Have you paid for next year's box, Mr. Papiri? Everyone wants boxes, you know."

"I will be here, Madam. I have no place to go. I have no desire to revisit my childhood. I can look at photographs of my mother. They do not move me. I will stay here until Felicity returns. We will continue this conversation until one of us dies, which ends the subject. I could outlive everybody. Rooted to a spot a man can."

But I am lying. In reality, more than anything I long for a pair of wings. A beautiful, elongated, white pair of wings (streaked with soft brown) jutting from my shoulder-blades straight up into the air (Fra Angelico). Instead of a cursory relationship to birds, a junior partnership ... If I had only traded my heart, exchanged it lucidly for a pair of wings ... or for a healthy head of lion hair (mane) even. My powerful heart with the Maserati build! But no, I had it

181

filched, pocketed, ripped off, rolled away, spirited by a ...
Yes, a pair of wings would do. I am longing, not a single
miracle to my name, not even a slight foretaste of the day or
night of her return. I expect nothing. The light shines over
neglected objects. Where are you, Felicity? Where are you
tonight, sweet Felix? And now that it is morning, where are
you, and how far?

"Later, Mr. Papiri."

"Goodbye, Madam Postmistress."

I watch her dumpy figure disappear into the cement
cube of the standard small town USA Post Office. Not
quite an old lady bent like a question mark (so many old
women dry up in this interrogatory posture: inquiring from
the sky? Do they—as Questions—point to the earth or to
the sky? Or are they merely the graphic emphases of an
Inquisition which has already begun?), but not a young
woman or even a middle-aged one, our Postmistress hovers
between ages like a sack of Christmas cards in the hold of a
plane. From that box, which is the only bombshelter in
town, she (the government) watches the stark rainy winters,
the olive mountains with snowy peaks, the forgetful
inhabitants, and thinks to herself: Why do I lose so many
sheriffs here? One sheriff was found floating face up in the
river like an armed Ophelia. Another had his eyes gouged
out as he slept; he wandered screaming through ravines of
blackberry, tearing himself more, before help came in the
form of a poacher who mistook him for a lovesick wolf and
shot him between the eyes. No one knows why, there are
mysterious aspects to Wits End, the natives spurn the laws,
some are violently allergic to authority (reality), many are
registered parricides. Only during their Identity Festivals
can they be spoken to at all.

The Postmistress is a double agent.

In the day, she spies for the government (patriotism).

At night, she is the terrestrial informer for the Aztec

gang that scoops up hearts. Squatting in there, protected by her cement womb, she opens all letters and reads the town's secrets. These tell her which hearts are broken. She tells the Aztecs. And the spoon comes down.

The Postmistress is vulnerable. She is human. She has a daughter. The extra she earns from the government she puts away for Aura's education (Civil Service? Taxonomy? Apiculture?). The reprieve she obtains from the Aztecs is also for Aura. So far they have left Aura alone. Aura has a heart.

Δ

A rabbi once asked his disciples this question: "What should a man most value in life?"

The first disciple answered, "Good eyesight."

The second said, "Good friends."

The third declared, "Good neighbors."

The fourth replied, "The vision of things to come."

The fifth, "A good heart."

The rabbi agreed with the last speaker, for what he said embraced all that had been said before. (*Talmud*, Pirke Abot, 10)

Δ

Does Much ever move from the rotting boards of his shack porch? Others have asked. No, he does not move. Abundance requires stability. Only after birthing the neon tube did Much stand, excited. He saw the lit billboards of the future, and stood. Immediately after, he squatted down again. The neon dimmed and he knew that he must be careful not to spend his life shuttling between the extreme cold of the mountains and the extravagant sun of the

183

tropics, an activity that earns a man nothing except the contempt of swings, seesaws, teeter-totters, jugglers and balls, which do it much better. Like a Swiss lift, a life like that will not outlast its hate of tourists.

Much is a native. Tourists visit him. They pull his hair to test its strength, they poke him under the arms to see if he is really as skinny as he appears, they stand on him to have their picture taken. Some go inside and have sex with his wife. All this is breeze on Much rock.

Δ

Once Felicity woke me up before dawn.

What are you afraid of, Rafael?

A hand, I said.

Partially hidden in the dream, the hand was still there when Felicity, to calm me, airbrushed me with her hair. As it went I looked at it: a beer-can ring on the index finger, a rubber band wound tightly around the pinky, a rusty silvery thimble on the thumb. The hand was relaxed, leaning languidly as if over the side of a cruising car. Go away!

Don't, she said, don't reason with a hand, it's a waste. Of all the organs we know, it is the most definitive. It changes the world yet the print on the palm stays almost unchanged from the beginning. The hand does not listen to reason. It has its instructions direct from God even as I do.

Felicity, I begged her, bury me between your breasts. Suck me inside your vagina so I can be with Captain Nemo. Let me be a small scar on your cheek. Take my prick in your hand and squeeze it until it bleeds: with what comes out of it, write **MADE IN AMERICA** on the walls of the night.

She did. There was nothing inside it, it was only an empty tube, a hollow weenie, a broomstick, a tube of Crest

184

filled with air through which did not come the race in flames looking for home.

There was a gush elsewhere however. A fountain opened in my skull and a piece of bone flew up when a geyser of light forced open a passage through the top of my head. The organs we know had given in to the organs we didn't. Almost. Briefly.

Felicity rocked me to sleep, until I fell in it.

The street is empty. There is no Felicity. She does not come as she once did, a swaying auburn lamp with electrically disheveled hair riding atop her favorite animal, Aura. She slaps the side of her beast of burden with a brisk hot palm which has her shiver and Aura scream, shaking red hair. Aura is naked and slashed. There are whip marks on her ass. Felicity's eyes are in shadow, she is fierce and cruel.

Something I don't have to feel:

A man with a heart, missing his girl thus, will do desperate things. He will stand on some stairs and howl like a wounded wolf until they take him away. He will play Russian roulette with the sun. If it comes out, he says, I will kill myself. If it doesn't, I won't. The sun spares him by staying hidden in the clouds but next day he finds a new reason to howl, a new incitement to madness. Life is unbearable, his knees bleed, he sways to and fro between hermeticism and communism; flesh rises and falls according to the trading in the ideological market. There is no solution, one has to be sentimental. The heart wills creation that way.

Felicity staggered in, patted her Aura on the sensitized behind and dropped her knit bag (made by spiders) at my feet. She then fell to sleep like a stone (with dreams) smelling of night with wisps of orgy smoke still clinging to her, the milk of dawn all over her body. Aura too fell asleep beside Felicity.

I then fell upon her bag, tearing it in my haste to get

185

to the ritual objects of her life. The mirror, ah! Streaked by the remains of cocaine, minuscule crystals reflected the greed in my face. A topless black lipstick glared at me with its suggestion of oil and dark fur... I applied it to my lips, almost biting and then biting deep into it... The bottom of the case from where it had lewdly slid out into my mouth, was made of engraved gold. Naked Aztecs battled conquistadores at Uxmal. The wrinkled gold sky above the battle was a repeating pattern of half-opened clams, trillions of minuscule gold folds descending through the warriors in a barely perceptible mesh, a disappearing logos... In it, set incongruously and crudely, was a cheap, unpolished, milky blue turquoise. Sticking from under it was a single black hair. Felicity's hair was red and curly, my heaven (paradiso) was made out of it. I lived in her red hair like a jaguar in the rain forest. There were others there, I knew. The people she saved.

Through her hairpin I saw the shining cupolas of the heavenly Sophia higher up, a city like Rome at sunset, woven also from Felicity's hair. A child, looking through the V of his slingshot at the sun, sees the future thus. Felicity's hair is so fine a man could fix a watch with a swift stroke of a single hair, feeling at the same time that he is Spinoza come to collect God from the promises of his childhood.

There is only one child in the Playground, with a slingshot, aiming to bag a sparrow. It is the cowboy at the very beginning of his conscious life. His mother is leafing through a magazine, with her legs crossed. Her nylons are askew, their lines wave. On the cover of the magazine is a small furry demon leashed to a gold chain from a beautiful wrist. Travelling up the wrist one sees a superb arm, a creamy round shoulder, a long gracious neck and, installed firmly in it, a flaming red tongue. The furry thing wags his head (of a pig) and his tail, the tongue urges him on, the child bags the sparrow.

186

Δ

Here is the Postmistress with a letter.
"Good morning, Madam."
She hands it up.
It is from Felicity.

My dear: I am on a train. The suspicion gnaws at me that I have been chosen for something. Alexander the Great wanted to have three daughters at regular intervals of one thousand years each, and to this purpose he preserved his sperm in milk, so I may be one of these daughters. Enclosed is a song I wrote. Choo Choo. Do not italicize.

I hummed the song in there. The night fell. Walking home, I leaned for a moment against a car—equidistant between the General Store and the Post Office—and relaxed briefly in the arms of the folklore of my male nation, humming Felicity's song. Do the people we are swoon? From behind the fortified walls came the sound of a swan blowing a bugle. Or are we a swoon-proof nation? Erect Tatars lift tent flap to stare at the moon(s). Swooning, the moonlit penis takes its seat in the onyx chair. The rows of backs sporting in an immense V before him give off a humble and terrified red light. But the penis is only part of the Being in Charge. A ritual part, like the scepter. It is, in fact, the scepter which is now firmly gripped by a vast Presence, coming closer. When it is close enough, I see that it is a train coming in at full speed from the moon. On top of the locomotive, standing with her head thrown back, is Felicity. The train stops and the lit penis is now in her hand, a brakewoman's torch (Tvardovski Lenin). She signals with it and her hands are velvety claws.

She speaks, for instance:

*To one amortized as I am to the lures of place, indifferent to
the trappings of belonging, hateful of nationalism, peevish
regionalism, indigenous depressionism, and that supreme pet-
tiness of natives of all kinds, the train is the only home!*

*To those dull to the click of the wheels I wish the click
of their watch! I condemn them to be buried inside their clocks
and timers!*

*I will go on record with poet Salamun that "important
organs are: the brain, the heart and the joy in life. The rest is
sfumatura"!*

*I will board trains everywhere! Like a contraband
parcel I will appear phantomatically from behind the rain in
one place or another! I will be the spirit of this continent! Look
for me in Lima, Rio de Janeiro, Bogotá, Tlatlico, Panama,
Chicago, New York, Chichicastenango, Santa Fe, La Paz! I
will be smoke! The chains of weather and time will not hold
me! Back and forth from hemisphere to hemisphere!*

Felicity's voice rises straight up and she addresses me
directly across the gulfs of frozen moonlight. Her eyes light
up, she aims the phallus light at my chest, it inscribes a circle
there where my heart had been:

*Rafael Papiri! I now erase the word SET from your program!
You have set fire to the Bank of America, set up impossible
situations, set yourself in the world like a jewel in a theft, set
yourself up, set yourself as an example, set yourself in a
cement block and moved no more, set thin steel spikes at
regular intervals, set the cops on someone's trail, set your
shoelaces in such ways that bombs went off in newspaper
offices, set cats up with dogs, dogs up with cats, set a pair of
scissors in the heart of a wheel of cheese and set all this in
front of me, and said, "This is a feast for you, Felicity!" I
now free you from your set, your setting and your settee ... I
set you free, Rafael, into smoke! Smoke, ah, smoke, this
does not set except in the lungs of railroad workers where*

188

technology has gone beyond grammar. Strike! In smoke you can find yourself, and out of it weave a volatile fiction, a profound lament on the immorality of our time, as well as a dirge for all the lost hearts and a whipping post where you can atone for your miserable being! You can deeply regret being human! You won't be one for long!

Felicity stretches one of her silk-stockinged feet forward to feel for the ladder and I see the leg and paw of a jaguar forming under the moonlit silk. Before she leaves she turns to her audience once more:

I am the train beast that runs through the lives of the millions who are either kneeling or have the word SET on their foreheads. I will make these millions of you lose respect for each other's arbitrary claims! The only law will be the certainty of its opposite! I will go through you from Old Nairobi to Zozer, watching the metamorphic vortex from which, shoulder high in goo, you will be praying to savage gods for a towel!

Having said this, she goes.

The folklore of my male nation I realize when I begin to walk home, stops in the Nineteenth Century. After that, we have no more folklore. Everything's written down. The only way to ride through my unconscious—and here I speak for you too, men—is on a train. Jets do not fly through the unconscious. The air space is closed. Composed of tunnels and rails, the folklore of the male cannot emerge into light without disappearing. Repeatedly, men on airplanes become clichés and vanish. At the center of our secret world is Lenin standing on the locomotive in Petrograd. Except now Felicity stands in his place.

After hatching the train, Much knew that he had signed the death warrant of the native in America. This is why, in penance, he became one. The rest he knew had either lost it (the displaced Indian) or would lose it (the sense of being here). No one around him had a nesting instinct, hence the constant name changes; if they had new names perhaps they had just arrived (so they can stay a little longer). Syrius became New, New became Space, Neon became Phallus, Electric became Dead, Selectric moved Away. Even in the old-timers where one might expect the regular repose of a regular heartbeat, he could hear only the broken car keys (the fluttering rail tickets) of an ancient impatience. Barely in topsoil, their roots thrashed like dying eels. The fumaroles dragged them to and fro. Heartless, the people had eyes only for the vast chilly spaces. Frantically, they used his rockets as soon as he gave birth to them, pointing them outward, to the stars. The few who still had their hearts did not let a day pass by without offering them for sacrifice: "Will Mr. God breakfast now or later?"

"You are doing so much penance for Seeing!" Much cried. "You pretend interest in earth and trees and beach balls" (rubber products) "but you are interested in Death only . . . a refuge for those who have Seen. All the clinging to each other you do" (Enough moaned, the brief unthawing flared through the wall), "all the marks and stamps you make flower on each other's flesh" (the star-and-flower sheet continued stamping the writhing denizens), "all the post-sacrificial reason of post-sacrificial beings" (the conch shell echoes, sperm is a metal), "all this is only to form a cluster, I know, a cloud of humans to start spaceward together, through the cosmic chill. Pass the spaceship hat. And for all that you still think that you are home."

Much birthed a shadow in the shape of a large black

190

dog which curled at his feet. This was the first "no-thing" in the long series his black hole required.

Much has time. He is immortal. Only overproduction can kill him.

Δ

When the Postmistress passed I said, "How much is a box for a whole year?"

"Six dollars, Sir."

"So if I'm not here for a year you will continue to stuff mail in my paid-for box every day until it bursts? Then what do you do, when the box bursts? Do you set interpreters to work on summarizing the messages which are, mind you, only from official and mercantile sources? Translators? To put the appeals in the various languages of the planet? Or do you perhaps simply deepen the box a few inches? Elongate it a few more? Cut a couple of corners?"

I didn't say that. All I said was:

"All I ever get is ads for camel soap."

"Yesterday there was a postcard with a train on it. And the day before, when everyone got tax forms, *you* had a lovely card with a cowboy on it! Who are you trying to fool, Mr. Papiri? Not only do you get mail from acquaintances, you get mail in secret too, through couriers, illegally ... I see you picking up folded messages from the sidewalk ... it is my business to know, Mr. Papiri, and I do. But tell me ..." (voice becomes plaintive) "where is that sweet lamb, Felicity? I am asking you as a mother, not as a Postmistress ... My daughter pines for her so, it breaks my heart. Poor Aura, she sits at the attic window all day, looking at the street, trying to make the runs in her stockings sound like jews' harps ..."

The Postmistress breaks down and weeps for a full hour, while I wave at the pinkish pyramid under a roof at the end of the road, a blurred shape I know to be Aura. We wave at each other often, like this, but we do not speak, preferring to nurse our sorrows separately.

"Maybe I'll go look for her," I spoke softly.

Clutching her mailbag fiercely, the Postmistress sprung like a steel coil from the pool of her tears. She rose above me like a statue:

"You *cannot!* I am the guardian of this town's permanence! Everyone who moves wounds my person!"

The broken mother passing into a question mark (in a field of poppies) was gone. In her stead stood a fat exclamation point wedged in the soil. She tore the scarf from her neck. On her neck was a violet triangular warning: *No news is good news! Nothing for you! Death to movement!*

"I am the living tree of this town, Mr. Papiri. On my body, see ..." (she tore the uniform from her left shoulder) "are engraved with red hot needles the names of everyone who ever left this zip code. These names are the names of my ENEMIES! I will not rest until I have them *here!*" (She slapped the side of the General Store; cans rolled from shelves; comics flew into detergents; the cowboy steadied the building from the other side.)

After a pause, her face became suddenly joyous, a fire spread through her cheeks. She looked at me expectantly, patriotically:

"We are thinking of hiring someone ... to carry on *his* body the tattooed names of all newcomers so that, between him and me, the permanence of Wits End will be ensured for one generation ..." Her face darkened again. "But if you leave, they will burn your name into my breast and I will have no choice but to turn the bloodhounds loose on you!"

The tattooists, with their hot needles, must always be at work on the poor woman's overwritten body. Every time someone changed their name (as we spoke, twenty people did, first, middle and last) it had to be recorded. When I squinted hard I thought I saw several fingers holding needles swarm under the severe postal uniform. Minuscule fumaroles (whitish steam) shot out of her body from thousands of red hot pricks.

"Think of Aura," I said.

"I am. If I don't, they'll take her heart."

Held up by pain, the woman seeped into the cement cubicle. The sun was a flute. I waved and Aura waved back.

Δ

"Señor, I am the best. I will not rest until I match a man to his hopes. I married the railroad. I sent tulips from Holland to Rio by train. You ask me how?" I did not. I trusted him. He beat the railroad map with his fist, making a dent in the Panama Canal. "Well, then, I have the train for you. This one ..." He traced a trench with his thumb the length of South America. "This train, Señor, spans every major crack in the American continent from the Grand Canyon to Tierra del Fuego. It crosses every slash of earthquake as well as the countless rifts cut by wind, carved by time, forced open by volcanoes, torn wide by the ships of our cosmic brothers, hollowed out by meteors, ripped by dynamite ... This train, Señor, is on the world's most exacting timetable: the jungle closes promptly behind it. Nature reclaims the tracks as soon as it passes, and only nature can reopen them. Of course, nature doesn't have long. A unique train at a unique time! Against this bacchanalia of cracks spanned only by thin steel rails, only the most jaded Englishman would keep his losses secret. The others will speak. They will be seized by an overwhelming need to reveal what they know. One of them will tell you what *you* need to know. One hand washes another, everybody gains in the end, buy now, pay later, as you people say. There is a scale of civilization, see, embodied in progressively more terrifying scars in the earth: Aztec, Maya, Inca, the Amazon. The train will run counter to the movement of the earth and you will be able to watch with your eyes the earthquakes moving north toward California. A straight line of cataclysmic restlessness runs from Tierra del Fuego to Wits End, Señor. In climbing the arrow of this restlessness you will go to the source, to the utmost tip of the continent..." He leaned in my ear and whispered, "There is a cave there, the headquarters of the continent..."

"And that," I exclaimed, swept by the movement, "is where Felicity stands, surrounded by mythical beasts, combing her long red hair!"

"Yes, possibly. I'm sure."

Exhausted by his own vision, the agent (Carlos Freud, Travel Agent, Las Americas) closed his eyes and examined the mandala behind them: spread like the rays of the sun over a round belly, the railroads of the planet flowed through the hands of Walt Whitman into those of Blaise Cendrars. These huge poets (grown men) played with the toy trains which shook when they exchanged booming transcendental jokes. A hundred thousand trains, Blaise? Walt was losing count. A million wagons? A trillion cabooses? A heart in each locomotive? Cattle, prisoners, merchandise, male, female, ghostly, smooth, bearded, the passengers filled them to bursting. I'm getting sleepy, Blaise, said Walt, allowing his mind to let go of its fabrications which then slid on the shiny rails. Which of these will get through two world wars and two hundred small ones? And which of these, having done so, will meet up with Felicity to hook her by the hair and bring her back to Wits End like a spider pulling in his net?

Walt Whitman, poet, dreams several false endings to the drama initiated by his century, behind the closed eyes of

194

Carlos Freud, Travel Agent, Las Americas. I do not want to disturb the poor man.

I clutch my Amerail Pass and go.

Δ

There is a bottomless 125-mile crack ahead of you. It is raining, in the aftermath of a tremendous earthquake which hurled the bones of Huitzilopochtli and Xipe Totec into the air, killing 100,000 people. But the mountains are fairly quiet now, only Tlaloc, the rain god, pisses monotonously on the doings down here to show his displeasure at the slowdown in the number of sacrificed virgins.

Engulfed in gloom, two Quiche women hide their faces in shawls representing the last battle between Xecotcovach and Tucuumbalam, respectively called the Heart of Heaven and the Heart of the Sky. Their husbands are likewise buried in a corner of the compartment, asleep, like stones.

Immense zeroes of land and sky are pierced by condors. The rain curtain parts occasionally to let in a pair of burning eyes which come close to the train window, looking in for a long time, then disappearing suddenly in the rain.

I look back. I see, behind the pupils, two black candles burning on a mud floor. These are the eyes of one of the brides of Tlaloc, floating out of the *cenote*. One eye is mischievous and friendly, the other is somber and strict. Mercury rises in the glass tube of the seductive eye, shedding a lusty light on me. I reach for Enough and she raises her hips, pulling down her silk panties. In the other eye, Death looks at me squarely like a Catholic martyr. I withdraw from the middle of this; Enough, with her hips in the air, grins at Death, who leers back. With his paws in his back pockets, the rawhide man advances

195

toward his children, with his eyes on his sister.

He is close.

Humans fill drowned fields and crevices, occupy the hollows in rocks, walk and canoe through flooded gorges, squeeze their faces to lightning-lit patches of window in crumbling adobes. The face of Tlaloc is black. I touch the cold window with lips and forehead where the eyes were. "Have you seen Felicity?" I shout (silently) at the rain.

On the luggage rack are my belongings: a faded red valise in the shape of a heart full of letters from Aura to Felicity; an instance of the postal system of mothers being unable to deliver the letters of daughters save through the "trystero" of menfolk (studies in the interior); my paper hat; my paper overcoat; my paper gloves (on which I had written: "Toward Felicity. Half-baked thoughts hurtle through space like seed. Re: moist black-red soil"); the fountain pen (Pelikan *cenote*) with which I had written it; my paper shoes; two jars of murky, natural honey (purchased from a masked man at the station, produced by black bees for the palates of the tortured); two pair paper socks; a Japanese umbrella (to spread over picnic we were going to have, Felicity and I); a paper alarm clock; one fifth Old Crow.

Felicity eats like an abandoned violin in an attic: mostly stardust and drops of water. A drop of honey—rarely—to help her remember. All around her, Wits End revels in orgies of meat and fat vegetables. Armed with oversized cloves of garlic and hunks of doughy bread, the natives reach for their weaker brothers and sisters ... and all strangers are food, automatically, when they acquire a Post Office box. The price for homesteading is an arm, a leg, a runty child. Most Wits Enders sport gashes and stumps as well as large, round bellies. Vegetables grow with a meaty fierceness from every crack, offering bountiful bulbs and stalks to everyone. It is not unusual, during an Identity

Festival, for instance, to find a person smothered in wild cabbages with a neighbor's leg hanging from his mouth (Goya). In the midst of this, Felicity is in perpetual dietary fronde, a distinct rebel, fierce and red.

Δ

Dear Madam Postmistress:

I cannot explain myself.

Felicity may elude me forever but not the logic of my travel agent.

I know, of course, that a man without a heart can always go shopping in the nearest neon dump where poisonous lumps of scorched earth are sold, and wait home for his darling to return, from hunger (Ha ha). He could wait there, on top of his pile of bubbling aluminum, and draw curses from the grease pit of his race.

Why did I leave Wits End, that creamy basket of clouds, when all over the world trains carry the wrong people to the wrong places? Good question, Madam.

I could tell you that I was given notice by the elements: lightning was going to hit, tornado was coming, tidal waves, bleeding, darkness, flood, an endless streak of disaster aimed at my puny person; or that Felicity is the clock by which my personal time goes; but I would be lying.

Closer to the core of the matter, is my fear of your Hand. Only Felicity could keep your Hand from strangling me in sleep. Her presence was the brace holding your Hand in the pocket of your uniform. When she went, I heard the click of the handcuff falling away.

Which Hand? You only have one, the left.

At this very moment, I know, it is following this train swiftly with all five fingers outstretched, through fog and drizzle, never more than a few yards behind the last wagon

... When and if I fall asleep—I'm not going to, I promise ... it will—if it finds me, ha, ha—reach deeply into my stomach, take hold of the tight ball in my cortex (spinned experience) and begin to unwind it ... to make me follow the thread to the womb to lose a whole incarnation ... Go to hell! Here, I spit, sign with the cross, with my familiar, this is my M.O., here is my I.D., this is a magical icon of the *Virgen,* this is spook oil from Haiti, I burn a nasturtium, goodbye.

To think that once upon a time, with Felicity home, I could fearlessly rock (improvised womb, wicker chair), even delight in seeing your Hand buried deeply in a pocket full of telegrams you pulled selectively on your co-citizens. At those times, I could look smugly at my portion of the universe with the Playground full of fatherless children describing odd sun orbits, and think to myself: Only a heartless man can evolve!

Everyone wanted to camp out on this peak of positivism (Disney mountains) ...

unfinished   unsigned

Δ

I fall to my knees on the carpet of cigar ashes of the Second Class Mexican train. I look up.

Who is the god of this place? I ask.

The Indios rise and walk into the rain.

Whoever you are, keep the Hand from me until I find Felicity! Then I will surrender another heart to you, I promise! I will surrender Felicity's heart!

I bang my head against the map of Mexico fastened with screws under the seat. Sparkling rattle, shedding bronze serpent under us. The map of Mexico with train routes slashed in it by somebody's spurs, is my Wailing Wall. Again and again I hit it.

198

When it comes, the god's voice booms:

*Keep on truckin' brother! Don't stop until you find Felicity!
Don't give in to Historicity! Forget Ethnicity Ethnocentricity
and above all Psychologicality! And no Descriptivity! And
then I'll see what I can do for you you you ... This is the
Great God Tezcatlipoca the Soul Brother direct to you from
Texas via WZYZ.*

I promise! I shout in the now silent compartment. If
the train dies under me and they retire the engine and tear
up the berths and the seats, I will move to another train!
And supposing, if I live that long, that one day trains will be
used no longer, I will board a frigate! The canoe, though I
have to carve it from the last standing tree, will do in the
end if nothing else would carry me! And if supposing that
an anti-motion madman conquered the world and ordered
all locomotion stilled, all passports revoked and everybody
chained on a fifty-yard chain in a vegetable plot, I would
still find a way to keep going until I find Felicity!

*You seem to have covered it! Uncovered it! Vowed it! But
would you still stick to your rails if it was proven that the
native shall inherit the Kindom of Heaven and the wanderer
the fire holes of Hell?*

I will! (Tear streams down ashy cheek.) This is the
chance I take, Tezcatlipoca. I see us humans in the future,
without electricity, discovering our feet with a shock. Like
legendary mammals, our feet emerge suddenly as the most
important organs of our new consciousness. Women's feet
prove their curved superiority by being well equipped to
walk the distances from house to well, from well to the next
village and from there to the ruins of an ancient shopping
plaza to catch lizards for breakfast. And men's feet assume
again the ways of crouching, plowing through mud, pulling
carts. Yes, the future is an opportunity for feet everywhere.

199

But I promise! If the future comes before Felicity … My feet will do the same! Walk! Longer and farther! Until I find her!

In that case, replies Tezcatlipoca, obviously impressed,

> *you will rid yourself of sin and you will find the place you pray and I pray for, the place where between the ages of six and seven you wore out ten shovels digging a hole to heaven! You quit this when they kidnapped you and put you in school! And when you find this place and escape the temptations, the Communists and the lights of Sodom, you will hear the choir of angels and will see the White Wall which will then open for you and God Himself will let you roam free in the Freezer of All Human Actions where your heart waits for you—to shake your hand! This is WZYZ and your Citizens Band!*

What about Felicity? I cry (for instance).

No further comment from Tezcatlipoca. Sound of train wheels. To the train it makes no difference who talks to whom; it does not matter to the train that somebody's chasing somebody who is running from somebody. All that matters to the train is that you dig the rhythm, and keep time with your head drumming against the map of Mexico, screwed under the seat.

The Herald

"He hasn't calmed down yet!" The Editor slapped the day's pile of sister papers. In them were his models and his enemies. The lingering fantasia of an alternative reading. Ten years ago the pile had reached the ceiling. Now the ceiling had come down and the floor had risen.

She nodded. In some ways he was a man. In the same ways she wanted to be a man. Only being a man made it easier for him to be a man in those ways. He'd already been halfway up those ways when he started being a man in those ways by simply being a man. But she had started at the very start of those ways to be that sort of man. The start, which was also the bottom for her, was Obituaries for the Big Paper. But this was the Little Paper and her man was the editor of it. Sometimes when she despaired of being, she thought the bottom job at the Big Paper was equal to the top job at the Little Paper. When she thought that she lost sight of the pile of sister papers, and she saw the editorial attic as the little attic that it was, and the house housing the Little Paper as a little house on a provincial street in a moth-eaten town in a lost part of America, and her boyfriend, the editor, as a pimply college kid consumed by an antiquated ambition. At those times she paid sudden attention to her fingernails which she painted bright black, and to her body, which she bent in ways recommended on television, and then she took these nails and this body and offered them to the business manager of the Little Paper, who at those times seemed to her to be the authentic man. Her obituaries at those times became masterworks of precision, little prose poems bemoaning, alongside the deceased, the death of her illusions. But just when her masterful obituaries reached the point of poetic insight from which she could have soared into genuine ambiguous mortality, the Little Paper would publish a story that shook up the Big Paper. Watching the colossus tremble immediately restored her faith which, acting like Clearasil, purified her boyfriend, the editor, of his acne, and modified his dimensions to make him appear gigantic. Closely following on the footsteps of the Hulk on television, this psychic change was something she had come to expect.

"He hasn't calmed down yet and that's it! I don't care who he is!" Anger was tonic. He saw her gape and felt her desire for him steam off her frayed jeans. But there was a rub, a hitch and a kink in his madness. He not only cared who the man was, but was in fact mortally afraid of this man, who made him so angry and so mortally afraid. He also knew that he had no idea who the man he so hated was, and that made him angrier and more afraid. Everything about the man pointed to huge holes in the sky, crevasses full of goopy void. The man had been introduced to him as a rare and famous creature from outer space, who had landed by mistake in his little town and, due to an improper functioning of his wings, was unable to return to the glittering world he'd left behind. As soon as the man had landed in town, he had been advised by several witnesses to the phenomenon, to take full advantage of the illustrious stray by employing him on the Little Paper. The Big Paper too had been alerted instantaneously, and was employing the lost alien as much as it could. That under these circumstances the alien would consent to also work for the Little Paper was nothing short of miraculous. But here was the rub: While the stray seemed to fit perfectly into the Big Paper he was completely ill at ease in the Little Paper. For the Big Paper he wrote about his travels

through space, his many years of wandering lost in the Universe in search of his home. But for the Little Paper he wrote exclusively about the smallness of his present habitation, the innumerable little details of miniature irritation with the lack of life on the streets and other small matters. His entire stance ran contrary to the ambitions of the Little Paper which had managed—or so he thought—to give the impression that it was only a matter of time before it too would become a Big Paper. The alien pricked the painfully enlarged balloon of the very essence of his conceit. And when the editor respectfully pointed out the damage, the alien exploded, causing a scene which in its profound meanness threatened his entire sanity. The Little Paper, the Editor had carefully explained to the man, was against slavery, servitude and servility in all its forms, and was thus the only hope the current generation had of having those principles upheld.

"Yes," the man had replied, "The Little Paper is the only hope the current generation has to have those principles upheld and to have espresso too. The Little Paper is what holds their top quality stereo speakers together with their principles. For each item purchased through the advertising in the Little Paper, the Little Paper slips a little principle into the package. Streamlined to near perfection, minus a couple of kinks like me, the Little Paper has combined purchasing and upholding to a high standard. For each full-page ad there is a full page principle. Fall-in-the-Gap Jeans are covered by news of an anti-nuclear demonstration in faroff Utah. When finally planted in those jeans, the reader's flesh has a conscience. Stereos come with proposed sewers, home computers with gay rights, French wines with Agent Orange, modular furniture with toxic shock syndrome. The moral payoff is instantaneous and it has the added advantage of short-circuiting the connection of the market to the ills of society. Eventually, as in the case of an ad for tractors followed by a story on the rape of the Amazon, the process is circularized and the buyer buys the product with its specific guilt attached. Your goal, obtainable in a few years, is to match each product to its specific regret in the time it takes the reader to get from his home to the store. The potential is there, dear friend, for attaching the guilt-causing reasoning to all products directly along with the assembly instructions thus saving time and paper. Instead of being forced to waste their guilt-desiring organs on several sheets, your readers will be given only the dose necessary at the time of purchase."

In spite of himself, the Editor was curious. "And how would you propose to bring together purchaser and product in that case?"

"In the near future," the man said solemnly, spitting a pomegranate seed on the purple rug, "our present advertising methods will be obsolete. Unable to leave their houses during extended air pollution alerts, the people of the future will be watching constant parades of products going by on wall-to-wall screens. When deciding to purchase, our future customer will push a button and the object will descend from the wall wrapped in its sheet of specific moral opprobrium. The lucky buyer will then proceed to work off the debt, spurred on by coded guilt. You will be able to assign writers directly to products rather than events, since the products will in any case be where the events are and will often produce the events. This novel and orderly way of approaching the world will produce immediate profits. You will, for instance, follow doughnuts to an anti-nuclear demonstration where, stale and soggy, they will be distributed gratis by a drug manufacturer. You will follow a machine gun directly to war. All reporting until now has been done ass backwards from event to product. You will have a chance to straighten things out."

"What's more," exclaimed the Editor, swept off his

feet, "the time will come when we won't need writers at all … The product itself in the normal process of its functioning … will zap the user with a moral charge directly. A ninety-volter straight to the cortex …"

He was immediately sorry for having allowed himself to dream along those lines. Especially since the Alien finished his thought for him: "Yeah. You might as well sell the paper immediately and invest in voltage from the manufacturer. You can go straight to the brain. And one day, of course, there will be no need for the product either. The consumer will plug himself into the energy source and receive as much as he's willing to work for. Invest in sockets … and kill yourself," he concluded.

"Why don't you fire him if he bugs you so?" asked the girlfriend. "After all, the sky's the limit in this business. We can get a hundred writers for the price of this one …"

She loved his anger, but it was spent. Her jeans cooled. Her thoughts returned to the obituary of a powerful man who had died that afternoon. It was going to be a great obituary, she decided. Crystal clear and soaring. For each listed accomplishment she was going to inject a final note of the irremediable. An eagle had passed. She pulled out the black lacquer and began to do her nails.

THE OLD COUPLE

He touched her there. He was it, she was the city and there was the bus.

"Have you noticed how the transit system is worse in towns where there is no café life? I propose putting espresso bars and jukeboxes on buses, to remedy both situations."

He was her equal.

He was irony, she was subjective mysticism.

"The ironist is a vampire who has sucked the blood out of her lover and fanned him with coolness, lulled him to sleep and tormented him with turbulent dreams," said Söoren.

He was stoned and she was straight.

He was there and she was after it.

Both of them were dizzy.

They were behind something, a bright object, a dictionary on fire careening through the industrial sky.

"There goes Amy Vanderbilt," he regretted. "Now how am I ever going to learn the latitude?"

He was an adept of depth and so described himself to the nun who wanted to know why, of all things, the Virtue of Prudence?

She was nun, no one, numen, to him.

To her he was fat and she advised more lines of thought whipping through his mug to restore the native intelligence that surely must bust through porcine desire.

Thought whips redoing sensually ethereal flesh.

Compassion filled them both to about the size of a normal person. A person, that is, unused to the brain with ready receptors for history.

Various "esprits" chased each other down the virgin psychic highways of their double cerebrum Autobahn.

But only when they touched their heads together.

Apart, their heads gave each one minute's thought to "the sad fact that ... the confusion of two realities, one in single, the other in double quotes, was a symptom of impending insanity," transtextualized Vladimir.

In the news, at this point, liberal democrats committed mass suicide in a jungle in Guyana. It was the first recorded act of premarxist leftwing psychosis in history. One would have expected the vacuum left by the death of Stalin to be filled by excuses. But no, the "esprits" had their way here, signalling as they were willing to listen, that the final hole had been made in scientific rationalism.

He was the one expecting. She was baffled by the mangled circuitry.

"How could such a blatant ghost phosophorize in such a clean, determinist, metonymic, structural and atheistic household?" she explained.

"What do you expect in a world where the only God-lovers left aim to make anthropologist?" veered the bus driver.

"What's the last war you remember?" he asked of the man at the wheel.

"The code says be civil to your passengers. The Civil War, of course."

People's sense of history is how well they remember their wars.

Here is the last war he remembered: Having made so many sinister jokes over the years, he had been infected with a residue of terror which is, invariably, left over by successful black humor, like a coating of grease on the bottom of a well-used pan, apt to flavor the simplest snacks with a dark primal flavor. Throwing away the pan, which in this case was his brain, was clearly impossible, so he went to war instead with the proddings of residual malevolence in even his cleanest or most sincere moments, as when viewing a baby or smelling a flower.

Wrestling with a demon, in short.

Improper balance between wit and generosity had resulted in an amount of muck sufficient for demonic animation. It was this he had last fought, preventing his poetic instinct from slipping into institutional proceeding.

He was glad he remembered this much because he couldn't, otherwise, see himself going very far with himself as a character, because he could not escape viewing himself *sub specie aeternitatis,*

rolling timelessly through the city,

on a shelf full of similar monads, individual cereal packs lined shoulder to shoulder in the Safeway, various contents of eternally simultaneous conception.

She would have gladly conceded time to the nineteenth century where it belonged, if it weren't for the fact that she hated grammar and wasn't ready for religion. "Limbo is an interesting condition," she mused at the intersection of Melville and Frisby, consisting, as it does, of sheer inattention. If she were going to pay attention, she would have to become religious, and if not, she would have to put in time, as in a slot machine. Going out on a limb, in proper limbo, was a tightrope walk between an askew glance and a corresponding—hopefully or she would fall— twitch in her soul.

He said, "The future is not historical."

The youth of the country shared his opinion. They were not having children.

She had children. She believed in the future.

There were no children on the bus.

He believed in the future too. "It's my opinion and I'm sharing it."

He used to have a guaranteed neurosis in the clear

opposition of his ideas, growing quite independently in his head like tomatoes in a hothouse, and his feelings and perceptions, the real weather as it were, when tomatoes might or might not grow, but as he grew he went more and more with the weather. The considerable health gained thereby was only occasionally interrupted by obsessive ideas, so it was a shock when one did come along, as in the aforementioned "last war he remembered," and had to be fought, as it always must, with all the superstitions in his arsenal. Unfortunately being healthy had cut down on his arsenal and the weapons remaining were either too powerful or too rusty for effective retaliation. Mythical battles fought with childhood weapons owe their clarity (as the fog clears) to memory.

She still had the immunity conferred by regular practice of superstition. She brushed her teeth with witch nipples. At the same time she was perfectly familiar with the computerized abstractions behind the images, and could wage fantastic energy war, let me tell you.

When two senior citizens were voided into the night, the driver, Vladimir, said: "*Partir, c'est mourir un peu, et mourir c'est partir un peu trop.*"

Eh bien, that transportation should behave this way.

"What yoga do you practice?" he asked of her.

"Overhearing. She prefers overhearing to monasticism," said the man in uniform.

"Consider this man. The breakdown of his days into shared psychic units, a consequence both of industrialization and of his own schedule, has led to the banalizing and perhaps disappearance of mythic time. But since he *is* a mythic man ..."

"*Merci, mademoiselle.*"

"... he must now invent a myth for every known quantity of time. As seconds and microseconds, as well as the increasing sophistication of what he drives, become

210

more and more important, his mythmaking must match his driving speed, long ago over the official limit."

The Bionic Driver offered that the task was made ever more difficult by the fact that the conversational mode (outside of New York) was utterly alien to everyone. The fear of talking had spread to such extremes it was about to overtake America's primary fear which was the fear of not going to sleep.

"At ten o'clock the streets are dark. Afraid not to go to sleep, the Americans sleep. Add to that, that wit today is more terrifying than sperm, and that people would rather talk with sperm. Why, I remember when society was voluble, we were moral."

The two of them said nothing.

We, the silent people, hold sperm to be self-evident ...

In Reality he was a raving demon.

In reality he was a plumber.

In 'Reality' he was her.

In 'reality' he worked for her.

In "reality" his demon was her plumbing system, and he her plumber.

In "Reality" there was no one.

But just as he preferred a mask to a carefully doctored face, he preferred a face to the thought-out nothingness.

She preferred the fall turning to winter, out the window, a clear night of gentle, windy sweetness, filled with the *materia mystica* the exuberant hands of her childhood had so easily thrown into the air of other such nights.

Surprised to see the extremely personal become so subversive, he saw the narrowing shaft, the cone tunnel, the parachute. Extreme personalism is being everybody (yeah,

211

but do you have Blue Cross?) and only women can be extreme personalists. Of himself, only his penis was personalist.

The penis is a woman.

Being there—standing on your head.

Imperious old fart, berated the bus driver, you've parlayed seven inches of schlong into twenty-five years of slavery!

Was it true?

He touched her there

Demented wit *en face* a cemented slit.

PETRA

The medium stopped my boyfriend at the door. "She wants to see you alone," she said.

She? For three days I'd been trudging to Madame Rosa's fifth floor walkup in Prospect Park. We'd been conversing *à trois* with a bizarre character named Gustav. Not only was he not a she, but he went out of his disembodied way to make a point of it. Gustav loved strategy. He'd been a Habsburg officer during the heyday of Franz Josef, stationed in the dusty garrison in Hungary where he'd played cards and done cavalry drills, until one day, when he was called to stand guard for Archduke Ferdinand in Serbia. Leaving Sarajevo with the Duke, he remained his companion through at least three Stages. Their favorite thing for fifty years or so had been to play astral pinochle and discuss the many ways in which the Austrian Empire could have won the First World War. The Archduke was quite bitter about it, especially after he met von Metternich and the great soldier had totally agreed with his ideas about the war. Gustav's job on Stage Two had been to catch the generals and strategists of that event when they entered the astral plane, and to bring them by the scruff of their souls, so to speak, before Ferdinand for a dressing-down. But this year, to Gustav's dismay, Ferdinand had joined Stage Four, and he was left with no one capable or interested in discussing strategy, which had compelled him to that ultimate of desperate ectoplasmic acts: making conversation with embodied creatures. The florid, flower-nightshirted, pom-pom-slippered body of Madame Rosa hadn't been his first choice, but everywhere he went in the Circle of Mediums (which looks from the other side like a deep cauldron with little circles of lights in it) he found most of them taken by snarling entities in deep communication. So he plunged into the first available one like a man finding a vacant stall in an airport lavatory, and that was Madame Rosa.

I didn't exactly like Gustav. Most of the time he seemed to be speaking to Jack, anyway. Never mind the fact that it was I who paid the madame her twenty fat ones each time, and that it was I who had committed herself to foolishly writing a Sunday magazine feature on it. At times, I felt that I was watching two boys talk toy soldiers, and once I did my fingernails and went to Madame Rosa's incredible bathroom (there were *five* shrines in there, each one with a votive candle and dead flowers under oily lithographs of muscular madonnas, and hundreds of bottles of variously colored liquid labeled "luck," "money," etc.; two black velvet Azteca paintings behind the shower; a *velvet* shower curtain; a shag rug of plastic black curls resembling not a sacrificed sheep but a murdered car seat; and *glued* on the toilet were *hundreds* of pictures cut from magazines, making the whole an indescribable collage and a most unsettling place for lowering one's behind, which then seemed to fit into a puzzle only God knows what it meant to spell; and on the back of the door hung large terrycloth towels with appliquéed images of the Vatican and of every pope that would fit; the toilet paper was perfumed, lavender and had little crowns in filigree) and when I came back, Gustav was still talking as if nothing had occurred.

So I was rather relieved when Madame Rosa said "she," and told Jack to wait outside. I could barely imagine that Gustav had decided to change sex and have a *tête-à-tête* with me. Something else was going on.

"OK," said Jack, "I've waited for women before."

214

Madame Rosa wasn't exactly her usual self. She seemed a little unsettled. With Gustav she had been perfectly comfortable. She sank at once on her enormous floating pillow embroidered with primitive theosophy, and started talking. It was a clear, young voice. I remembered it at once.

"Petra!" I blurted.

"Long time no see, Jockey!"

"I still don't see you. But if you see me, that's enough. How do I look?"

"Bored, tired, losing a chunk of your soul every time you sell another stupid article."

It was Petra all right. I felt suddenly afraid. She *was* dead then.

"I didn't know you were dead, P."

There was a pause. Madame Rosa groaned and shifted hams.

"Well, I'm not. I'm just tripping. I'm part of an astral corporation I formed with Armanyi. It's hard to explain." She didn't have to. We'd both been a little in love with Armanyi in our school days, but she had become quite obsessed later on. She read occult meanings in his slightest gestures. We'd fallen out over him. But Petra! How well I remembered her, her sleepy voice. We'd met in grad school in Chicago. Armanyi taught the course in comparative religion. I'd begun collating the myths of the Aleuts with those of their Siberian brothers when my roommate suddenly quit. I couldn't afford any distractions, and this business of finding a new roommate was a distinct pain. I didn't want a man, especially a handsome one. I meant to avoid chatterboxes. No smokers. No airheads. I hate rock 'n' roll. I think I rejected thirty people on the phone. Then Petra called.

"Petra," I said, "if you're not dead, why do you have to bump into me this way? Couldn't you use the telephone?"

"I can't use the phone," she said in her sleepiest voice. "I can't take buses. I can't take trains. I don't have a burro. I don't know how to use a Telex."

I didn't understand. "This astral corporation you and Dr. Armanyi formed, it isn't something fiendish and debilitating, is it?"

Madame Rosa made a cackle sounding like the boingg! of a spring deeply buried in a couch. I remembered Armanyi well. He was bald and his eyes were bottomless, black, filled with India ink. I surprised him sleeping once in his office. He faced forward in his chair, with his eyes open. I passed my hand in front of his eyes, and he woke up. "I'm sorry," he said, in that charming Balkanic tobacco voice, "I have been sleeping in my clothes as if at the beach." That image had an eerie effect on me, and when I met Petra and heard her voice, the first thing I thought was: "She sleeps in her clothes as if at the beach." After she became involved with Armanyi, and she started spending little time in the apartment, her voice deepened and she started sounding sleepier and sleepier. The day before she disappeared, she looked thin and helpless, as if she were waiting on a beach for a wave to come and undress her. Cosmic. Strange. Vague outlines. But very pretty, enticing, nymphic. Oval, dark, silky, sleepy. She'd scared me.

"Petra," I asked, "where did you go when you left the house on Jarvis?"

"To Tibet," she said.

"With Armanyi?"

"Sort of. Listen, there is something I want to tell you. When I left, you were still struggling with your thesis. I knew that the only way you could finish it was if I helped you. So I gave you the idea for a second version."

"What are you saying, you semi-dead ectocreep? That you did my work for me?" I recognized in this the tenor of some of our less subtle instances of life together.

216

"No, no," hastened the astral Petra. "Only the *idea!*"

I'd written two versions of my thesis. One strictly for school, in which proper methodology was used and common myth themes were described, classified and dismissed; and another, a poetic version, expressing my bleak disgust at the present situation of native peoples below the Arctic circles. This version, called *From Russia with Love,* was about the fragmentation of spirit caused by the bristling weaponry, nuclear warheads and deadly toys that now separate brother tribes from one another. Unable to scale the rotating radar dishes and blinking electronics of the Polar cap, the Eskimos and the Siberians gaze longingly at each other through quickly disappearing legends. I submitted the first to the Masters' Committee, the second to a literary magazine. I got my MA and the poetic polemic was published. I was much taken with myself for it, and still am.

"Really," Petra was saying calmly, as if we were still sitting on the sunny living room floor of our young womanhood, "I didn't have anything *substantial* to do with it ... I only saw your dilemma and cleared your mind for its own work."

But I wouldn't have it. Disembodied or no, this was the same Petra I once—in one of my moments of uncertain reason—fiercely desired one afternoon, only to be reasonably turned down. Her disembodied voice seemed suddenly full of that body, and I filled with the memory like a sail with a spring breeze. I shut my eyes tightly and rocked a little back and forth. The stab of embarrassment came as expected. It came every time I thought about it.

"What's wrong?" said Petra's sleepy, faraway voice.

I opened my eyes. "Then you can't see everything?" I said.

"I can see everything connected to a certain plane of thought. I have little insight into desire. That was part of the deal. But I see that you are tired, that you are falling into a routine. A real danger to spiritual life. You used to be so adventurous."

I didn't remember being particularly adventurous. I'd gone to school for too long. The most adventurous thing I remember was getting drunk in a Black jazz joint on the South Side of Chicago, the day Petra had gone. She'd gone, leaving this message on the refrigerator with magnetic letters: **G O N E   T O   I N D I A**. I sat in that joint, having accepted the protection of a flashy dude with a gold tooth, scrambling that message in my mind, until I came up with **ONE GOAT IN ID**. Satisfied for the moment, I let him take me home in his pink Cadillac, and didn't answer the phone until graduation.

But she had a point. Routine was getting to me. Jack, outside the door, was an engineer, and the house was full of blueprints.

"If I go to Chicago and ring Armanyi's Tibetan bronze bell, will you be there, Petra?"

"Armanyi?" she said. "He's been dead for years."

"Then ... you ... why not you?" I shouted.

Madame Rosa opened her eyes. Sweat streamed down her volumes of flesh, her library of flesh, her *Encyclopedia Britannica* of flesh. She looked exhausted. "Wot speereet, Miz Jokey!" she groaned. "I should you pay me feeftee for dis!"

I looked at the fire-escape window painted Giotto blue. A teenager was smoking a pipe on it.

When I went out, Jack said: "I know why Gustav wanted to see you alone."

"Why?" I said.

"He wanted to propose. You always listen so patiently to him."

JULIE

A bar for the newly bearded opened on the corner. Club
Moderne. *Club. Moderne.* The first is typical of the ambitions of the newly bearded: to club up, to be among their
own, to club anybody strange, to be British, if possible. The
second is ironic and named after the style of 1950s lawn
furniture—the first mass-produced plastic—which is be-
coming collectible now. "Moderne" also stands for chic-
tacky, which counteracts a little, the stuffiness of "club." In
any case, the name is perfect and the newly bearded flock to
it like flies.

Above analysis is the work of my girlfriend Julie. I was
studying the mysteries of the street from the window, with
a cup of coffee. A bag lady was stopping traffic. A stuck
clock over the newsstand said 11:32. Stupid. There isn't a
clock in the vast literature of stopped clocks ever stopped at
11:32. In Russian novels they are always stuck at 3:00 PM,
which seems to be the hour when most Russians search
their souls for some reason. Maybe because that's when it
gets dark in the winter in Russia. In French novels, clocks
stop at 6:00 AM, an hour all the more mysterious insofar as
no French man or woman has ever been awake at that time.
It is the hour of children, the hour of concierges, milkmen,
and guilty adulterers. The hour, in other words, when the
French feel horrible. In Prague and in Czech-German
novels, the big clock in the tower is always stuck on the
midnight hour by the figure of Death with the scythe. For
Czechs, as well as for other Eastern and Southern
Europeans, midnight is political. In English novels ...

"There is a fly in your coffee, your apron is backwards, your hair is a mess and what's with all those assistant professors across the street?" asked Julie.

I looked. Next to the entrance—tan wood with a bulging porthole—three newly bearded men stood rigidly under a streetlight—on in the daytime—looking pyramidal and hieratic. They formed a frieze, a monument of Graeco-Roman embarrassment. They looked as if they'd just shaken hands and felt bad about it. They looked as if they'd gone to school for an eternity and that they would continue to do so for eternity. They looked very defensive.

"Life has dealt them a mortal insult," I spoke.

Whereupon Julie analyzed the name of the club.

I could be in love with Julie, because she will say, apropos of nothing, after reading a *Time* magazine article: "The flowers have syringes." Of course, I could reconstruct her thought, retrace her path, find how a notice about Fernando Arrabal and an anti-drug poster in the subway contributed to it, but it would be useless. I would rather she went on, as she usually does: "And the flowers had frozen food, and we had the flowers. Criminal." To which I would add: "My cousin Eddie's little girl Blue doesn't go anywhere without flowers. Their car is full of dead flowers. The lawn is devastated." But I am not in love with Julie, I'm just not sufficiently inclined in that direction.

After a few hours, there was an ashtray full of her white-filtered Carleton butts and my yellow-filtered Camel Lights, two cruddy cups of coffee and milk no sugar, two glasses of sweet wine and an empty bottle of same.

"Well, should we try it?"

"Let's."

I twisted my hair in an unravelling climber's rope, stabbed at my lips with a black lipstick and put on a long sweater that would do fine for top and bottom. Julie put on some Jackie O. sunglasses. Just in case, I put my diaphragm case with the yin-yang sign I painted on it one night, in my pocket, next to my Camels. We were ready for the nouveau hirsute.

I felt neon-nausea from the start. Blinking blue signs on the other side of the bar. Expensive leather jackets. Women like labels peeled from Sunkist oranges. Mixed drinks the colors of tourist brochures. Swizzle sticks with skulls on the ends. Bumping against people I couldn't help noticing the hard square of plastic set in their behinds like a little window for the cogitative dwarf inhabiting them to look out from and reflect. And I heard: "What makes it work?" "What makes it go?" "That a way to go!" to which Julie added: "What makes it fly?" and I: "What makes it float?"

It's getting easier and easier to put people in poems without them noticing a thing. I can take this fat creep right here touching my elbow and put him between the lines of a couplet, thus: *Creep:* "I coulda had it just like that," *Me:* "I ate the barracuda's cat." See if he'll ever get out of there. Caught behind the bars of that couplet, he'll be calling for mercy, but only Julie and I can let him out. I ordered another Jim Beam on the rocks, and Julie got a green green Chartreuse.

We sat there when they said: "Sit here, ladies!" Where we sat, the black leatherette was still warm, having been vacated by two rather peeved females. Like the rest of the neo-hairies, our beaus had cornsilk-in-moonlight, amethyst-in-milk, brand-new, first-time-ever beards. They rustled and trembled like virgins shaken by moonrays. The sandpaper of the underworld waiting patiently on the other side of the mirror hadn't gotten them yet.

"According to Fourier," said Julie, "human beings should have six orgasms a day: three with friends, and three with strangers."

"We're friends," hastened the left one. "We work for

Channel 4 ..." He extended what appeared to be a friendly arm but was in reality a dead stick of petrified wood from a California petrified forest. Like many other young professionals he had not enough life in him to reach through all his extensions. There was barely enough life for the beard and part of the lower lip. The rest of him was without gloss, mostly petrified, and some dead wood. The limb fell with a thump on Julie's very thin arm, nearly cracking the bone.

"We're strangers," said the right one, exhibiting for all the world a bit of humor. In him, wood, beard, flesh, stone and even bits of metal like those vague veins of copper in certain stones, mixed rather indiscriminately. "But why would this guy, Fourier, say that?"

"He was a Socialist," Julie explained. "He believed that insufficiently loved people, like politicians, young people on the way up, middle-management people and the plain disgusting, ought to share in the erotic wealth of the community."

"You some kind of intellectual?" said the petrified forest.

And now Julie did something very strange, which only she can do. She looked straight into his beard and made herself soft and desirable like a siren and she was almost impossibly hard to look at. She oozed the substance of the night and the air became palpable and wet, and she said, "Wittgenstein attacks diseased questions with healthy questions. We usually *know*, you see, but when we ask what it is that we know, we don't know anymore. An education based on asking questions about things we already know is not an education ... it is a slow unravelling of the mind. *Comprende?*"

Lost in her, he had no choice. He said, "You're probably one of those types that sits up at night asking 'What is time?' " he feebly insisted.

"Time is a magazine," said Julie, pulling her arm.

"And what do you do?" said the right, to whom I "belonged." "Keep her in ears?"

I liked that. I laughed. Keeping Julie "in ears." What a delicious image. I saw her standing as a steady stream of attentively perked ears passed by her like small animals at Christmas at the SPCA. Eventually, Julie needs more and more ears to satisfy her voracious appetite for intelligent listening. I transform my body with the aid of surgery into an immense Ear, a human-sized Ear. But one day I meet the Nose, and we leave Julie and Gogol behind ...

"I go to acupuncture class. I watch."

"I watch too," quoth he, "I watch the wires. Something comes through, I rip it and redo it in my unique style."

"Men are machines," I say.

"Love machines," he quips.

I like him. I take out my Camel Lights and start shaking them. The finely bearded wire man looks at my hand, puzzled. I look too. Instead of Camels, I'm tapping my diaphragm case. I probably blush, but I brave the sea.

"It has the yin-yang sign on it," I explain, proffering it. He recoils slightly from it, as if it were a snake. I regain my cool, and go on: "It's the first, actually, in a series of designer diaphragms I'm working on. Another says, 'Will you still love me in the morning?' Stuff like that, you know." I snap it open and then shut like a cigarette case. Slip it back in my pocket. Find, pull out and light a Camel.

Julie explains to "her" bimbo: "Absolute process is absolute terror. What exactly is my interest in you? Your self? I doubt it. A life, anybody's, is a literary form to be used in the same way as a sonnet. You know, fourteen lines and *bam!*"

"I tell you one thing about reading," says the hapless, petrified gent, losing some of the silky sheen, still hoping for approval, "it doesn't help you get around in the dark ..."

I can see that we are working apart, that soon there will be a rift, then a canyon, then a river will rush through it, and Julie and I will be standing on opposite shores, she with an enemy, me with something lukewarm like a glass of milk, and probably not too unpleasant either. I try to cross over while the crack is still only imaginary, but my burro trips and falls in.

"Julie," I speak, "I'll cast myself in an ancient myth and scare the pants off of both of them!"

"Not for my sake, I hope," the tart replies tartly. She is a language fiend, capable of swallowing a mass, a room full of people, a Third World country between the gaping words. "I don't hear you anymore," she says. "This limp, nerveless batch of new, bearded yes-men makes me puke." She gulps down her drink, exits.

"My," says the left, "how many shrinks does it take to change *her* lightbulb?"

"You're a growth," I tell him, and nudge his friend. But his friend doesn't laugh. "Screw you both," I declaim.

When I shove off, I notice the petrified and coppery arm of my beau trying to lift itself and fly to me and rest like a heavy bird on my shoulder. But it picks up a glass instead, and turns to the now completely still left.

Julie is nowhere to be seen, the street is full of commerce. The newsstand sells dirty magazines. The joint dealer on the corner does the boogie to internal rhythm. A dog regards a ruined Cuban sandwich. A PR gigolo I'd noticed before licks his lips as I pass. Back at the window, I call Julie. No answer. The gigolo looks up. I light a Camel. I look up.

A certain shackled limpidity is in his eyes next morning, like a flower on a window still. The day is full of clouds and through the open window pours street jazz.

THE BABYSITTER

M y husband was home on one of those rare weekend
visits from his teaching job two states away. "We
need the money," etc. Which is true, we always need *the* or
money, in general, but going away is as important to him as
food is to all of us. So *money* is one of those euphemisms for
separation and silence, and it is a symbol as well for being
"grown up," "that's how the world does it," etc. These
notions are important to Mark. He would like to be
perceived as a "man-in-the-world" (and when I'm not
around, as a "man-of-the-world"), something solid, substantial, a "cube." He wants to (and sometimes does) project
matter, thingness, substance, a thing light does not go
through. He wears black or brown wingtips, baggy creased
pants, nearly square ties, shirts with much collar. He quotes
the classics, writes poems to Virgil ("O Virgil, your children
have taken to the streets!") and has a job translating Racine
for a scholarly house, in iambic pentameter. (Well, not a
"job," really. The advance was $250.)

Instead of our usual fight, which always ended with
our daughter banging her head on the piano and calling for
Peter Pan, we decided to have people over for dinner.
Mark's weekend visits didn't allow for much social life
together, as you may imagine. Our fights took up all our
time. "Having people for dinner" was something Mark
took seriously, because "that's how people do it." I was
reading it more in some who's-afraid-of-Virginia-Woolf
sense, literally having them for dinner. Instead of pasta and
white wine.

The unfortunates we chose were chosen in characteristically tactical fashion. One couple, with child (this way, the "child" would "play with" Becky), was new in town. The man was a Big Writer, a Visiting Professor in Fiction at the University. His wife was his wife. The Big Writer was from California and he was visibly wilting here on the East Coast. The wife was not known to have strong feelings, although it was generally assumed that she too was "wilting."

The other couple were our friends, the Alexanders. Alexander the Man was a poet and local firebrand who would think nothing of dipping his pen in venom to attack anything that appeared to have just insulted his sense of beauty and disorder. Fairly famous, he was continually sabotaging what would have, in time, become an awesome reputation, by biting all the hands that fed him, without exception. He could also be loyal and embarrassingly affectionate at times. He was the very opposite of the kind of Jew Mark was. Mark was the totally gentilized Jew who wished to appear Southern and Republican. Alexander was the violent partisan of whatever ideas he was wearing at the time.

The female Alexander was an artist. Quiet but shrewd, she gave things a thorough Midwestern look that approved if the thing looked or was sincere, "honest," "made of wood," "sterling," "brassy," "real." In her eyes, Mark appeared as the scarecrow he really is, and few others passed the test, though I think she had a certain affection for me.

It was a dinner made in the more ironic reaches of heaven, where the planners have real fun. I objected in vain. Mark thought that the prose writer and poet should meet, and that the "children should play." This is the kind of logic the Chinese erected around their Empire in order to keep the Mongolian orgies out of sight. Eventually, I was amused by the idea of the mix, and decided to keep

226

observing as much as my role of hostess would allow. And to keep filling glasses.

BW was thin, cocained, tan, nervous. The BW Wife was anorexic, long-haired, suffering, creased downward, harried and ironic.

But their Babysitter, who hadn't been invited, was the real surprise. She was pleasingly teen-plump, chestnut-haired, blue eyes, all California. She paid absolutely no attention to Baby, who was only five months old and a mix of unchanged diaper and ready howl.

"Just give her some scraps," BW said. "In California we always bring extra people."

"That's because we only eat salad there," said the Wife.

I showed them around the living room, called Becky in to show her Baby (she turned her nose up in instant disgust, ran into her room and slammed the door through which vague TV sounds could be heard for the rest of the evening), and went to the kitchen to tend to the pasta sauce.

I heard Mark say that the Alexanders, who were due any minute, had been living for years solely on the proceeds of his published literary works, without teaching. BW, whose literary earnings must have been eighty times the size of Alexander's, said thinly, "Big deal!" In addition to those earnings, BW had a fat university job in California, and moved around the country and abroad, exchanging semesters with other professors.

"He's got another wife to support," observed the Wife apropos her hubby, "and another set of kids, both of whom are junkies."

"I don't think Myron is a junkie," the Babysitter said firmly. "He fires but he's not hooked."

"He's a weekend junkie," agreed BW.

This was already more than our little world could

safely take. Mark changed the tack, as tactfully as he could, which can be brutal.

"Translating high classical French," he said, "can be extremely difficult, but the rewards are great."

Usually, at this point in our provinces, someone calls for a recitation and Mark is only too happy to oblige. He reads in a stentorian voice, picked up from God knows what old record, maybe from the first poetry reading ever, Lord Alfred Tennyson reading "The Charge of the Light Brigade."

But the Wife said, "Bullshit. Anybody who's been firing as long as that is a fucking junkie. If he couldn't get it for a week, he'd turn into a snivelling little worm, begging for what's left in a whore's cruddy cooker!" The pasta sauce was bubbling and I swear I saw a thin-lipped smile in the tomato red. It was like the triumph of language over pasta, or the "Comeback of the Wife" or something. In any case, something glorious and exhausting. Mark, I knew, was speechless.

But just as calmly as if that had been only a normal quip in the course of the many sets of quips that keep our social lives in shape, BW said, "I don't suppose you mean to point out our similarities with that metaphor? Like father like son, and all that. Sort of like, 'The son will lick the crud in the whore's spoon, while the father will go for the rest of the whore.' Very good, dear. Excellent."

Echoed by the Babysitter: "Just as you said in your book *Language and Manners*, page 28, 'second-strike language can devastate *leisurely* ...' "

Which is when the front door started banging furiously. Alexander didn't believe in doors. He thought they should be knocked down. I went to let them in. Passing on my way through the living room, everyone looked peaceful and sunny, sipping wine. Could I have hallucinated all those words? Mark was standing by the

228

bookcase with an early edition of *Phèdre* in his hand.

Alexander kissed me hard on one cheek, and would have liked to pat my behind, I'm sure. Alexandra pecked me too and appraised me coolly, down through the tomato spots on my apron. She said, "I'll help you," and Alexander advanced right into the middle of the living room, zeroed in on BW, held out his hand and said, "I hear your new book's making a shitload of money!"

"I can't complain," BW said sourly.

The Wife and Baby were then introduced to the new couple, but not the Babysitter.

"Who are you, the Babysitter?" asked Alexander.

"How did you know?" said the Wife.

"Blue eyes, pug nose, adoring smile," said Alexander. "We used to live in California."

At this point, Alexandra and I went into the kitchen, and I took out the plates, and she broke the spaghetti box and dropped the noodles into the boiling water.

Alexander's vehement voice said, "How much did you make?"

I couldn't hear the answer, because Alexandra said, "They brought a babysitter all the way from the *West Coast*?"

BW's new book was called *The Boys' Room*, and it was being touted as the season's hottest property. In reality, the hype had to do with the success of the earlier *The Women's Room*, by Marilyn French. It was commonplace in publishing circles that the first man to write a similar roll of toilet paper would make a wad. And now here it was, *The Boys' Room*, the story of four or five guys getting drunk and spilling all the male-chauvinist-pig beans that had been simmering in them for years, ever since women's lib had been going around with razor blades looking for balls.

"Dinner is on," I said, advancing two steps into the room. Everyone came in, except the Babysitter.

"I put out a plate and chair for her," I said. "There is plenty for everybody."

"I will take her plate to her," said BW. "She's the Babysitter." The Baby, last I'd seen him, had curled up in a corner with Becky's large felt monkey, and had gone to sleep in a puddle of feces and urine.

My protest went unheeded, and BW filled a plate heaping full of pasta, poured a lot of sauce on it, and went into the other room. There was a fork planted in the top of the mound, and, just as he exited, he grabbed a *second* fork.

"Now what do you suppose that *second* fork is for?" asked the wife.

Mark refilled the glasses with wine, and we sat down to eat. Passing the Parmesan, rolling up the noodles, swishing the wine and getting ready for that first bite took a little time. Nobody said anything.

"Good food," said Mark to me, the first words he had directed my way since coming home for the weekend. "I miss home cooking," he said to everyone else.

"We eat out," said the BW Wife. "BW eats out too."

"I could review *The Boys' Room* for the underground paper," said Alexander, "if he gives me a copy."

"*The New York Times* will review it on the front page," came BW's voice from the other room, "as will all the other big places. But I would be very interested in what a place like *that* would have to say!"

Now he'd done it. Alexander put his fork down slowly, and said to the invisible BW, "A place like *what*?"

There was a giggle in the living room, coming from the Babysitter, and BW, his mouth full of pasta, said, chewing, "Underground, those kinds of people ..."

"And who the fuck are those *kinds*? Do they matter less than the riffraff who read the bourgeois sheets?"

There was more giggling, and then the Babysitter said,

"That's not what he meant. On page 78 of *Language* there is a quote from Walter Benjamin ..."

"Why doesn't he come in here?" said Alexandra.

"He's feeding the Babysitter," the wife said.

Good hostess that I am, I said, "Let's have a toast for *The Boys' Room*, may it prosper!" Everyone raised their glasses, and clinked, except for Alexander who made a point of drawing out and then sucking in a very long noodle.

"Chin-chin," said BW from the living room, and there was a clink of glasses out there.

After that, we ate quietly. Alexandra noted the pretty mugs for coffee, and she said that you could get a similar red wine cheaper at Frank's. The Wife closed up like a shell, opening up only to suck in noodles. Mark brought Racine up two more times but dropped him for lack of interest. Alexander puffed a few times as if he were going to say something, but disgust soon showed on his face and he tended to his food. Occasional giggling came from the other room.

Afterwards, everyone took their coffee back into the living room. BW was sitting in the rocking chair with his eyes half-closed, rocking a little. The Babysitter was changing the baby from an oversized box of Pampers I hadn't noticed before. The soiled diaper lay next to her like a flag captured in battle.

"I think he's sleepy," she said to the wife. "Maybe I should take him home."

"Let *her* take him home," said BW, meaning the Wife.

"I will," she said, and caught deftly the car keys BW threw suddenly at her.

"OK," said the Babysitter. "I'll see that BW gets home safely," and she took out a stick of gum.

The Alexanders left soon after the Wife did. Mark tried to make some kind of conversation, but BW and the Babysitter started making out on the floor, next to the diaper no one had bothered to throw out. There seemed to be some kind of invitation for us to join in their petting. Some kind of California manners, no doubt. But Mark and I don't do that kind of thing. I went in to put Becky to bed, and Mark went to his office to read or pretend to read.

When we left the room, BW and Babysitter turned off the light.

A Bar in Brooklyn

My search for anonymity took me all the way to Brooklyn. I saw a Happy Hour sign in the window of a teeming watering hole and went in. I took the only stool in the sea of suits and imagined myself to be a slim sloop maneuvering the straits between bulky tankers in the Gulf of Aqaba. A bubbling office siren to my right was emptying the contents of a coconut shell into her hold through a pink straw. But at my left—I had to do a double take. At my left was a priest.

His left hand, next to me, was planted on the bar at the elbow and a smoking cigarette bloomed from its fingers. Next to his other hand, which lay limply and ecclesiastically (as in "a holy hand") on the bar, was a Manhattan in a tall glass. The cigarette hand had a ring on the matrimonial finger. His fingernails were rosy and well clipped.

I ordered another (it was two drinks for the price of one) in order to steel myself for conversation with the man of the cloth. But as I involved myself in ordering, another floozie, born no doubt from the ground oyster shells that littered the floor of the establishment, took the father on. I say another floozie because when I search for anonymity, *I'm* a floozie. She was a chestnut-haired, ruby-lipsticked nymph with a bottle of Bud in her hand. The business suit gave in to all kinds of topography.

"Taking refuge from the sanctuary?" was what I had planned to ask him.

"Seeking asylum from the eternal verities?" was what she asked him.

That wasn't bad. And then she said, "I don't mean to impose." And that *was* bad. Quite plainly, she was imposing.

The priest was young. Forty at most, blond, pale, handsome and sensual, if not downright corrupt around the mouth.

"Not at all," he said. "The thing is, God is fairly indulgent. He's forgiven people for more than a Manhattan."

"And cigarettes?" the floozie asked.

It's exactly what *I* would have said. Maybe floozies are generic. I looked a little closer at my competition. Her sneer reminded me of one similar in a pic of myself, taken at Ocean City, Maryland, when I was fifteen and had just lost my cherry.

"That's a sin, I admit," the father said sadly. "Tried to kick it several times but every time it gains on me again. I wake up at night and see a little glowing tip inches from my face, tempting me." He half-closed his pale, weary lids in the likeness of a suffering man.

"The fathers of the desert should've had it so hard," laughed the hussy.

Father opened one eye, then the other, and switched gears. His voice took on the upper edge of the pulpit basso. "And you? Have you no vices, friend? Are you not stereotyping me in your mind, right now, quicker than I can dissuade you?"

"I try not to," she said, allowing a kind of velveteen chill into her voice. I felt it, and people must have felt it three stools away, because there was suddenly that silent bubble in the place, that sometimes opens abruptly in a noisy room and everybody can hear clearly the last thing said. Everybody looked at the priest, and then at the girl, and the understanding that surpasses all knowing gripped everyone, and then the noise resumed.

I was most intrigued by her at this point. I took her

234

proportions mentally, using my palms to measure her in my mind from her moderately high high-heels to the part in her hair. She was about my height, and built similarly if one allowed for exaggerations and costume differences. It was a little spooky, and I decided to play avant-echo, to see if we did resemble each other all that much. I decided to say quickly to myself whatever seemed appropriate, before she made her replies.

The father, embarrassed by the silence but now relieved by the noise and on his second Manhattan as well, said, "Any man's reputation can be ruined here, leave alone that of a servant of the Lord."

"Let's get back to your sins," I said to myself.

"We left off at the glowing tip," said she.

"Now, now," teased the priest. "Let's not get carried away. I'm a man, I have feelings."

"What kind of feelings?"

"What kind of feelings?"

I shifted uncomfortably. I said, "Jinx. You owe me a Coke."

"What?" said the floozie.

"Nothing," I mumbled. "Just thinking."

"Seriously though," she said to him, "don't you find any contradiction between this bar and your duties?"

That was quick, I hadn't had time to get in an avant-echo.

"Not to delve too deeply, dear, but God is bigger than His contradictions. He really does forgive. He may in fact preside equally over picket fences and tanks, over His Left and His Right, if the truth were known."

"Thanks," I said, because I was his left.

"I'm Episcopalian," he continued, "but in the Catholic Church God is divided between the rich and the poor, and between men and women. The clergy, the theologians, the wealthy prefer Jesus, while the poor and women and most of South America worship the Virgin of Perpetual Sorrow. The strong wield theology like a nightstick, the poor yield their tears like little bombs of grief. In any case, it's bound to end badly."

The father stopped short. Emotion had crept into his voice about halfway through this speech, and he'd surprised himself. I don't think he meant to say all that. He flushed and a number of freckles appeared like a strange constellation beneath the pale skin.

"That's some kind of revolutionary Manichaeism," I said to myself.

"You sound like a left-wing Nicaraguan," said she.

Now that was definitely out of her league. She just wasn't dressed the part for those words. Where would a lipsticked bimbo working in an office in Lower Slobovia get that kind of quick grasp? I looked closely at her, and as I looked I thought that I discerned dark lines under her eyes, barely covered by makeup. Her hands were shaking a little too, and on the wrist of one of them, just under the flowered sleeve of her blouse was a black mark. It could have been a speck of dirt or it could have been the outermost edge of a tattoo that began on one of her breasts and went down her arm to end just below the sleeve.

"And I didn't mean to upset you," she was saying.

Her bluster turned quickly into an apology. I was beginning to lose interest, and was just turning toward my right where, for the past few moments I had become aware of a massive bulk of horny meat, when I saw the father reach under his tunic.

From under there he extracted a Pelikan fountain pen. He took off the top and the gold nib glinted for a moment in the light refracted through my whiskey. He pulled the half-soggy napkin between us quickly toward him and scribbled a few words in rapid cursive. He handed it to her.

She put it in her skirt pocket without reading it, and

held the priest's gaze in her own. Between them, ionized particles and magnetized atoms rushed to form an intense field. It was blinding. My heart fluttered like a dove.

"OK, then," I said to myself, but she said nothing.

Printed in June 1999 in Santa Barbara &
Ann Arbor for the Black Sparrow Press by
Mackintosh Typography & Edwards Brothers Inc.
Text set in Bembo by Words Worth.
Design by Barbara Martin.
This first edition is published in paper wrappers;
there are 300 hardcover trade copies;
100 hardcover copies have been numbered & signed
by the author; & 20 copies lettered A–T
have been handbound in boards by Earle Gray
& are signed by the author.

ANDREI CODRESCU was born in Sibiu, Romania in 1946. Since emigrating to the U.S. in 1966, he has published poetry, memoirs, fiction, and essays. He is a regular commentator on National Public Radio, and has written and starred in the award-winning movie, *Road Scholar*. His novel, *The Blood Countess* (Simon & Schuster, 1995), was a national bestseller. He teaches writing at Louisiana State University in Baton Rouge. He lives in New Orleans. His most recent books from Black Sparrow are *Alien Candor: Selected Poems 1970–1995* (1996) and *Thus Spake the Corpse: An Exquisite Corpse Reader 1988–1998* (1999).